Angel glanced up from the newspaper he'd been examining for more information on the bizarre murders.

Kate Lockley entered the office. Before Angel could even rise to greet her, she dropped a box of case folders on his desk. "These are copies," she declared, "but I'll want them back. All of them. Don't make me regret this, Angel."

"I won't."

"I forgot to mention one thing that puts us on the whole cult angle. One of the bodies was missing." She held up a hand to stop the obvious question. "We found a pile of clothes in an alley, along with personal effects, white . . . bone powder, and a few patches of torn skin. For God only knows what sick purpose, somebody wanted those remains."

Wanted? Angel wondered. *Or needed?*

Angel™

City Of
Not Forgotten
Redemption
Close to the Ground
Shakedown
Hollywood Noir
Avatar

Available from POCKET PULSE

The Essential Angel Posterbook

Available from POCKET BOOKS

ANGEL™

avatar

John Passarella

An original novel based on the television series created by Joss Whedon & David Greenwalt

POCKET PULSE
New York London Toronto Sydney Singapore

Historian's Note: This story takes place during the first half of *Angel's* first season.

This book is a work of fiction. Names, characters, places and incidents are products of the author's imagination or are used fictitiously. Any resemblance to actual events or locales or persons, living or dead, is entirely coincidental.

An *Original* Publication of POCKET BOOKS

POCKET PULSE published by
Pocket Books, a division of Simon & Schuster, Inc.
1230 Avenue of the Americas, New York, NY 10020

ISBN: 0-7434-0698-2

First Pocket Books printing March 2001

10 9 8 7 6 5 4 3 2 1

POCKET PULSE and colophon are registered trademarks of Simon & Schuster, Inc.

Printed in the U.S.A.

For my sons, Matthew and Luke,
because all the time in the world
would still never be enough

Acknowledgments

My thanks to Keya Khayatian for putting me on the map in Los Angeles as well as in Swedesboro. My editor, Lisa Clancy, and her assistant, Micol Ostow, for making it fun. My agent, Gordon Kato, who is as excited by stories as I am. Jean Wipf and Mary Moyer for their continued local support. Jeff Richards for the virtual beer. Max Etchemendy for speaking in tongues—i.e., the Latin lessons. And Andrea for all her love and that little push when I needed it.

Special thanks to Joss Whedon and David Greenwalt for creating *Angel* and to David Boreanaz, Charisma Carpenter, and Glenn Quinn for breathing life into the characters.

PROLOGUE

Elliot Grundy's demon was becoming impatient.

Shouldn't be too surprised, Elliot thought, *patience being a virtue and all that.* Even so, his computer's modem had barely stopped grumbling over its irritatingly slow connection, when the demon demanded to know where she was. "Don't worry," Elliot assured him, although the "him" aspect was still up for grabs. Elliot wasn't really sure the demon had a sex, but referring to the demon as "him" rather than "it" just seemed more natural. Well, once one got beyond the completely *unnatural* concept of dealing with a demon in the first place. "She'll show."

Elliot sat at his computer desk in the bedroom of his one-bedroom apartment wearing a sleeveless T-shirt stretched over his considerable paunch and threadbare sweatpants. He'd settled in with a party-size bag of cheese curls and a chilled two-liter bottle of Pepsi. In no time at all, the orange powder from the cheese curls coated his entire keyboard. Nothing his minivac couldn't clean up later.

He fired up the Internet chat software and connected to the chat room, one of many he'd bookmarked. Before actually logging in to the room, he started his text-to-speech utility program, which spared him the eyestrain he'd experience from staring at text on the screen for long hours. He assigned a generic male voice for room announcements. It was a singles chat room with no moderator. Come and go as you please. No censorship, no rules. Anonymous. His favorite kind. Next he assigned a male voice to his log-in name and a female voice to the woman's.

Since this was a graphical chat room, he had to pick an avatar in addition to a log-in name. The available avatars ran the gamut from cartoon animals to caricatures of classic movie stars like Bogart, Mae West, and James Dean. All the avatars tended to have large heads over miniature and basically unmoving bodies, as if part of some bizarre casting call for the television series *South Park*. Elliot selected his avatar, the Frankenstein monster, and entered his screen name, FrankN9, to log in.

The chat room screen was a two-dimensional representation of a bar, with stools, tables, and booths. All the depth of Colorforms. An animated bartender avatar, endlessly cleaning a beer mug with a white cloth, served the nonhuman role of room announcer. "FrankN9 has entered the bar," said generic male voice number one through the computer speakers.

Several avatars bobbed aimlessly around the bar, including a cowboy, a red bulldog, a showgirl with a high-kicking stick leg, and, demonstrating another annoying looped animation, a hula dancer. To avoid any confusion that duplicate avatars might cause, each had a name tag underneath it. Comic book–style word balloons appeared above the cowboy and the hula girl. "Hi, FrankN9." Grundy hadn't bothered to assign them text-to-speech voices.

Behind Elliot, the demon spoke in a voice that would have made Barry White think he had a shot with the Vienna Boys Choir. "Where is she?"

Elliot resisted the urge to look over his shoulder at the demon, whose neutral state he found a little unsettling, especially on a diet of cheese curls and cola. By rights, it shouldn't have disturbed him since, as the demon had explained, he was only able to manifest on the physical plane with substance borrowed from Elliot, a result of their pact. "She'll show," Elliot repeated, wiping the orange residue from his damp palms onto his sweatpants. "She's just . . . fashionably late, is all."

Elliot typed a question for his avatar to speak in

the digitized voice of generic male number two: "Anyone seen L8Dvamp?"

A few quick replies. Bulldog: "Not tonight." Cowboy, in character, no less: "Out of luck, pardner." Then the group resumed chatting among themselves, word balloons sprouting and popping like soap bubbles.

Behind Elliot, the demon rumbled ominously. He wasn't quite sure how the demon made that sound, but it made his gut vibrate uncomfortably. Elliot cleared his throat, "Look, she's probably just—"

"L8Dvamp has entered the bar," said the voice of the announcer.

Elliot heaved a sigh of relief and began typing. His assigned computer voice came through the speakers: "Hi, L8Dvamp. I've been waiting for you."

L8Dvamp came as her usual avatar, a lady vampire with black hair piled high, red eyes, a drop of blood dripping from each curlicue fang, wearing a shirred white dress with a plunging neckline. "Good evening, FrankN9," spoke generic female voice number one. "Were you afraid I'd get cold feet?"

Having recently faced that precise fear, Elliot took a long slug of Pepsi. After a resounding belch, he said to the demon, "Annoying bitch. Deserves whatever happens to her." But he typed, "Never entertained the thought."

A small window popped up in the middle of the screen. The message read, "L8Dvamp has invited you into a private room." Next to it were two buttons. "Accept" and "Decline." Elliot uttered a sigh of relief. *Good, she's skipping the preliminaries.* He clicked on "Accept," then said to the demon behind him, "What I tell ya, big guy? She can't resist our collective charms."

"Proceed," the demon instructed.

A new window overlaid the bar. This one had a two-dimensional love seat in one corner and a brass bed in the other. Things could get kinky in here, if the chat turned into a computer sex session, but Elliot had other plans. Besides, L8Dvamp's avatar had already wobbled over to the love seat. He leaned forward, his cheese curls all but forgotten, and typed his end of the conversation into the keyboard: "So . . . ready to meet in the real world?"

"You really think we'd make a good couple?"

"Remember, my psychic told me I'd have a serious relationship with a Pisces, and you're a Pisces. Seems like fate."

"Okay, but one favor first."

"Crap! What now?" Elliot said. But he typed, "Anything. Name it."

"Describe yourself again," she said in the robotic approximation of human speech, "so I'll recognize you when we meet."

When, he noted. Not *if.* "Just last night I asked

you to describe your dream guy. You said it was amazing how close I fit that description."

"Yes. And that seemed like fate too."

"Okay. Describe that dream guy again."

"Mid-twenties. Athletic build. At least six feet tall, dark blond hair, blue eyes, natural tan."

Elliot was five-eight with rust-colored hair and a few acne skirmishes around a pale, round face. His skinny arms bracketed a pear-shaped body. Elliot began typing: "I'm six-one . . ." Then he turned to face the demon. He had to, so he could get the rest of the description right.

Standing less than an arm's length behind Elliot's chair, the demon looked like nothing more than a man-shaped lump of yellow wax about six feet high. The demon had no facial features and only spatula-shaped hands and feet, no fingers or toes. But now the waxy shape stretched up to a height of six feet one inch. The head sprouted numerous spikes, that flopped over and became blond hair. Blue eyes appeared and seemed to focus on Elliot. Nostrils and a gaping maw opened, then sculpted themselves into a narrow nose and full-lipped mouth. The lumpy wax surface took on the consistency of skin over an enviable musculature and finally deepened in color to a surfer's tan. As the demon continued to resolve into a human shape, complete with fingers, toes, and body hair, Elliot finished typing the demon's physical characteristics into the private room, followed by a question. "Well?"

"Picture's worth a thousand words."

"Meaning?"

"If we're gonna meet, I need to be sure. Do you have a Web camera?"

"Great," Elliot said to the demon. "She wants to see your mug."

"Do it," the demon said, his perfect teeth flashing.

Elliot sighed. "Think you should put on some clothes first?"

"Right," the demon said, extending his arms. Elliot's clothes would never fit, so the demon created his own illusion: basic white shirt, jeans, and boots.

Elliot turned back to the computer and typed. "I'll show you mine if you show me yours."

"Ha-ha."

"Hold on. I really want to meet you before it gets too late." *Yes,* Elliot thought. *I have a very impatient demon breathing down my neck.* The chat room had an option for cameras and videoconferencing, which was too formal a term in this situation. Elliot lifted his spherical camera off the top of his monitor and passed it to the demon, who held it before his face. Elliot turned the camera on through the software. In moments, a postage stamp–size window appeared in the corner of his own monitor and he saw a grainy, color image of L8Dvamp. She had dark hair and a plain-looking face, accentuated with dark red lipstick.

"Thanks for being so understanding, FrankN9."

He switched off the video link. "No problem, L8Dvamp. Where should we meet?"

"I'm at CyberJoe's," she told him. "How soon can you get here?"

CyberJoe's was a new Internet coffee bar located in West Hollywood off Melrose. At one time it had been a popular dance club, with an encircling upper tier that looked down upon an expansive dance floor. Although the balcony level had probably once been at eye level with the obligatory spinning mirrored ball, the tables and booths that had replaced the balcony now allowed for more intimate conversations. While the interior architecture hadn't been overhauled extensively, the mirror ball was long gone and the music—now piped through camouflaged speakers—was electronic, New Age, and subdued. Booths and tables everywhere sported computers with sleek and expensive flat-panel displays. The stairway and balcony railings were outlined in blue and yellow neon lights, perhaps to simulate information coursing through the place and out into the world at the speed of light. Otherwise the lighting was as muted as that of a posh restaurant late in the evening, but instead of candles casting a warm glow on the faces of the customers, flat-screen monitors bathed the computer acolytes in a ghostly pale aura.

For a place that had once vibrated with dance music cranked up well beyond the hearing-impairment threshold, CyberJoe's became, on occasion, eerily quiet. The only sound emanating from the tables of actual Internet researchers tended to be a steady clacking of keys. So the managers of CyberJoe's, in addition to supplying over thirty varieties of coffee and tea, had instituted in-house computer trivia challenges and chat night topics to foster camaraderie among their clientele, having lost sight of the simple fact that it was hard for patrons to interact while staring into a computer display.

Ginger Marks (a.k.a. L8Dvamp) agreed with Eddie (a.k.a. FrankN9) that the best way to interact with each other would be to leave CyberJoe's and go for an evening stroll. They walked for a while in comfortable silence. Ginger couldn't help glancing over at him every couple of moments, then smiling. "I have to say," she told him. "You're exactly how I pictured you."

Eddie smiled, taking the compliment in stride, almost as if he'd expected it.

Ginger thought he was simply too good to be true—exactly as she'd pictured her dream guy, in every detail. Yet her first photographic impression of him as he walked through the door of CyberJoe's and greeted her was that his nose was a little too thin for her liking, his eyebrows a tad too bushy. Then, within moments, those same features seemed just right. He still looked basically the same as he had a half hour ago . . . only better. *Was it a trick of the imagination?* she wondered. *Nobody's appearance changes just because you want it to.* "So what about you?"

"What about me?"

She grinned, spread her hands expansively, causing her silver bracelets to clink together. She wore a wine-colored blouse and black Capri pants. Around her neck was a pendant in the curved *H* shape of the Pisces glyph. "Am I exactly how you envisioned me?"

"Physical appearance isn't nearly as important to me as what's on the inside." He flashed a dazzling white smile, took her hand in his, and kissed it. "But I must say you are delightful in every way."

She laughed. "Why, thank you, Eddie. It's strange. I want to keep calling you FrankN9, or at least Frank."

"That's better than plain old Frankenstein."

Several teenage boys were walking down the street, intentionally banging into each other, perhaps reminiscing about a mosh pit. One gave another a playful shove in the back and started to run away, toward Ginger and Eddie. The others took off after him. Eddie grabbed Ginger and pulled her aside, shielding her from the stampede of youth. "Hooligans," he said.

"Just kids goofing off."

Eddie glanced over her shoulder, down a narrow side street. Then he looked deep into her eyes in a way no other guy ever had. The intensity of his gaze actually gave her chills, made her a little weak in the knees. He was incredibly attractive and athletic, and he seemed so passionate. She wasn't sure exactly what was coming over her, but she knew she had every intention of giving in to it.

He said softly into her ear, "Mind if we step off this expressway for a moment? I have something . . . important to tell you."

Lost in his deep blue eyes, she nodded once.

After he led her a few steps into the alley and placed both hands on her shoulders, she found her voice again. "Okay. We're alone now. I seriously hope the important thing you're about to say is not that you're married."

He chuckled. "No. Actually, it's not something I want to say. It's something I've wanted to do all night. And I required a little . . . privacy."

She tilted her head back as he leaned down for the kiss. "Oh . . . I understand completely."

As his hands slid across her shoulders, their lips met. After only a moment, she felt the moist tip of his tongue and parted her lips. "Ginger," he whispered, "I'm afraid you don't understand at all."

That was when his hands, near her neck now, clamped down over her collarbone, pinching her flesh. His fingers lengthened and hardened, and his nails extended, digging into her flesh, then piercing it, stabbing into her chest, neck, and back. Ginger tried to scream but his tongue had elongated as well and was probing down her throat impossibly far, scaly as a snake.

She tried to push him away, but her hands quickly became too heavy to lift. Her arms dropped to her sides. One by one her silver bracelets slipped off her withering hands, clinking on the asphalt. Her body convulsed, thrashing in his grip until, finally, she succumbed to the rising tide of darkness that swept over her.

While they were joined, the demon convulsed as well, as if he were connected to a live wire. But far from damaging him, each jolt of energy that flowed from her body to his, engorged him with the stuff of her life essence, each pulse a dizzying thrill. Yet the euphoria only lasted for about thirty seconds. Then she simply had nothing left to give. When he withdrew his fingers and tongue from what was left of Ginger's body, they whipped around like agitated eels. All eleven appendages had become segmented, tapered to hollow points, still shiny with Ginger's gore. While the erstwhile fingers and thumbs were long enough to reach the ground, what had passed for his tongue was only eighteen inches long. The demon threw back its head and retracted its tongue with a contented slurp. Then he held his arms up, palms facing inward like a doctor who had just scrubbed for surgery, and willed his eel-like fingers back to human dimensions.

With a parting glance at what had once been Ginger Marks, Eddie the demon strolled out of the alley with a newfound spring in his step. Though fully charged, crackling with energy and vitality, he knew the feeling wouldn't last. Ginger's essence was just one step in the fateful dance to complete him, to make him whole.

What he left behind—inside the crumpled wine-colored blouse and black Capri pants—resembled a shed snakeskin, but it was human-shaped with tufts of dark hair. All the internal organs, blood, and viscera that had made it possible for Ginger to live and breathe were missing. Even her bones had been reduced to a fine white powder.

The same cool evening breeze that nudged an empty soda can down the deserted side street also fluttered the delicate, translucent flaps of skin that had been the fingers of Ginger's right hand.

CHAPTER ONE

"Everybody's using the Web now," Cordelia Chase explained to Doyle as if he were an inattentive child. "Even people who have a life."

The moment Angel stepped out of the office she'd begun her campaign to win Doyle over to her plan to drum up some business. Namely, to create a Web site for Angel Investigations.

"So that's it, then," Doyle said with his pronounced Irish brogue. "Put up a Web page and all the poor downtrodden masses will flock to our door."

"Of course not," Cordelia replied. "The poor don't have computers. We need more paying clients. Emphasis on the paying part."

Cordelia was sitting at her desk in the reception area of Angel Investigations in a sleeveless red crop top, black jeans, and stiletto heels. Doyle leaned on the corner of her desk, slouching in his old leather jacket over a green shirt with a rumpled collar. Even though Cordelia complained about her inability to keep up with the latest fashions on her meager receptionist's salary, being around her always made Doyle feel as if he'd slept in his clothes, out on the street, in the rain. Not that he was complaining. At the best of times, Cordelia took his breath away. The rest of the time, she put a lump in his throat. And while he had yet to work up the nerve to tell her he had feelings for her, well, hope sprang eternal.

Though Doyle imagined that Cordelia made most men feel unworthy of her company, he carried the extra burden of having a father who was a Brachen demon. Sure, he was one hundred percent human on his mother's side, but how far would that get him with the former Sunnydale prom queen. Cordelia had made it abundantly clear that she had relegated all demons to the enemy column. So it was no surprise that he'd neglected to tell her about his Brachen side. Someday he would convince her that being a half-demon didn't necessarily make him one of the bad guys. *Until then,* he thought, *no sense dashin' the dream.*

"We help the helpless," Doyle countered. "It says so right there on our answering machine. In your very own voice, I might add. And generally the helpless aren't known for their stock portfolios."

"We'll still help the helpless," Cordelia countered. "But would it kill us to find some helpless people with disposable income?"

"I suppose not."

"So are you with me? Can we present a united front?"

Doyle thought about uniting with Cordelia and had to clear his throat. *Better get beyond* that *visual image before you stuff your foot in your mouth, boyo.* "Fine. I'll play devil's advocate. Though, for the sake of this example, I suppose that'd make me Angel's advocate. What about the expense?"

"We can do it on the cheap," Cordelia assured him. "Lots of free stuff on the Internet I can use. It would be like—like another utility bill. And so far we've managed to keep the electricity and phones working." She rapped her knuckles on the desk. "Knock wood."

"Next problem, then. Do you even know how to design a Web site?"

"I figured out how to print invoices," Cordelia said. "Not that I get a lot of practice. How much harder can Web site design be?"

"I'd wager good coin it's gonna be harder than printing invoices."

"That's your problem. You wager too much," Cordelia commented. "This is more like a sure thing."

Doyle cleared his throat. "I've lost more than one shirt on a sure thing."

Cordelia opened a desk drawer, removed several

thick computer manuals, and dropped them with a resounding thud on her desk. "That's every book the library had on Web site design, except for *The Complete Simpleton's Guide to Web Site Creation,* which is a title I found a little insulting." She frowned. "Although encouraging."

"I still think you're insane to try."

"Doyle, they even have software wizards to do this for you," Cordelia said. "It won't be that difficult. And the Web site will be like having another office, with even cheaper rent than this dump. I'll even set up a subscription service for access to our demon database. I'd bet a lot of people will pay good money for that information."

Doyle gave a wry grin. "And you say I'm the one who wagers too much."

"Doyle, some of these sites get ten million hits a month," Cordelia said. "That's like . . . the population of L.A. or something."

"But don't you find it a bit depressing? All these people parked in front of their computers, ignorin' their loved ones?"

"They invented chat rooms and instant messaging for that."

Doyle rolled his eyes. "Oh, brother." Finally he sighed. "You really believe you can do this?"

"Right from my desk," Cordelia said, flashing her lovely smile. "In between answering the phone, mailing invoices, and all my—um, auditions."

It had been a while since Cordelia's last audition. Doyle wondered if she was tackling this project to take her mind off the lack of chances at stardom. When Cordelia left Sunnydale for Los Angeles she'd assumed it would only be a matter of time—and not a lot of time at that—before she was discovered. Meanwhile, she needed her job at Angel Investigations just to make ends meet.

Since Doyle could offer no help in jump-starting her film career, he figured the least he could do was to offer his moral support in her Web site project. He saw just one problem: "Angel will never go for it."

"Which is why I've decided to keep it a secret from him," Cordelia explained, then held up her hands as he started to protest. "But just until all the extra income starts rolling in. So are you with me?"

"I'm with you, Cordelia," Doyle said. "But I've got a bad feeling about this."

"Okay, Mr. Doom-and-Gloom," Cordelia replied. "But you're worrying over nothing."

Angel worried that he was too late. One of the big problems with the visions Doyle received courtesy of the Powers That Be, aside from the splitting headaches they gave Doyle, was that they tended to be vague—brief glimpses of people in dire need of being rescued from what often turned out to be a fate far worse than death. Angel reviewed the tidbits Doyle's vision had given him this time. A video arcade and a teenage boy in danger from a card-carrying member of the Creatures-of-the-Night Club. And not many helpful details about the exact nature of said creature. Just that it was big.

Leaving the bright lights of the Santa Monica Pier behind him, Angel recalled another detail. Doyle had seen the word "one" in red neon outside the arcade. A telephone-book check had come up empty. Thinking it might be a new arcade, as yet unlisted, they'd called information. Again, no luck.

He was about to climb into his convertible to check out the Beverly Center, when a group of teenagers crossed the intersection. In the direction they were heading, was a blue neon sign that read "Warp" in slanting letters. On impulse, Angel walked several steps across the street. More of the sign came into view. The word "Warp" had a large yellow lightning bolt symbol after it.

Bit it was not a lightning bolt, he realized as he walked faster toward the sign. It was the letter Z. He ran toward the place, knowing what he would see next. His instinct was confirmed as red neon letters eventually spelled out "one."

Doyle had only seen part of the sign. The place was called the Warp Zone.

The group of teenagers who had led him to the arcade entered a few steps ahead of him. Amid all the beeping, blooping, zapping, and blasting sound effects, he found it hard to concentrate. There were at least a hundred teenagers in the place. Those who weren't already mesmerized by battles with space aliens, fighter squadrons, tanks, zombies, mutants, and, yes, even vampires, were feeding dollar bills into machines that spat out tokens needed to begin or renew the mayhem. Hardly any of the teens interacted with one another. Even those arriving in groups would split up and look for an unoccupied pinball machine, video game, or virtual reality helmet. *If the Pied Piper of Hamelin ever makes a return visit,* Angel thought, *he'll come bearing handheld video games.*

Aside from misspent youth, Angel noticed nothing sinister in the arcade. Granted, some creatures of the night were good at passing for human, as he should know, being a vampire himself; even a vampire with a soul had to hide his true nature in public. Yet he doubted a vampire would make a move inside a crowded arcade, so Angel stepped out into the cool night and looked for the shadows. Toward the rear of the arcade, the white exterior walls were riddled with a mosaic of graffiti. With all the beeping and zapping still echoing in his ears, he couldn't be sure at first if he'd really heard the sound of shoes scuffing cement. Nevertheless, caution won out.

Crouching, Angel peered around the back of the arcade and saw what appeared to be a large, bulky man in a dark overcoat and crumpled fedora ambling down the poorly lit street behind the arcade. The man had one arm wrapped around a teenage boy with straggly blond hair who was wearing a World Wrestling Federation T-shirt over apocalyptically frayed jeans. Judging by the way the boy's sneakers dragged and flopped along the ground, he was unconscious or worse. By supporting the teen's weight, the big guy made it appear as if they were walking along together. Near the back wall of the arcade, Angel spotted a fresh pack of spilled cigarettes.

Step outside for a nicotine fix and walk into a supernatural ambush.

Careful not to make a sound, Angel climbed atop a Dumpster against the side of the building. From there, he leaped gracefully to the arcade's roof, then ran along the length of the building, quiet as a shadow, his raincoat flowing behind him. As he neared the edge of the rooftop, he veered toward the corner, adjusting his angle on the fly, then launched himself toward the ambling figure clutching the boy at his side. At the last moment, Angel lowered his head, brought his elbow up, braced it with his other hand, and drove it like a wedge into the back of the creature.

The creature stumbled with the impact, dropping the boy and crashing into a chain-link fence. Angel felt as if he'd attempted to tackle a tree—a very large tree, with an extensive root system. He rolled and sprang to his feet, marveling that he hadn't dislocated his shoulder. Still, it hurt like hell. Proverbial hell, anyway, he thought. He'd spent time in literal hell. And nothing hurt worse, by far.

Instead of fleeing or turning to fight, the creature simply lumbered over to the unconscious teen and picked him up again. In the dim light, Angel was still unable to tell exactly what he was dealing with, but the creature seemed to be wearing sunglasses under the floppy hat. And black leather . . . mittens?

"I need to see some I.D.," Angel called, "because, frankly, I can't figure out what the hell you are."

The creature all but ignored him.

So Angel charged, this time leaping into a kick. He caught the creature square on the jaw, the sole of one boot snapping its head back and dislodging its hat. Once more the teenager slipped from the creature's grasp, slumping to the ground. Angel saw that he was still breathing. But now Angel had the creature's complete and undivided attention. Not really a good thing, just a necessary thing.

With the hat gone, a pair of twitching antennae were now exposed. And what had looked like sunglasses turned out to be bulbous, multifaceted eyes, like those of an insect viewed through an electron microscope. Below a flat nose, the creature had protuberant mandibles, which upon cursory inspection might have been mistaken for a dark beard. All of which meant the creature wasn't actually wearing leather mittens over its hands. It had no hands. Instead, its arms terminated in crablike pincers. With a quick backhand blow, one set of those pincers struck Angel alongside the head, staggering him as he was climbing to his feet.

Angel shook off the blow and moved in close, striking the creature's broad gut with a flurry of punches. When that proved ineffective, he tried to chop the side of its neck with the edge of his palm. A pincer came up and caught Angel's hand, squeezing painfully, grinding the bones of his hand together. Blood dripped down his wrist. Before the creature could crush the bones, Angel drove the heel of his free hand into the creature's face. If it had a nose, he might have driven cartilage back into its brain, assuming its brain was in its head. But it had no nose, and all Angel managed to do was drive its head back a few inches. Mandibles clacked inches above Angel's face.

He morphed into his vampire mode, displaying creased brow, yellow eyes, and fangs. Then he flexed his wrist, releasing one of the spring-loaded wooden stakes he kept hidden in the mechanism up each sleeve. First he drove the stake into the creature's wide midsection, but, as he'd expected, it had little effect on what seemed like an armored hide or carapace. *Let the eyes have it,* Angel thought and tried to pound the narrow end of the stake into one of the glittering eyes. The point skidded off the rounded surface of the eye and over the head, giving Angel another idea. Dropping the stake, he wrapped his free hand around the left antenna. It was rough and bristled with short spikes, like tiny thorns, but the pain of clenching it was nothing compared to what his other hand was experiencing in the crushing grip of the creature's pincers. Angel yanked hard on the antenna.

The creature shrieked horribly.

Through gritted teeth, Angel said, "Here I thought you were the strong silent type."

The creature tried to hurl Angel away, even releasing his hand from its pincers. Uninterested in a stalemate, Angel held on to the antenna, though the blood drawn by the tiny spikes made his grip slick. Because of Angel's momentum, the creature had no choice but to stagger forward bent over. Even as it continued to lumber forward, gaining speed, the enraged creature clutched Angel around the waist and hoisted him into the air.

I have a bad feeling about this, Angel thought about two seconds before the creature slammed him into the back wall of the arcade. It stepped back and lunged forward again, repeatedly ramming Angel into the wall, using its own weight in an attempt to crush Angel in the process. At some point, Angel's vision dimmed and he must have sagged in its grip because the next thing he knew he was sailing across the back street, bowling over three trash cans full of rotten garbage. Yet he doubted the crashing and banging of metal trash cans would be heard above the otherworldly electronic din flowing out of the arcade.

Angel rolled onto his hands and knees, ready to resume the fight. As he climbed to his feet he realized he must have been groggy longer than he thought because both the creature and the unconscious teenage boy were gone. Shaking his head to clear away the cobwebs, Angel bent down and picked up his stake. He was about to put it back into the spring-loaded mechanism when he noticed the end was discolored, coated with something pale green.

Blood, he realized. So he had hurt the creature after all.

Angel's face reverted to his human countenance. All the pounding to his head must have dislodged some information stored way back where the synapses were dustiest. He recalled reading something years ago about a beetle-like creature—a Sakorbuk demon! What else did he know about Sakorbuk demons and their—as Detective Kate Lockley might say—modus operandi? Only one thing came immediately to mind: they preferred to eat the flesh of recently dead humans. This demon's current victim was still alive, but for how long?

Knowing the shambling creature couldn't have

traveled far, especially carrying its prey, Angel loped down the back street in the direction it had been heading before he'd attacked it. Every few strides he glimpsed a droplet of green, almost glowing on the asphalt. *Even better than bread crumbs,* he decided. Abruptly the trail ended. Either the creature had stopped bleeding or Angel had missed a turn. He backtracked, looped in a circle from the last drop of blood and was about to give up when he noticed a manhole cover in his path. No stranger to the Los Angeles sewer system, Angel removed the cover and was soon underground. As he dropped from the bottom ladder rung, he heard rhythmic splashing to his right.

Just ahead of him the beetle demon lumbered along with its limp prey, heavy feet sloshing through the thin stream of foul-smelling water that trickled along the base of the sewer tunnel. A luminescent green substance—a bodily secretion of the Sakorbuk?—had been smeared in an uneven line on either side of the sewer tunnel, eerily lighting the way. A thought nagged at Angel: he was forgetting some vital bit of information regarding Sakorbuk demons.

Following at a discreet distance, he stayed to the side of the water stream so as not to alert the Sakorbuk to his presence by splashing. The demon seemed to have a destination in mind, and Angel suspected it would be some sort of hive or nest.

Less than fifty yards farther on, the Sakorbuk dropped its burden. Angel counted four beetle demons waddling around a T-shaped junction in the sewer system, all wearing roomy overcoats to disguise their appearance from casual observers. Besides the demons, Angel saw three more teenage victims, one of them a girl with dark hair and a pale complexion. Fortunately, all were breathing. They were all upright, propped against the tunnel wall, arms crossed over their heads, hands glued to the wall with some sort of sticky white substance, like the mother of all discarded bubble-gum wads.

Angel crept forward as the Sakorbuk he'd trailed hoisted the unconscious boy again, then engaged in some sort of chittering, mandible-clacking dialogue with the nearest beetle. The second one lurched forward and raised the boy's arms, crossing his hands together against the wall. Once they were positioned, the first beetle raised its head, spread its mandibles wide, and emitted a sputtering, hissing sound. Clear fluid sprayed over the boy's hands, quickly congealing and turning white. Now all four victims were lined up like ducks in a row. Or platters on a buffet table?

The lumbering beetle demons positioned themselves so that one stood in front of each victim. In unison, they tilted back their helmet-shaped heads and emitted a gurgling sound. Their pale throats swelled and seemed to split open vertically as something moist and maggot-white pushed its way out from the flap in each beetle's skin.

Angel edged closer and saw they were teardrop-shaped beetle larvae, about a foot long. Each one plopped to the wet floor of the sewer tunnel and immediately inched its way, using twin rows of tiny feelers, toward the nearest victim. That was when the other bit of information clicked into place. The four larvae did not intend to feed off the teenagers' flesh; they wanted to incubate inside them until the humans became beetles themselves. That was how Sakorbuks reproduced, for want of a better word. All the hormonal changes running rampant inside human adolescents was conducive to better beetle raising. The relationship was more parasitic than symbiotic, as the demon larva eventually took over the host body and mutated it into the adult Sakorbuk form. Angel had seen more than enough to know he'd better put a stop to it and fast.

Each of the four larvae had already made its way over a shoe and onto a pant leg of its chosen victim. Inch by inch, they worked their inexorable way up the bodies of the unconscious teens.

"You're having a party and I wasn't invited?" Angel said as he stepped into the center of the tunnel and approached the four startled beetles. The one Angel had trailed emitted rapid-fire clicks and squeals to the others. They clicked and shrieked in turn, moving to intercept Angel while their offspring continued to climb.

All the commotion roused the teenage girl, who was farthest from Angel. She took one look at the glistening lump of translucent white flesh wriggling and squirming its way up her shirt and screamed loud enough to rouse the three other teenage hosts. In moments they were all yelling, kicking frantically, and flailing their bodies from side to side in an attempt to dislodge the climbing larvae.

Less than twenty feet away from them, the four Sakorbuk adults had surrounded Angel. He launched himself at the first one, the one he'd already injured, propelling himself off the side of the tunnel for maximum impact. Possibly because it was standing in water, unsure of its footing, or because it had been weakened by Angel's earlier attack, it went down, rolling on its curved back. Angel somersaulted through the stream of foul water and took the open lane toward the teenagers. He would never be able to defeat all four adult Sakorbuks before the larvae committed whatever unspeakable atrocity they were attempting in order to obtain host bodies. He ejected a stake into his hand from his wrist device and swept it over the WWF boy's chest, impaling and dislodging the larva. He whipped the stake, flinging the larva across the sewer tunnel, where it landed with a wet splat. But in a moment it simply rolled over and scuttled across the tunnel again, returning to its chosen victim.

"Talk about a one-track mind," Angel said.

"Look out!" the WWF boy yelled a split-second before Angel was clubbed by a hard set of pincers, knocking him against the wall.

Angel lashed out with a snap-kick that staggered the beetle a step. Before it could recover, Angel swung a powerful backhand, stake point extended. It struck the hard carapace of the creature without penetrating it or even slowing it down long enough for Angel to rescue the teens.

"Oh, God!" cried the second boy in line. His neck was tilted all the way back as his designated larva moved from his shirt collar up to his neck, leaving a trail of slime on his throat.

The third boy gritted his teeth and continued to thrash, attempting to yank his hands free of the gummy substance gluing them to the sewer wall. His larva was also making its way up his neck.

The girl, farthest away, was the shortest of the four victims, which meant she presented the shortest climb for her larva. Hoarse from screaming in terror, her voice was now just a harsh whisper as she shrieked, "Jesus! Get it off me! Get it *off!*" Then, abruptly, she fell silent. The larva was over her mouth, which she had snapped shut at the last instant. She appeared to be foaming at the mouth until Angel realized the larva was secreting a bubbling substance across her lips and up her nostrils. Her eyes rolled back into her head, and her whole body relaxed, becoming completely slack, including her mouth, which sagged open. Immediately, the gelatinous larva began to squirm into the opening between her gaping lips. Apparently boneless, it would have little trouble working its way into her mouth and down her throat.

Angel reached down and pulled a dagger out of a hidden sheath in his boot. The blade was six inches long and perfectly balanced. He flipped it in his hand so he held it by the tip, prayed his aim was true, and flung it toward the girl's face. The blade sliced through the fat, wriggling larva's body, and the force of the throw dislodged it from the girl's mouth with a loud, wet *plop*. The skewered larva rolled several feet down the tunnel end over end—or side over side, it was hard to tell—squirming on the knife blade until, finally, its glistening white body became dull gray.

Then Angel was struck down, but not before he saw the second boy in line actually attempt to bite a chunk out of the larva climbing onto his face. But it, too, started to froth. The third teen in the line whipped his head around, mouth clenched shut, but foam was already starting to form around his mouth.

Angel braced his hands on the wet floor of the tunnel and kicked out with both legs, knocking the first beetle into the others behind it. But unlike a row of dominoes or a set of tenpins, none of them went down. Their outer shell was simply too hard for him to inflict much damage. However, as that first beetle had tilted precariously backward, Angel caught a glimpse of the pale flap of skin under the mandibles, the flap that had expelled the larva. If the Sakorbuks had a tender spot in their armored hides, he was betting that was it.

Two of the beetles attempted to flank him. Angel caught the one on his left with an uppercut, striking directly under the flapping mandibles. Even as the blow landed, Angel flexed his wrist to eject his other stake. He drove it home, right into the center of the pale flap of skin. To his surprise his hand went in as deep as the stake was long and a sound not unlike a walnut in the wooden jaws of a nutcracker prefaced the creature's head ripping free of its broad thorax. It toppled over with one last twitch of its antennae.

Before the beetle on the opposite side could react to the beheading, Angel drove an elbow into its head, rocking it back a step. A roundhouse blow with the stake went into the flap on an angle, but the damage was done. Angel backed up two steps, then launched a wheeling kick that ripped its head off. It fell with a crash.

While Angel fought the adult beetles, the WWF-promoting teenager he'd followed into the sewer waited until his appointed larva was just about to climb up his foot again. Then he launched a preemptive kick. The larva sailed away and slapped against the far sewer wall where it stuck for a moment before oozing down to the floor again. If not dead, at least it was stunned. The boy twisted sidewise and kicked high, managing on the third attempt to kick the larva off the biting boy's face. The biter then attempted to use the same kicking maneuver on the third larva, even as its victim was slowly succumbing to the foam secretion. But the biter was woozy himself, having swallowed or inhaled some of the debilitating foam and his kicks weren't reaching nearly high enough to help the third teen.

Now that Angel had dispatched two of the beetles by exploiting the weak spot in their armored skin, the third beetle protectively lowered its head and charged Angel, ready to wrap him within the grip of its widespread pincers. Angel dropped his remaining stake, jumped high and curled his body, grabbing one antenna in each hand, planting his feet against the beetle's midsection, and using his own weight combined with the Sakorbuk's momentum to take it down, roll it over him, and kick it away. And he never let go of the antennae. The creature's immense weight pulled against the spiny antennae, and they ripped free of its head. It shrieked and thrashed on the floor of the sewer tunnel, then quivered, almost still.

"I love it when they roll over and play dead," Angel said.

The last beetle, the one Angel had originally followed, collapsed on top of him as he lay in the sewer water, attempting to pin him or crush the life out of him. Angel whipped his head out of the way of snapping mandibles, even dodging a hacking, hissing stream of the clear glue-like fluid aimed at his eyes. His right hand swept the floor of the sewer, fingers struggling to get a grip on the stake he'd dropped. Instead he knocked it farther away, completely out of reach. Undeterred, he watched the snapping mandibles, waiting for the exact moment when they clacked shut. With lightning-quick vampire reflexes, his left hand shot out and clamped over them, squeezing and holding them shut. That gave him the leverage he needed to pry the creature's head back just far enough to reveal the vulnerable flap of skin. Angel morphed into full vamp mode. This wasn't going to be pleasant, and he thought he'd face it better as a vampire. "Open wide," he said and rammed his fist into the flap. His arm went in up to the elbow and broke through the other side. His knuckles were coated with green blood and Sakorbuk brain matter.

Angel rolled the dead beetle off him and sprang to his feet. As he passed the quivering, antennae-challenged beetle, he paused just long enough to drive the heel of his boot through the exposed flap. The pincer arms fell back, the head sank into the water, and the creature lay perfectly still at last.

Squashing bugs underfoot had never been so much fun.

The third boy in line had finally succumbed to the foam drug secreted by his larva. He slumped against the wall, his mouth gaping open. Well, it would have been gaping if not for the squirming larva bulging out of it. Angel reached in distastefully, slipping a finger into either side of the boy's mouth to get a grip on the glistening, jiggling lump. He squeezed hard until it squirted out of the unconscious teen's mouth into Angel's hands. It wriggled in his grasp, like a greased piglet. Worse, it began to secrete foam all over Angel's fingers. So he dropped it to the floor of the sewer tunnel and slammed his boot down on it. Its skin membrane ruptured, splattering viscous white goo all over.

The last two larvae were making determined progress back to their intended victims, but still a few feet shy. Angel retrieved his knife from the dead gray larva and made short work of slicing the last two right down the middle.

Finally, Angel hacked through the bonding agent that pinned the teenagers' hands to the wall. Only the WWF teenager seemed fully alert. Although he had enough facial piercings to set off even the most forgiving metal detector, his wide-eyed look of fear caught Angel's attention.

"What—what are you?"

Angel realized he was still in full vamp mode. No

doubt the boy thought instead of being rescued he'd simply become prey for something higher up the demonic food chain than hell's own tapeworm. *We all have faces we don't show the world,* Angel thought. *Some are just worse than others.*

"What *are* you?" the boy repeated, edging away in terror.

"Believe it or not," Angel said, "I'm a friend."

The words hardly seemed to comfort the boy. The others began to stir. The larvae's narcotic had probably induced a short-term stupor, incapacitating the victim just long enough for the larvae to squirm down the esophagus and set up shop in the stomach. Angel decided to make himself scarce.

"You should all be okay, considering," Angel said. "But I wouldn't advise loitering down here. I hear there's strange stuff in the sewer."

As he turned away, Angel shifted his features to look human once again, hiding the darkness that lurked within. Never before had his human face felt so much like a mask.

CHAPTER TWO

"I'm looking for . . . Angel?"

"This—this is Angel Investigations," Cordelia said, having slammed her bottom desk drawer shut after hastily dumping the pile of Web design books into it as soon as the door started to open. Still not ready to tell Angel about her Web site plan, she was sure the computer books would be a dead giveaway. Or an undead giveaway, Angel being a vampire detective, after all.

"Have I come at a bad time?" asked the attractive auburn-haired woman, a curious and slightly amused smile lighting up her face.

"Wait a minute! I know you," Cordelia said. She turned to Doyle, who had hopped down from his perch on the corner of her desk at about the same time she was dumping the books. He too had expected Angel to walk through the door and probably didn't want to appear too relaxed after Angel had spent the better part of the evening in pursuit of the arcade demon. "Doyle, I don't believe it! This is Chelsea Monroe."

Doyle offered his hand, which the woman shook while he spoke. "A pleasure to make your acquaintance, Ms. Monroe. Any friend of Cordelia's, naturally, is a friend of mine."

"Doyle, you jackass," Cordelia said. "She's not my friend. She's Chelsea Monroe . . . from *L.A. After Dark.*" She stared at him, waiting for recognition to dawn. *Am I the only one in this entire firm who hears opportunity knocking?*

"Now you're just statin' the obvious."

Chelsea Monroe raised her hand to her mouth to cover a chuckle. She was model tall—obviously, since she'd been a runway model until three years ago—and wore an expensively tailored suit of shimmering gold that revealed a lot of cleavage and a lot of leg. Black heels and a matching clutch purse completed the outfit.

Cordelia sighed. "Doyle, if I lend you a dollar would you *please* buy your first clue. She's the host—hostess—of the television show."

"*L.A. After Dark?*" Doyle guessed, and Chelsea gave a brisk nod.

"Late night," Cordelia said. "Her local ratings are right up there with Leno and Letterman. Entertainment industry reports, exposés, studio confessions, insider gossip, club tours, everything. Any of this ringing a bell, Mr. Leprechaun?"

"No, but I'll take your word for it."

"Chelsea Monroe," Cordelia said again, with a wide grin and a shake of her head. "And you're here to do a story on me—I mean Angel. You are here to do a story on Angel, aren't you? It's about time this firm got some first-rate publicity." She frowned. "Wait—I said that last part out loud, didn't I?"

"Loud enough to make the neighbors pound on the walls," Doyle said, not above getting in his own little dig after the leprechaun comment. "If we had any neighbors."

Cordelia just ignored him and addressed Chelsea. "I'll warn you right up front about Angel. He's not much of a talker. World champion brooder, yes. But he's a vam—I mean, a man of few words. Take my advice and . . . draw him out a little. You won't be disappointed. He has presence, real presence."

"Actually I'm not here to *interview* Angel," Chelsea Monroe explained. "But I do have a proposition for him. Is he around?"

"He called not too long ago," Doyle said.

"To say he was heading back. Should be here any minute," Cordelia added, thinking, *Actually, we thought you were him.* "If you'd care to wait in his office, I could make you a cup of coffee or something."

"Spectacular," she said. "If you don't mind. I'll review my notes until he shows."

"It's a plan," Cordelia said.

Chelsea looked around the office. Cordelia cringed, seeing the dingy office through a stranger's eyes, all secondhand furniture and peeling file cabinets. But Chelsea just nodded. "I like the effect," she commented. "Period ambience. Really captures the whole noir private detective genre so well."

"That's exactly what we were going for," Cordelia said, immensely relieved. "Wasn't it, Doyle?"

"Oh, absolutely," Doyle agreed. "Spade, Marlowe. We're big fans."

Chelsea entered Angel's office, leaving the door open a bit.

Cordelia whispered to Doyle. "Did you notice? I'm sure it was Louis Vuitton."

"Louise who? Oh, you mean Chelsea Monroe's a stage name."

"No! I'm talking about her outfit. I have an eye for these things. Not that it does me any good, since I can't afford to buy clothes like that. Not that you'd care, but I'd swear that was a Prada bag."

"Not that I'd care, no," Doyle said. "Me, I'm interested in the real woman underneath all those fancy clothes."

"Leash your hormones for a minute," Cordelia said. "And tell me what you think she wants with Angel."

"Ha! Isn't he the one, having beautiful women stroll in off the street with propositions and such."

"Somebody talking about me?" Angel said, having entered the room so quietly neither one of them had heard a sound. Vampires could definitely *do* stealthy.

"Any luck?" Doyle asked.

Angel nodded. "I found out where the bugs go when you turn on the lights. Very big bugs. Sakorbuk demons, actually."

"I'm sure that's fascinating—and probably disgusting," Cordelia said. "But time out. Chelsea Monroe is here. She wants to talk to you."

The name wasn't registering on his face. "She had an appointment?"

Cordelia rolled her eyes at the hopelessness of it all. "Of course not. She's Chelsea Monroe!" Then she noticed his disheveled appearance. He had his coat draped over his arm, along with his spring-loaded stake contraptions. His gray pullover and black pants were torn and soiled with bits of garbage, some sort of white goo, and a clotting green fluid. And his hands were a foul mess of blood and goo as well.

"Look at you," Cordelia said. "You're a mess! A filthy, disgusting, and might I add, pungent mess."

Angel ignored her. "What should I know about this Chelsea person?"

Doyle jumped in. "That she's a remarkably beautiful woman with a proposition for you."

"A business proposition," Cordelia amended.

Doyle looked at her from under raised eyebrows. "And our boss here wouldn't be the first one to mix a little pleasure with his business."

"She's on TV, Angel! She wants to put us—you—on TV."

"True or not, I'd better get cleaned up before I talk to her." Angel dropped his stake gizmos on an empty chair and tossed the raincoat over them. Never know who might walk into the office. Then he pulled off his gray shirt, revealing his broad, though vampy-pale chest. "And I should probably burn this. Dry cleaners never seem to have much luck with beetle-demon brains."

He held the shirt out to Cordelia, who raised her hands in a clear "no way" gesture. She pushed a wastebasket out with her foot, refusing to get any closer to demon brain matter than was strictly necessary. Angel dropped the shirt into the wastebasket.

"Am I interrupting a business meeting?" Chelsea asked, leaning casually against the doorframe of Angel's office, one hand on her hip. "If so, I must congratulate myself on my impeccable timing." She strolled across the room, giving Angel a quick but thorough appraisal from head to toe and back up again. "I take it you're Angel?"

He nodded, looking a little like a deer in the headlights, if Cordelia was any judge.

Chelsea offered her expertly manicured hand. "Chelsea Monroe, *L.A. After Dark*."

As he was about to grasp her hand, Angel remembered its current condition, thought better of it, and retracted it. "Better wash up first."

"When something's worth waiting for," Chelsea said, "I'm a very patient woman."

Doyle leaned toward Cordelia and said, sotto voce, "Is this the part where she offers to scrub his back?"

Just as casually, Cordelia whispered, "Second date."

"Could you two keep Ms. Monroe entertained while—"

"Please, call me Chelsea," she interrupted. "Ms. Monroe is so formal, especially when one of us is half undressed."

"Right," Angel said. And cleared his throat. "Give me a few minutes. Cordelia, could you . . . ?"

"Oh, right, complete mind block," Cordelia said to Chelsea. "I totally forgot about your coffee."

After he'd gone downstairs to his private rooms, Chelsea commented. "Great physique. A little sun wouldn't hurt, though."

Loud enough so that only Cordelia caught it, Doyle muttered, "I seriously doubt that."

Five minutes later, Angel stepped into his office wearing a fresh burgundy shirt over black pants. His right hand was wrapped in white gauze, although he expected the pincer cuts to be completely healed by morning. As he settled into the chair behind his desk, he noticed Chelsea Monroe grinning at him, index finger poised against her lower lip. "What?" Angel asked, wondering if he'd missed a spot of green goo or Sakorbuk brains in his haste to clean up.

"Nothing," she said quickly, to put him at ease. "It's just that . . . you're nothing at all like what I pictured."

"Were you expecting a halo and a tiny set of wings?"

She laughed. "No, it's just that, this part of town, these . . . surroundings. I envisioned a sleazy, cynical, world-weary misanthrope in a rumpled raincoat. Maybe an ex-cop with a beer gut and a bad comb-over, chomping on a cigar, racing form tucked in his pocket, maybe late forties, early fifties."

First, you need to add about two hundred years, Angel thought. "Sorry I don't fit the stereotype." *No gun and not even an official private detective license, not that an* unofficial *license would accomplish much.* "Guess this means I don't get the part."

"No need to apologize. On the contrary, I'm delighted." She smiled warmly. "Oh, you'd be in real trouble if I were casting the role of private detective. But that's not why I'm here."

"Why, exactly, are you here?" Angel leaned back, head against intertwined fingers, relaxed.

"You're direct. I like that."

"Saves time."

"Oh, I couldn't agree more," she said, then took a sip of coffee while maintaining eye contact with him over the rim of her cup.

Angel had the impression they were talking about two entirely different things. *Maybe we are.* "How's the coffee?"

"It's . . ." She chuckled and shook her head. "Let's just say the coffee is exactly how I imagined it."

Angel quirked a smile. "Wouldn't want to disturb the natural order of things too much."

"Right," she said. "Terrible coffee can be comforting that way. But you obviously want to know why I'm here."

"As much as I'm enjoying your company," Angel said. "Yes."

"Here goes. *L.A. After Dark* is doing a special report for sweeps," Chelsea explained. "Sweeps are certain times during the year when ratings are very—"

"I'm familiar with the concept," Angel assured her.

"Right," she said. "Good. Well, needless to say, it's an important time for television shows. So this special is going to be called *Your Cheating Heart*, like the Hank Williams song." Angel nodded, he was following her so far. "We're looking for some provocative footage of spouses cheating on each other. Not exactly hidden cameras in hotel rooms. Nothing pornographic, just . . ."

"Provocative," Angel supplied.

"Exactly," she said. "Basically 'caught in the act' stuff without actually showing anyone engaged in the act, if you get my meaning."

Angel leaned forward, placed his elbows on his desk, hands curled together. "I understand," he replied. "I just don't see where I fit into this special report."

"We're hoping you and some of the other investigators we plan to contact can provide us with leads. Our crew will tag along on your surveillance."

"Not gonna happen."

She leaned forward, physically reducing the distance between them. "We are prepared to compensate you handsomely for your services and—"

"Compensation isn't the problem."

"We will also have your clients sign releases," she added quickly. "Or their faces will be digitized out on camera. Names will be protected. Rest assured, we're not interested in ruining lives over this."

"Points for you," Angel said dryly. He stood up. In his mind, the meeting was over.

As he walked around the desk, she rose and approached him. "Tell me what your concerns are," she said, placing her hand on his arm.

"Just another stereotype shattered," he said, glancing down at her hand. He could feel the warmth of her fingers through the cloth of his long-sleeved shirt. In her high heels, she was only an inch or two shorter than he was. Several inches taller than Buffy. *And why did I just make that comparison?* "I don't take on the type of cases you're interested in."

"If I sounded judgmental, I apologize. Everyone has to make a living."

"No apology necessary," Angel told her. "I'm just stating fact. Angel Investigations is not about catching cheating spouses in the act."

"Really?"

"Really."

She looked into his eyes for a moment, as if expecting to see evidence of a lie there. "You know what? I believe you."

"No reason you shouldn't," Angel said. "It's the truth."

"Okay," Chelsea replied. "Then I thank you for your time." Angel reached for the door. As he turned the knob, Chelsea reached out abruptly and held the door shut. "Mind if I ask you a question?"

"Why don't we have better coffee?"

She smiled and shook her head. "That is a good question, but not the one I had in mind. I was just wondering what Angel Investigations *is* about."

"We help the helpless," Angel replied.

"As simple as that?"

"It's never simple, but it's what we try to do. It's the reason we're here."

"Tell me, is it true what Cordelia said?"

Angel smiled. "That all depends on what Cordelia said."

"Right," Chelsea said, reading between the lines. "She said that you take on a lot of cases without getting paid."

"We *help* the helpless. We don't run credit checks on them."

"You see, that answers the other question."

"What other question?"

"Why the coffee is so horrible," she replied, releasing the door.

"Electricity or good coffee," Angel said. "Not a tough decision."

As they stepped into the reception area, she offered her hand, which he took. "Well, it has been a pleasure, Angel. Do you have a last name?"

"Just Angel," he said. "That seems to be enough."

"I'm sure it is."

Again he had the feeling they were talking about two different things. "Good luck with your special report."

"Thank you," Chelsea said and walked to the door. Before stepping out, she turned back, her expression thoughtful. Then she flashed a dazzling smile. "Don't be surprised if you haven't seen the last of me."

Before Angel could reply, she slipped out the door and was gone.

"That was interesting," Angel said, more to himself than to Doyle and Cordelia, who were both looking at him expectantly.

Cordelia said, "You know, I never really considered a job as an entertainment news reporter. But it could be glamorous. Don't you think?"

"Oh, she's a glamorous one, all right," Doyle said.

"Spill, Angel," Cordelia said. "When should we expect the camera crew in here? We'll have to work around—"

"There won't be any camera crew."

"What?" Cordelia's jaw was threatening to become unhinged. "Are you telling me you turned away Chelsea Monroe? You turned down *L.A. After Dark*? Angel, you can't buy that kind of publicity."

"For once I have to agree with Cordelia," Doyle said. "Would have been nice to get some traffic through that door. Other than the bill collectors, naturally."

"She's doing a story," Angel said, staring at the door even though Chelsea was long gone. He turned to Doyle and Cordelia, both standing near her desk. "It's not our kind of story."

"Guess you're right," Doyle said. "Can't very well shine television spotlights on the kind of cockroaches we have to deal with."

"I don't know," Cordelia said. "The way she was looking at you, Angel, she might have a completely different type of undercover story in mind."

Angel frowned. *What difference does it make*

what Chelsea wants? Angel thought. *I know what I can't afford.*

Being a vampire cursed with a soul also meant he was cursed with the memories of what he had been and done before his soul was restored, and what he had become again after experiencing a moment of true happiness with Buffy Summers, the Vampire Slayer. Though he was guilty of more crimes than a human being could atone for in a lifetime, he was not human. He was a vampire, and a vampire could live forever. He wondered again if that would be long enough to make amends.

Silently, Angel took the stairs down to his living quarters.

Cordelia looked innocently at Doyle. "What? What did I say?"

CHAPTER THREE

Jenna Kershaw, an attractive young woman with sandy hair, wore her blue silk blouse open to the third button, revealing a hint of cleavage and the merest suggestion of a lacy black bra, along with a knee-length pleated skirt. She sat comfortably on the white sofa, legs tucked back and crossed at the ankle.

In front of the sofa stood a large glass-topped coffee table, a serpentine twist of chrome piping its only support. Atop the table was an oversize volume promising incredible views of the world's greatest suspension bridges. Jenna figured if you'd seen one suspension bridge you'd seen them all.

Hanging near the living room window was a pair of anemic ferns, victims of improper direct or indirect lighting. Certainly she would never have claimed to have a green thumb.

Against the far wall stood a massive entertainment center with at least a dozen stereo components, including a VCR and a DVD player. A massive television set dominated the unit, its screen so large the life-sized people on it appeared to be one interdimensional portal away from invading West Hollywood. In the near corner, beyond the sofa, stood a small desk supporting a fashionable blueberry-colored computer.

Greg appeared, carrying two wineglasses and a bottle of white wine. "Your libation of choice."

"So I see."

He sat down on the sofa beside her and handed her a glass before setting the bottle down on the table. As he leaned back, he sighed easily, elbow resting on the low back of the sofa. Sporting a full head of wavy brown hair, he had pale green eyes, a long nose, and a meticulously trimmed mustache. He wore a gold chain under a green three-button pullover, khaki Dockers, and brown Rockports. *Mr. Casual,* she thought. Easy enough to believe he'd been in three beer commercials. Far easier to believe he was a valet at the Blue Fountain in Beverly Hills.

"I can't get over it," Greg said. "I watch the *Today* show every morning, and I swear, you're the spitting image of Katie Couric. But you probably get that all the time."

She took a sip of her wine. "Not as often as you'd

think." Indicating the suspension bridge book, she asked, "You actually read about bridges?"

"No. I just look at the pictures," he replied. "Actually, I'm between books right now. So tell me, what do you think of the entertainment center?" Without waiting for her to comment, he added, "Wait till I dim the lights and slide in a DVD. You'll swear we're in a theater."

She placed her glass carefully on the table, put a cool finger on his jaw and turned his head back toward her. "Greg, we're not in a theater."

"No, but it's the next best thing."

"Think for a minute, Greg," she said, curling her lips in a provocative smile. "What would be the *best* thing?"

Greg chuckled. "You're not talking about the movies anymore, are you?"

"Clever boy," she said.

He set his wineglass on the table beside hers. But instead of reaching out for her, as she was expecting, he twisted around and flipped open the padded arm of the sofa. From a hidden compartment, he fished out at least six infrared remote control units. "Marvels of the modern home," he said, using one remote to turn off the TV set, another to turn on the stereo receiver, equalizer, and CD player, and a third to dim the lights. A slow and romantic jazz instrumental began to play, and the placement and separation of the surround speakers made it seem as if they were on stage in the middle of an invisible combo. "I'm still looking for that killer universal remote."

Jenna slipped her hand inside the collar of his shirt, ran her fingers along the gold chain until she found the flat scorpion medallion hanging there. It had tiny diamond eyes and a ruby chip for a stinger. She inched closer to get a better look. Her knee pressed against his thigh.

"Like it?" he asked, a little short of breath.

"Mm-hmm." She looked up into his eyes. "Greg, what are you thinking right now?"

By way of reply, he leaned in close to her and kissed her lightly on the lips. "That, obviously."

"That was nice," she said, closing her eyes, waiting for him to kiss her again, knowing he would.

His left hand touched her knee, slid under the edge of her skirt as he leaned in again and kissed her deeply this time, sliding his right hand down to her waist. She opened her mouth for him, reaching up to place her hands around his neck, thumbs stroking his collarbone to find just the right angle.

Greg moaned softly as her tongue found its way into his mouth, pushing his own tongue back. Then his eyes opened wide in disbelief, and he started to gag. Before he could pull away, her fingernails dug painfully into his neck, chest, and back, holding him firmly in place. Her fingers became something else, something sharp, flexible, and long as they burrowed into his flesh. By then he could barely breathe. Her tongue and finger-tentacles were suctioning out everything the convulsing Mr. Casual had to offer.

His muscle mass shriveled, his lungs withered away, and his eyes pulled back into his skull even as his ligaments snapped and his skeleton collapsed into fine powder. And through it all, the frantic rush of sound as his life force was sucked from its mortal shell into a new receptacle.

In less than a minute it was over. Jenna's bloody tongue retracted, as did her slime-covered finger-tentacles. They whipped about as they shortened, speckling the white walls of the apartment with droplets of blood and bits of viscera. She stood, once again looking remarkably human and just as Greg had desired her. It was less physically demanding for her to simply retain the last human form.

"It really is the *best* thing, Greg." She slipped out of the apartment, almost glowing with the energy that suffused her so soon after absorbing the matter and essence of a human. This time she thought she might retain her substance long enough to walk all the way back to Elliot's place. Then again, the demon always felt invigorated right after an absorption. But it wasn't enough, would never be enough, until the ritual cycle was completed.

* * *

Ever since her second husband, Ben, had passed away, Lois Laulicht had had trouble sleeping. She managed to make ends meet, living off the widow's share of his pension and the rental income from the tenants in the renovated apartment house she owned and called home. It would have been more than enough had it not been for the second mortgage Ben had taken out on the place a few years before his death. As it was, she had to be careful with her spending and avoid extravagance.

Ben had lived long enough to see the renovations completed but not long enough to reap the rewards of the higher rents. Someday the second mortgage would be settled and she wouldn't have to worry so much. Yet she often wondered if she would live to enjoy those carefree days.

When she had trouble sleeping, she would take to the hallways, leaving her first-floor apartment behind as she climbed the stairs and moved, quiet as a ghost, through the building that had been Ben's life's work. Most of her tenants were young, for she loved to be surrounded by the vitality of youth. Somehow they made her feel just a little bit younger herself. Not that her nocturnal wanderings were meant to spy on her young tenants. No, on her late night walks, it was Ben she sought. Seeing his hand in all the loving details of paint, paneling, wallpaper, and baluster soothed her nerves, made sleep fall within her grasp again, if only for one more night.

As Lois climbed the stairs to the third-floor apartments, she noticed something out of place. Dim lighting spilled across the hallway, reaching the top of the stairs and coming from the open door of apartment 300B.

That was Greg's apartment, Lois reminded herself, and Greg often entertained late at night. "Greg," she called, padding down the hall in her fuzzy bathrobe and floppy slippers. It wasn't like him to leave his door unlocked, let alone standing open. While her own generation had been unafraid to sleep with the doors unlocked and the windows open to catch the slightest breeze, Greg's generation had learned fear and caution at an early age. They welcomed powerful computers into their homes, watched in expectant awe as the riddle of the human genome was solved, yet they never forgot there were predators, human monsters roaming among them, ready to strike the weak, the defenseless, and the unwary.

Lois pushed open the door and heard instrumental music playing softly on the fancy stereo as she stepped into the dim lighting of 300B. "Greg," she called again. Then in a louder, more assured voice, "Greg, are you okay, dear?"

Her gaze was drawn to the bottle of wine and the pair of wineglasses on the coffee table. *So he* was *entertaining,* she concluded. Then she saw a pile of clothes lying on the floor in front of the sofa. *Dear heavens! What if they've retired to the bedroom?*

Deciding to back out of the apartment quietly and close the door behind her to avoid an embarrassing scene, Lois happened to notice something near the clothing, something . . . hairy.

With a cautious glance down the short hallway to the bedroom, she strode quickly to the coffee table to have a closer look at the hair. It sprouted above the collar of a green shirt. She dropped to one knee, determining that there was only one set of clothes on the floor, an outfit she'd seen Greg wearing several times. With trembling hands, she lifted the mound of hair and realized it was attached to something shriveled and translucent, which was stretching out of the collar of the shirt. A gold necklace with a scorpion medallion clinked, and fine powder sifted down from the . . . skin! It was Greg's hair that she held in her hands, she realized, and attached to the gray-streaked hair was his eyeless face, skin as thin as wax paper, stretching like warm taffy.

Lois screamed and kept screaming until Trish from 300A came to investigate and called the police.

With Angel downstairs in his living quarters, Cordelia had removed the hefty library books from her bottom desk drawer, stacking them one on top of the other on the corner of the desk.

A few more books, Doyle thought, *and the whole desk will tip over.* He grabbed one from the top of the pile, saw that it now sported a few bumps and nicks as a result of Cordelia's rough treatment, and flipped through it. He shook his head. "How can they possibly use the words 'made easy' in the title of a book over a thousand pages long."

"True, this is not exactly beach reading."

"I'd say they'd be a fine cure for insomnia if just looking at them didn't give me a thunderin' head—"

Doyle dropped the book and pressed the heel of his hand hard against his forehead. *Pain!* Overwhelming and sudden. He staggered back, eyes clenched shut as a vision, courtesy of the Powers That Be, nearly knocked him off his feet. Wouldn't be the first time. Images flashed though his mind faster than he could process them, leaving him breathless and stunned.

As abruptly as it had begun, the vision ended. Cordelia was at his side, steadying him on weak legs. He could smell her perfume. Jasmine. For the moment, at least, he was too rattled to entertain any pleasant thoughts about Cordelia. He let her help him to a chair.

"That's gotta hurt," Cordelia commented.

"You'll never know . . ." Doyle said. "Sorry I dropped your book."

"Lucky you missed your toe," Cordelia said. "I found that one on a shelf in the blunt-instrument aisle."

"Better hide it again, Cordelia," Doyle said. "I need to talk to Angel."

"Yeah, I pretty much figured it was the whole bat signal thing again."

Sitting at the computer desk in his bedroom, Elliot faced the fact that he wasn't much of a hacker, nor was he much of a programmer. All the cheese curls and cola in the world weren't going to make him something he was not. He'd suffered derision throughout his teen years despite his sure and certain knowledge that he was destined for great things. *Screw 'em all,* he'd often told himself. *Someday, when I'm rich and famous, they'll come crawling to me for a job.* Problem was, he would never become rich and famous on his own merits, and he wasn't about to luck his way into it since he never played the lottery. All that life, school, and endless days of torment inflicted on him by his so-called peers had prepared him for was beating the final boss in Super Dragonoid: The Ultimate Challenge.

Ultimate challenge, my ass, he thought. So he beta-tested a video game here and there. What had it gotten him except more video games? The Web sites that actually paid for reviews or tips paid so little it felt like charity work for the game-playing dweebs who couldn't even beat a level-one boss.

Now he was in his mid-twenties and stuck in a rut. Just about every paycheck he received from CompAmerica he spent on computer equipment purchased through his employee discount. Even after the discount, the bastards were still making money off him. He recalled with mixed feelings that fateful day when everything had changed, when an agonizing moment of humiliation at work had led to violent frustration and a sweet bit of inspiration.

Trudy Ryan, a nineteen-year-old redhead with a pale complexion and a fine spray of freckles over the bridge of her nose, had been a cashier at CompAmerica for less than a week when Elliot decided to ask her out. No easy thing. He'd been sneaking glimpses of her, waiting for just the right opportunity, since the day she started. She had seemed friendly enough, with an easy smile for everyone. Fooled him into thinking he actually had a shot. The day came when Elliot noticed a lull at the checkout lines just as Bernardo, the store manager, stepped outside for a cigarette break. With an armful of closeout items destined for the bargain bin, Elliot approached Trudy as she flipped through the pages of *People* magazine with only casual interest. After a few minutes of awkward small talk, Elliot mustered enough courage to ask the cute redhead if she'd care to have a burger with him and maybe catch a movie afterward.

In a sickening instant, Trudy's easy smile became a sneer. "Wait a minute. You're asking me out on a date?"

Elliot's burden of discontinued items shifted in

his arms. A generic box of floppy disks fell to the tile floor with a loud thud. "Only a movie."

"Sorry, Elliot, you're just not my type."

Elliot had to press. "So what *is* your type?"

"Non-losers."

"You don't even know me."

"What's to know?" she said. "Look in a mirror. Hop on a scale."

Bitch, Elliot thought, but bit his tongue.

"Get away from me, creep, before I charge you with sexual harassment."

Red-faced, Elliot flung the discounted merchandise into the wide bin and stormed off to the back of the store. Fifteen minutes later, while carrying a computer monitor box from the warehouse to the store shelf, he let out a scream of frustration and rage and tossed the box across the aisle, toppling and busting a computer system that had been running a game demo. Glass shattered, sparks flew, and Elliot kicked the debris.

Elliot heard Bernardo, the manager, shouting as he ran to the aisle. That was when inspiration struck. He clutched his back, cried out in fake pain, and staggered into a shelf. To add a bit of dramatic flair to his performance, he swept two dozen modems off a neatly stacked shelf.

Crippling back injury. Oh, yeah. He'd fooled them all. Even Bernardo. So for a while at least, he'd stepped out of the rat race, collecting disability checks in the bargain.

It was during Elliot's life time-out that the demon had begun to visit his dreams. The appearances were no more than dreams, Elliot thought initially. But then the voice began coming to him during the day, during his hours at the computer. And the demon voice made him an offer—an incredible offer. Maybe it wasn't too late for him to achieve fame and fortune after all. There was more than one way to reach the finish line. As the old adage said, when opportunity knocks . . .

Somebody was knocking on his door.

Elliot stopped typing, wondering for a moment if it was the police. No way they could tie the murders to him—obviously, since he wasn't responsible; the demon was. Let them try to arrest a demon! "Ha!" he said aloud.

More knocking, a little louder this time.

Elliot's attention was drawn to something on his keyboard, wedged down between the *Q* and the *A*. He reached in and grabbed it, realizing belatedly that it was a complete fingernail, his fingernail. It had fallen off his little finger, just like that. The skin where it had been was dry and smooth. And now that he examined his left hand, he noticed the fingernail on the ring finger had moved laterally. A little pulling and it lifted off, just like what happened to the guy in the remake of *The Fly*, but without the goo. "What the hell . . . ?"

"Anybody home?" a voice called from the hall, a woman's voice.

Elliot walked out of the bedroom, closing the door behind him, and yelled, "Just a minute." He crossed to the bathroom, opened the medicine cabinet, and took out two Band-Aids. After crumpling up the paper trash, he tossed it toward the small wicker wastebasket—and missed. With a silent curse, he strode to the door and looked through the peephole. "Oh, wonderful," he whispered sarcastically to himself.

He removed the chain and pulled the door open. "Hi, Shirley."

Shirley Blodgett was, in Elliot's eyes, plain-looking. Nothing hideous about her, but she seemed to go out of her way to look, well, plain. The most she ever did with her naturally frizzy hair was slip a headband over it. Never wore makeup because, she said, she was allergic. She had never had her ears pierced because the thought of the pain was "too much to bear." Never mind that five-year-olds had no problem lining up to have their ears pierced. Even Shirley's clothes were plain. She wore flannel or cotton shirts, sleeve length varying by season. The one time he'd seen her wearing a sleeveless shirt at work, he'd caught a glimpse of her bra and hadn't been surprised to see it was basic white. She also tended to favor cargo pants except on the hottest days, when she put on shorts—Bermuda-length, naturally. He couldn't remember ever having seen her in a dress or skirt.

In addition to living in the apartment beneath him—she'd been the one to tip him off when his unit became available—she still worked at CompAmerica, so it was necessary to keep up the fiction of his back injury whenever she dropped by his place. And she was always finding excuses to stop by. This time she was carrying a tall blue vase sprouting an assortment of flowers whose names, if told, he would never remember.

"Hi, Elliot!" In her perkiest voice, no less.

"What's the occasion?"

"I stopped at the Friendly Gift Shop after work and picked these up for you," she said, hoisting the vase higher, as if he might not otherwise notice.

"I can see that," he said bluntly. "Why?"

"To brighten up your apartment." She sidestepped him, entering his apartment without invitation. He rolled his eyes as she walked toward the kitchen. "And to add a little woman's touch to the place."

"It won't work," he said after closing the door and following her. "I'm bad with plants. I'll forget to water them. Or water them too much. They'll die. You'll cry. I'll feel bad. Spare me the inevitable guilt trip and take them down to your place where they'll receive all the love and attention they so richly deserve."

She laughed. "Stop being silly. They won't be a problem. They're silk."

"Silk? Then they probably need bottled water or something. I can't afford that on disability."

"No, you goof," she said, putting them in the center of his small, round kitchen table and fluffing them a bit. "They'll just sit here and look lovely. All you need to do is dust them every week or two." She turned to face him, smiling. "Think you can manage that, Grundy?"

"Well, I'm not completely helpless."

She sat down in one of the two wicker-backed kitchen chairs. "How's your back, Elliot?"

"Still sore," he replied and, as if to demonstrate, rubbed it with the knuckles of his right hand.

She shook her head. "When I first heard you'd hurt your back, I couldn't believe it."

For a moment he thought she was accusing him of faking the injury, but how could she know? It wasn't like he was moving furniture on the weekends or taking tango lessons. He hardly ever left his apartment, so unless the management had installed hidden cameras, he felt safe in his ruse. "Hey, those seventeen-inch monitors are way heavy," he said, to fill the silence if nothing more. "Accidents are bound to happen."

"Well, everyone always asks me how you're doing," she commented. "Because, you know, you live right above me."

Elliot seriously doubted if Trudy, for one, looked forward to his return. "Right," he said. "Only makes sense they'd ask you." *Sure,* Elliot thought bitterly, *I can hear them now: "So, Shirley, how's that loser Grundy these days?"*

Shirley nodded. "They know we're not soul mates or anything like that. Just because we work at the same store, live in the same apartment building, and have the same exact birthday."

"Well, you're the one who told me about the apartment," Elliot pointed out. "The birthday thing is just coincidence."

"Kinda freaky, though," Shirley remarked. "Like fate was drawing us together."

"I totally believe in free will," Elliot said.

Shirley stood up, looked around the room as a way of avoiding eye contact. "I'm sure they know we've never even been out on a date."

"You bet," Elliot said, quick to agree with her.

She nodded. "Well, if all's well, I'll head back downstairs. Let me know if you need anything. I can always—"

A familiar pain flared in Elliot's head.

A crash sounded from the bedroom.

"What was that?" Shirley asked.

She thinks I have somebody in there, Elliot realized. That wasn't a charade he wanted to create or maintain. Better she think he was simply up here alone all the time. Made it easier to play on her sympathy for the occasional errand. "Oh, that's—just a computer game. I guess I forgot to hit Pause when you knocked. My guy probably just got blown away."

"Oh, good," Shirley said. "I mean, not good on your guy getting blown away, but good on the nothing broken in there."

Elliot had to get rid of her. The demon had returned, and it might not realize he had a visitor. "You know, standing around is making my back throb," Elliot said. "I'd better turn off the computer and get some rest. But, hey, thanks for the flowers." As he talked he was ushering her toward the door. Since she'd been about to leave anyway, it was a simple matter of her following him.

"Hope they cheer you up," she said as he was closing the door. "And get some rest. I hate to see you suffering."

"Thanks," he called through the closed door, turning the dead bolt and attaching the chain.

Elliot hurried to the bedroom to confront his demon.

CHAPTER FOUR

Even with Shirley gone, Elliot shut the door as he entered his bedroom. The demon had reappeared on the far side of the bed, knocking over a table lamp. "Who's out there?" the demon asked, an incongruously deep voice rumbling out of the mouth of the woman form he had assumed for the evening's kill. Around Elliot, the demon used minimal glamour.

"Just Shirley from downstairs," Elliot said dismissively. "She's like a dog with a bone. Just because we have the same birthday she thinks it means something special or gives her the right to drop in unannounced and pester me." Elliot shook his head, as if the motion would dislodge her from his thoughts. He walked around the bed to set the lamp in place. "How'd it go?"

"I was successful."

Elliot edged past the demon, who still looked a lot like the national morning show news anchor even if his—oh, what the hell, *her*—hands were becoming spatulate. "Really? I mean, this won't go on forever, will it?"

"No, Elliot," the demon said. "When the cycle is complete, the ritual is over. I am nearing the end. My powers are returning in full. Once more I can sense any displeasure they have with my appearance and alter it at will. When I walk among them now, I sense their desires. They look at me and see what they want to see. I become what they want me to be, and so they become my natural prey again, even though I only have substance borrowed from you. Just imagine my powers when they are undiluted, when I am re-spawned."

"You know, I'm still a little vague on the 'borrowing of substance' aspect to all this."

"Simply this. Before we made our pact, our bond, I was but a detached psyche, raging thoughts without form. Now, when I need to manifest on this plane," the demon said, holding up arms that had become clay-like and dull, "I draw upon your physicality, literally borrowing *substance* from you."

"That's when I get the headaches?" Elliot asked. "And nausea?"

The demon nodded. "The temporary, though partial, loss of some of your essence creates a strain on your mortal body. And so, when I vanish, relinquishing your borrowed substance, you experience relief."

Elliot glanced down at his fingers, the ones missing fingernails. "And no permanent . . . side effects?"

"Any discomfort or . . . irregularities you suffer will not be permanent."

"Okay. So you borrow substance from me, then give it back when you fade out. But what happens to the bodies you consume, absorb, whatever?"

"With each absorption, my magical power grows more potent and I am able to retain physical form for longer periods. Once the ritual cycle is complete, I will attain new physical form on your plane. I'll have my own body, nothing borrowed—a permanent and powerful body even more powerful than my previous one."

"Okay, that's what happens when we finish the cycle. In the meantime, where do you keep all the substance you've absorbed? In a mystical meat locker somewhere?"

"The mechanism of the cycle is beyond your ken, Elliot. Just know that the substance acquired from my victims is held within the bonds of my magic, preserved until the cycle reaches . . . what is the human expression? Critical mass."

An unaccustomed feeling of regret overcame Elliot. "That's why you need so many victims?"

"Humans are weak, mortal creatures. Is it any

wonder I require the substance of many of your kind to construct a new vessel for myself? All twelve signs are required to complete the ritual cycle."

It would have been pointless to turn back, Elliot realized. The demon stared at him and Elliot wondered, not for the first time, if it could read his thoughts or simply sense his doubt.

"To prove the ceremony is progressing, Elliot," the demon said, "I will sense the person you desire and assume that form."

"That's disgusting," Elliot said, then thought he might have offended the demon. "Besides, what's the point? I know it's a sham. So thanks, but no thanks. I'll wait for the real thing."

More disgusting were the demon's sagging features, like a wax sculpture left too close to an open flame. Its eyeballs dripped like gray sludge down its cheeks, and the nose was collapsing into sagging, distorted lips. Usually by the time the demon returned to Elliot's apartment it had already returned to its pale, waxy state, a featureless man-shaped thing that shambled more than walked, sparing Elliot the stomach-turning dissolution from human to horror. Fortunately, the demon said, "I will rest now."

Beauty rest. That was how Elliot thought of it. After an absorption the demon had to magically process the life matter and life force of his latest victim. Each time he returned, it was with greater physical definition. Before the first few kills, the waxy features constantly ran, lips forming, melting, and re-forming. Now it could, at least, reach a stasis point, unchanging if bland. Not a real body of its own, yet better control of the substance he borrowed from Elliot. "Pleasant dreams, big guy," Elliot said as he returned to his computer.

Wind swirled in the room, scattering papers on the computer desk. The demon's form contracted, withering away with the speed of time-lapse photography until finally it winked out of existence with a loud pop.

Elliot felt his headache begin to ease. But his room smelled of ozone and something sour, a stench he'd come to associate with the demon. *Just gut it out a little while longer,* he told himself. *Then you'll have everything you ever wanted. Everything the demon promised.*

Angel arrived at 2707 Flair Avenue in West Hollywood less than thirty minutes after the police and less than fifteen minutes after Detective Kate Lockley of the LAPD. Most nights this would have been a quiet, subdued residential neighborhood. Not tonight. Angel counted three patrol cars with squawking radios, lights strobing the night in alternating swaths of red and blue. An ambulance had pulled into the driveway, and a coroner's station wagon was currently double-parked. A crime scene van had found a parking space on the opposite side of the street. In front of the crime scene van was a large news van with the mast of its microwave dish fully extended. Camera light in her face, a reporter looked as if she was ready to go live with a report.

While a small crowd had gathered in the street, other residents stood expectantly by their front doors. Angel parked his convertible a discreet distance from the gathering of official vehicles.

A small shingle attached to an old-fashioned streetlamp proclaimed 2707 Flair as the Coast View Apartments. If someone climbed to the roof of the three-story structure on a clear day, there was an outside chance that he might glimpse the coastline. Technically not false advertising. Still . . .

As Angel turned up the walkway, he saw Kate talking to two paramedics, one an intense looking young black woman, the other a lanky white man who looked as if he'd been on the job a few too many years. Angel had no need of acute vampire hearing to catch Kate's half of the conversation: "That damn body doesn't move till I say it moves. Understood?" The paramedics nodded vigorously.

A young patrolman intercepted Angel, catching him by the upper arm. "You live here, pal?" Angel shook his head. "Then move along."

Angel caught Kate's eye. "Let him through, Tompkins. But keep the press out of the building. I don't want them talking to anybody until we're done."

As the EMTs returned to their ambulance, Kate turned to Angel. "Been monitoring police scanners?" Kate came from a cop family and compensated for her good looks, blond hair, and blue eyes with a hard no-nonsense attitude.

"Not as a rule," Angel replied. "And not tonight."

"You have no business here, Angel. This is a crime scene. So who told you about it?"

"Let's just say I received an anonymous tip." *From the Powers That Be.*

"Why are you here?"

"To help."

"What makes you think we need your help?"

"You have no idea what you're dealing with here." In his fleeting vision, Doyle had seen the discarded skin of the victim, the shingle with the apartment name on it and something with tentacles or snakes growing out of its arms and mouth. Angel leaned forward and whispered. "What kind of killer leaves behind empty human skin?"

"How do you . . . ? We've never released—"

"So this isn't the first victim?"

"No," she whispered. "What else do you know?"

"First let me see the murder scene," Angel countered.

"Not gonna happen."

Angel shrugged, turned around and walked

toward his car. "Okay, then, I'll let you figure it out."

"Wait," she said. "I'll show you. Then you tell me everything."

"Everything," Angel replied. Unfortunately, he'd already told her as much as he knew. But he'd literally placed his foot in the door. No backing out now.

Kate led the way up the stairs to 300B. Along the stairwell, police were urging people to wait in their apartments until the detectives were ready to question them. Nearby, a beat cop stood with a young blond woman in the doorway to 300A. Across the hall, beyond the view of the interior of 300B stood an older woman in a bathrobe, face pale, hands trembling. Two policemen waited with her. "That's Lois Laulicht," Kate informed him. "Landlady. She found the corpse. Said the door was open. Went in to see if everything was all right. It wasn't." Kate nodded toward the other woman. "Neighbor. Patricia McGonigle. Heard the landlady screaming. Found her kneeling beside the body. Called 911."

Kate paused at the door to 300B and said, "Hands in your pockets, Angel. Look. Don't touch. Crime scene unit is still going over the place." Angel nodded, and she led him into the large living room of the apartment.

One crime scene technician was dusting two wineglasses and a bottle for fingerprints, another two were using a tape measure and sketch pad to record the dimensions of the apartment, while a fourth was taking close-up photos of the sofa, making notes in a small notebook after each shot.

Angel smelled the blood before he noticed the spray of bright red droplets across the back cushions of the sofa. He turned around and examined the wall, speckled with more drops of blood. *There should be more blood,* he thought. *A lot more.*

Blocking his view of the corpse was a tall, gaunt man in a charcoal-gray pinstriped suit. In one hand he held a small black bag; with the other he rubbed the gray stubble on his jaw. He shook his head and walked away, revealing the body. Or rather what was left of the human body. Remains . . . Remains seemed a particularly appropriate term in this instance.

"Our latest victim," Kate said. "We believe it is the tenant, Greg Schauer, thirty-four, single, no roommate, valet at the Blue Fountain in Beverly Hills, supposedly acted in a beer commercial or two."

"Believe?"

"Well, there's not a whole lot left on which to base an I.D. No face, no teeth to check dental records. We should be able to lift fingerprints from the . . . skin, but unless he was arrested previously or served in the military there would be nothing on file. Of course we can compare those prints to what we find elsewhere in the apartment, eventually get a DNA match. We do know those are Mr. Schauer's clothes, according to the landlady."

Angel crouched down beside the body, technically, the skin of Greg Schauer. And a lot of hair attached to the scalp. "Thirty-four?"

Kate double-checked her notebook. "That's what I got. Of course, we're in L.A. Everybody lies about their age. Why?"

"Lot of gray hair for a thirty-four-year-old."

"Landlady commented on that," Kate replied. "Said it looks like his wavy brown hair, but the gray is definitely new."

"Of course, whatever did *this* to him could have made his hair turn gray."

"Whatever?" Kate asked. "Don't you mean 'whoever'?"

"Whatever," Angel repeated, as if conceding the point.

Angel stared at the translucent skin poking out of the shirt and pant cuffs, out of the collar of the green shirt. And noticed something else: a fine white powder sifting down through the nubs in the carpeting. Even as people walked around the floor, tiny granules, finer than grains of sand, trickled down between the fibers. He glanced up at Kate. "What do you know about this powder?"

She shrugged. "First we thought it was drugs. Possible motive for the killings. We've had the samples from other crime scenes analyzed."

"Not narcotics," Angel guessed. "Human bones."

"We've kept the details from the press. Far as

they know, this was just a series of unrelated murders. But sooner or later they'll find out. And won't that be a circus."

"Can we talk somewhere?"

"Do we have something to talk about?"

Angel nodded once.

"I'll be a couple hours interviewing the landlady and the tenants."

"After that?"

She wrote an address on the back of one of her business cards. "Meet me here in two hours. I'll give you fifteen minutes."

By the time Angel left the Coast View Apartments, two more news vans had descended on the scene. Angel didn't envy Kate her task of keeping the details of the murders from the press. Too many people had seen the victims. Somebody would talk. Not that it mattered. Nobody would believe the details. And while traditional police wisdom dictated that some details be kept from the press to separate the real culprit from the handful of disturbed individuals who would falsely confess to the crime, that wouldn't help here. No way a human killer could have *shelled* a human being, leaving behind a complete, discarded skin like a candy wrapper, a skin still inside its clothes and filled with powdered bones. But if Angel hoped to pursue the case with Kate's help, he had to give her a rational explanation, something that would make sense to her and her superiors.

Angel sat in a rear booth at Shea's Tavern, tapping Kate's card on the mahogany table, an untouched glass of Killian's Red in front of him. He'd had to order something, and Shea's was fresh out of O negative. Not that he'd asked, but it was a reasonable assumption.

Kate came in, looking the worse for wear, and called out a greeting to the bartender before slipping into the booth with Angel. "Lucky me," she said. "I had to catch the first *skinny* murder. Next thing I'll be winning the Irish Sweepstakes."

"Any leads?"

"Guesses," she said. "Serial killer. Gangs or cults into flaying or cannibalism. Maybe an organ-theft ring."

"Connections between the victims?"

"All but one was single. We think that one was cheating on her husband. So what are your thoughts on Mr. Schauer's demise?"

"No forced entry," Angel said. "Two wineglasses. Stereo on. He was entertaining."

"Probably. Go on."

"What—whoever killed him was fast."

"Why do you say that?"

"No sign of a struggle. Glasses undisturbed. Killed right where he sat, probably before he knew what hit him."

"Okay."

"He brought the killer into his home," Angel said. "Willingly. So whoever it was appeared to be someone Schauer knew or someone he thought he could trust."

Kate nodded. "And since the victims apparently didn't know one another, we're still leaning toward multiple perps."

"There's more you're not telling me, isn't there? About the killer's appearance?"

She pointed to his glass. "You're not drinking this?" He shook his head, motioned her to take it. She took a sip. "Some of the killings have occurred near where the killer met the victim. Public places—bars, clubs, coffee places. We found witnesses who saw a couple of the victims leave with the killers."

"Plural?"

"One victim and one perp each time. But not the same perp." She took another sip and nodded. "Which is what led us initially to suspect possible gang or cult involvement. Multiple perps, same M.O."

Angel believed it was all the work of one demon, which led him to the inevitable conclusion. "The witnesses gave different descriptions of the killer."

"Yes," Kate said, watching him curiously. "That's what I said."

"You said one perp at each location," Angel

replied. "But the eyewitnesses at each place gave different descriptions of the *same* perp."

"Let me clue you in," Kate said. "Eyewitnesses are generally unreliable. Stress, panic, false memory conveniently filling in the gaps." Despite her doubts about eyewitnesses, Kate seemed unsettled by this aspect of the crimes.

"The victims were male and female, weren't they?"

"That's another guess, right?"

"But I'm right."

She sighed heavily. "Yes. And the eyewitness accounts are totally screwed up. Vastly different heights, hair colors, dress, even sex. Must be some kind of mass hysteria, group hypnosis, mentalism." She shook her head, disgusted.

"Mentalism?" Angel asked with a wry smile.

"We've found no evidence of psychotropic agents, so, yes, I'm grasping at straws," Kate confessed. "The eyewitnesses couldn't be more confusing if they'd formed a conspiracy to obstruct the investigation . . . Hey, now, there's an idea we haven't pursued."

"Kate," Angel began grimly, "you're looking for a monster—"

Kate arched an eyebrow. "A monster?"

"A *human* monster," Angel amended. "Or monsters, the likes of which you've never encountered before. I want to help you find him . . . or them."

"Again, what makes you think I need your help with this?"

"Are you any closer to finding the killer?"

Kate cleared her throat and glanced away briefly. That was answer enough. He continued, "I want to stop this guy as much as you do, but I have my own methods, different methods."

"Illegal methods?"

"Not necessarily. My connections won't talk to the police, but they will talk to me."

Kate quirked a wry grin. "After some friendly coercion?"

"Proper motivation."

"What exactly do you have in mind?"

"I need the case files."

Kate sighed and shook her head. "No. Sorry, Angel. Not on this case." She slid out of the booth and walked out of Shea's without looking back.

Angel crumpled her card in his hand. "Damn."

The next morning, Cordelia had two of the computer books open on her desk and was shaking her head as Doyle sat in a chair facing her. "What is it now, then?" he asked, a mildly sarcastic look on his angular features.

"Isn't java supposed to be coffee?"

"Ready to abandon the Web project?"

Cordelia frowned at him. "No way. We have a chance here to make contact with the millions of people out there who are glued to their computers."

"All those millions, shunning human contact," Doyle remarked with a shake of his head. "I'll never understand it. Call me old-fashioned, if you like, but I want to interface with a *face,* not a hunk of plastic and glass."

"Climb out of the Dark Ages, Munchkin man."

"That's *leprechaun,*" Doyle said. "And either way, I don't appreciate the insult."

Kate stormed into the office, looking perturbed and a little worn around the edges. She carried a box brimming with manila case folders. "Is he in?" she asked without preamble.

"Why, good morning, Kate," Cordelia said, flashing her most appealing and insincere smile.

"That's a matter of opinion," Kate said. "Well?"

Cordelia pointed to the closed office door. "Brooding ahead. Proceed with caution."

"Whatever." Kate walked into Angel's office unannounced.

"What's gotten into her?" Cordelia asked Doyle.

"Not enough shut-eye, that's for sure."

Angel looked up from the *L.A. Times,* which he'd been examining for more information on the bizarre murders, as Kate entered his office. Before he could even rise to greet her, she dropped a box of case folders on his desk. "These are copies," she declared, "but I'll want them back. All of them. Don't make me regret this, Angel."

"I won't."

"I forgot to mention one thing that put us on the whole cult angle. One of the bodies was missing." She held up a hand to stop the obvious question. "We found a pile of clothes in an alley, along with personal effects, white . . . the bone powder, and a few patches of torn skin. For God only knows what sick purpose, somebody wanted those remains."

"Wanted?" Angel wondered. "Or needed?"

CHAPTER FIVE

Several years ago an earthquake had brought down the roof of the Trinity United Methodist Church and the congregation had raised money to rebuild it. Three years later a fire gutted the church. Citing severe structural issues, building inspectors had officially and unceremoniously condemned it. Someday the congregation hoped to rebuild again, but the shell of the church was still waiting to be razed and it appeared, for all intents and purposes, that enthusiasm had waned.

Presently the outer structure consisted of four stone walls, the merest suggestion of a roof, and graffiti-smeared plywood windows. All the stained glass had either been destroyed in the fire or removed for safekeeping. Exhibiting various stages of water or fire damage were several rows of pews bolted to a mostly unsound floor. A charred pulpit and sanctuary overlooked a wobbly altar rail. For those inclined to embrace the ironic, as were the members of the Brotherhood of Vishrak, it represented the perfect location to bind a demon.

Vincent 74 had a shock of white hair, weathered features, and a neatly trimmed salt-and-pepper beard. He wore, as did all those present, a floor-length hooded black cloak with a blood-red lining. Black was the color for an existence, by necessity, in the shadows. Until the glorious day when they successfully bound a Vishrak demon, they were forbidden to wear the red side facing out. Once they had a demon under their control, they would emerge from the shadows and rule supreme.

As most senior brother, Vincent was in charge until the Omni arrived from San Francisco. The San Francisco Omni was the Brother longest alive, having taken the blood rite in 1939, if the rumors could be believed. Even without seniority, the Omni would have commanded the Brotherhood based on his office alone.

While Vincent waited anxiously in the middle of the nave, the others talked softly inside the altar rail, gathered around the makeshift altar. "Altar" sounded more impressive than "particle-board banquet table." The Brotherhood of Vishrak needed to be mobile, and once its folding legs were snapped up, the table fit easily into Willem 94's Taurus station wagon. Because of the accumulated heat of the three dozen black candles scattered throughout the sanctuary, all of the brothers had pushed their hoods back. All except Dora 99, their newest member, inexplicably a sister in the Brotherhood. Not that there were any written rules or guidebooks, just centuries-long tradition. However, Dora had been very generous with her favors and had been permitted to join through popular acclaim. Most times she kept her hood up to achieve some form of gender blending, but in this instance the raised hood actually drew unwanted attention to her.

Noticing Vincent's scrutiny, Dora left the group and approached him. "I've never seen an Omni before," she said excitedly, placing her hand on his arm.

"Be patient," Vincent 74 said, careful to remove her hand. He assumed she was trying to align herself with the most powerful member of their circle. "You will witness wonders this night." Vincent left her, walking down the nave to be alone. Dora trailed after him for a few steps, then squealed as a rat poked its twitching snout around the end of a splintered pew.

The rodents tended to congregate, appropriately enough, in the sanctuary or near the altar rail, simply because of the accumulation of junk-food wrappers and fast-food bags tossed aside by the cult members in the past couple days. Albert 97, who detested rats, had brought a baseball bat with him tonight. Occasionally, a loud *thwock* would ring out from the general vicinity of the charred pulpit, usually followed by a frustrated curse. It seemed the rats' reflexes were more than adequate to the challenge of Albert's batting speed.

Vincent stood alone in the cobweb-festooned narthex. After more than twenty-five years of faithful service in the Brotherhood of Vishrak, this would be the first time he'd ever witnessed, even indirectly, an Omni performing the re-spawning naming ritual.

Vincent's breath caught in his throat as a charcoal-gray BMW sedan pulled into the weed-strewn parking lot. A bald man in a black suit stepped out of the car, a black cloak rolled up under his arm. As the man approached the front entrance of the church, Vincent tugged open the wooden door hanging crookedly in its frame.

"Ah, Vincent, it has been a while," the Omni said as he slipped through the gap. Although it was forbidden to speculate about personal information within the Brotherhood, Vincent had overheard a rumor that the Omni was a partner in a successful law firm.

"Nearly three years."

"And now our time has come at last."

"We have patiently awaited your arrival, Omni."

Thwock! "Damn rats!" Albert yelled from the interior.

"Some more patiently than others, it would seem," the Omni replied with a frown. "Hold this." The man handed Victor a wooden case that had been wrapped within his cloak. Victor was curious to know what the Omni had brought for the ceremony, but he would never have dared to open the case without permission. Instead he waited while the elder slipped his cloak on and raised the hood so that only his pale face was visible—dark eyes, aquiline nose, wide mouth, and thin lips.

While the Omni appeared to be in his mid-sixties, Vincent knew he was at least twenty years older. Another rumor said that once each year every Omni over sixty was permitted to drink one droplet of preserved Vishrak blood and that, in so doing, he extended his life another year. Theoretically, with enough Vishrak blood an Omni would be immortal. Immortal but not invulnerable. That only Omnis were permitted to imbibe Vishrak blood was a sign of their importance to the cause of the Brotherhood. Only an Omni possessed enough lore and magic to locate and bind a Vishrak demon. The council guarded these secrets well, electing a new Omni only after another Omni had died.

"Let's begin," the Omni said. Long, confident strides carried him over the unforgiving floor. Scattered gaps revealed the dark basement below. Yet the Omni seemed to avoid the largest of the holes without conscious effort. He approached the bat-wielding Albert, whose face became instantly paler than normal. "What is your name?"

Albert stammered. "Albert 97, Omni."

"Lose the bat, Albert 97."

"But the rats—"

The Omni placed the fingers of his left hand against the side of Albert's face. Red energy sizzled and crackled there, sparking miniature crimson lightning bolts that spiked into Albert's scalp. Albert screamed, then crumpled to the floor in the fetal position, whimpering. "Never question my orders."

Dora 99 knelt beside Albert to comfort him. The Omni stared at her. "You have enlisted a woman in your ranks?"

Vincent cleared his throat. "She has proven her . . . devotion to the brothers—the Brotherhood."

Dora immediately fell to her knees before the Omni, pressing her lips to his shoes. "I will do anything for the Brotherhood, great Omni."

The Omni looked at Vincent, who said, "Dora 99 is obedient to the cause."

"Good," the Omni replied. "Rise, woman." She stood, looked up at him adoringly. "Do you know how to follow orders?"

"Oh, yes, Omni."

"Then stay out of the way."

"Omni . . . ?"

"This ceremony has never been performed with a

woman present, and I will not risk failure when we are so close."

Deflated, Dora whispered. "Yes, Omni." She returned to Albert's side. Still trying to obey the order for silence, Albert had clamped his hand over his mouth as he retched.

The Omni approached the altar, and the other brothers parted like clouds after a brief storm. On the table were the remains of Ginger Marks, a.k.a. L8Dvamp, last seen leaving CyberJoe's. Her gray-streaked hair had fallen out in clumps. Otherwise the skin was intact, bearing only a few nicks and tears. "Your people have done well, Vincent 74," the Omni said. "Now stand at my side." Vincent stepped forward, and the Omni continued, "We make the required thirteen." They numbered fifteen; however, Dora and Albert, near the scarred pulpit, were excluded from the ritual. "Join hands to form the circle."

Black candles had been placed around the stretched skin, one above the head, one below each hand and one beside each foot. "All kneel," the Omni intoned, a commanding hush to his voice. "Lower your heads before the sign."

With their hands joined, all knelt and bowed their heads. This was all new to them, and as exciting as a promise fulfilled. Vincent could feel the magical energies gathering. The Omni lifted his head. "Behold the clear and certain sign of the vindication of our faith. Behold the glory and the power of the Vishrak. As we witness the evidence, so shall we place a name to our faith, to that which would rise again and serve us in power and glory. In naming, so shall we bind. In binding, so shall we reign supreme. This is our faith."

The group intoned, "This is our faith."

From his lacquered wooden case, the Omni removed a small unused black candle and held its wick to the candle beneath the hand of the desiccated skin until it flared. He placed the small candle over the chest of the skin so that it would have been above the heart, had the skin still contained one.

The Omni removed a ceremonial dagger from a sheath inside his cloak. "We give blood to the heart." He pricked his bare left thumb, then held it out until a drop of blood fell onto the skin of Ginger Marks. "Follow as I lead." Each brother unsheathed his own dagger and dripped blood on top of the Omni's.

Next, the Omni removed a golden sphere the size of a tennis ball from his wooden case. He flicked a small latch, and the sphere split down the middle, popping open on miniature hinges. The padded interior contained a tiny glass vial with a screw top. Whispers raced around the table. "Silence," the Omni warned. "Behold the blood of a Vishrak, centuries old. I am only the third Omni to possess this vial."

The Omni unscrewed the cap, ever so carefully. To drop the vial or to spill so much as a droplet of Vishrak blood would be the greatest sacrilege. The last Omni to make that mistake had been compelled to immediately take his own life by plunging his dagger into his heart. Pressing the pad of his right index finger to the mouth of the vial, the Omni flipped it upside down for a moment, to stain his finger a red so dark it was almost black. Then he resealed the vial and returned it to the safety of the globe.

His stained finger held out for them to see, the Omni continued the naming ritual. "So that the glory and the power of the Vishrak may be ours, I touch the mind of his servant."

His unwilling servant, Vincent thought, but in dealings with a demon, the distinction was unimportant.

The Omni lightly pressed his index finger to the forehead of the skin. "And now I touch my mind with the blood." He daubed his own forehead, leaving a dark red streak. "For the glory and the power, I commune with the blood." He placed his index finger on his tongue and closed his eyes. After a moment he pulled the finger from his mouth. His eyes opened abruptly, showing only the whites. When he spoke again, his voice was deeper, rumbling through the rotted floor and booming off the charred walls. "As I know the blood of his kin, I will know the name of him who is without form. And with the name, so shall I begin to bind him in his new form. Thus we begin to bind the one named. . . ."

The Omni fell to his knees, head bowed. His body started trembling, and a faint red glow pulsated around his flesh, seeming to ooze from his pores. The Omni flung his arms out at his sides, whipped his head back, and roared, inhumanly loud, "*Yunk'sh!*"

The twelve Brothers of Vishrak shouted, "*Yunk'sh!*"

Even Dora, excluded from the ceremony, felt the power in the name. She whispered it to herself. Albert 97, however, just continued to whimper. Crimson blood fell like tears from his squinting eyes. Vincent feared that Albert had been driven mad by the Omni. If so, he was of no further use to them. Vincent would have to give the order or kill Albert himself, then toss the body into the basement and let the rats have him—an ironic end to their gloriously successful evening.

In Elliot's bedroom, the air rippled and the walls began to vibrate. Elliot dropped the stapled pages of the hacker FAQ he'd been reading and clutched his temples. The index and middle fingers of his left hand had fused into one leathery gray digit. Blood dripped from his nose. "What the hell?"

His demon was materializing, but this was unlike

his past manifestations. Always before the demon had drawn form from Elliot's body gradually. It had been painful but manageable. In no way was he prepared for the agony that now doubled him over, as if an unseen force were attempting to rip his spine out of his back while tugging his intestines up through his esophagus.

Elliot retched over the side of the bed, missing the wastebasket. He climbed to his feet. *Big mistake,* he thought. The room seemed to spin on a weird axis.

The demon stood at the foot of the bed, the waxy man-shape weaving drunkenly as spatulate hands clutched at the sides of his runny face. The demon's apparent loss of control unsettled Elliot. A moan escaped the demon's body rather than issuing from the melting mouth.

"What's wrong?" Elliot yelled.

In reply, the demon staggered around the foot of the bed toward Elliot, arms outstretched like a faceless mummy in an old horror flick. Elliot had no idea what had gone wrong, but his demon seemed about to kill him.

CHAPTER SIX

Elliot was wrong.

The demon harbored no murderous intentions. At least not toward his human servant. Rather, the demon needed Elliot. Wrapping its gooey, runny arms around Elliot in a grotesque bear hug, the demon trembled, siphoning strength, matter, and form from Elliot's human body. For Elliot, the bedroom began to spin again, his vision graying around the edges.

Abruptly the demon released him.

Elliot fell on the bed, feeling as if he'd been kicked in the gut. The demon, on the other hand, appeared steady and firm, his facial features distinct and well defined.

"Care to tell me what the hell that was all about?" Elliot asked, a little breathless. As he scratched at his left hand, he noticed his ring finger and his little finger were now fused together, as were his index and middle fingers. For the moment he was simply relieved that the demon hadn't meant to kill him, but later Elliot would have to ask the demon what was happening to his own body.

"A . . . cult that worships my kind has found the remains of one of my victims," the demon explained.

"But that's a good thing, being worshiped."

"Over the millennia, the elders of this cult have learned magical rites and have developed the ability to detect when one of my kind attempts a re-spawning ritual. They gather their forces. While they worship us, it is only to bind us to their will, to wield our power against all who oppose them."

"Don't they have to capture you to bind you?"

The demon pressed its spatulate hands together, and they almost seemed to meld together like soft clay before he pulled them apart again. "They know my name. That I am called Yunk'sh."

"Yunk'sh, huh?" Elliot said. "So what? So they know your name. It's not like they're gonna find you listed in the White Pages."

"Names have power. Have you not wondered why I never revealed it to you? To a mortal?"

Elliot shrugged. Actually, he'd never thought to ask. Now it seemed as if things were happening too fast. "This—this is all new to me. I'm trying to cope here."

"By knowing my name, their sorcerer, their Omni, has the ability to locate me. If I am bound, I will be in their control, and they will most likely instruct me to kill you. I will not risk being bound by the Brotherhood of Vishrak."

"Hey, I'm on your side, big guy," Elliot said.

"If I am to be re-spawned as unbound, and if you are to receive your reward, we must accelerate the completion of the cycle."

Before they had finalized the pact between them, the demon had asked Elliot what he most desired. "What is it? Power, fame, good looks, money, women?"

Elliot hadn't hesitated to respond: "Power. I want to be CEO and major stockholder of my own software company. Make me so big I'll make Bill Gates look like a pauper." With that power, he'd have plenty of money. And everyone knew the babes flocked to the guys with power and money. "But maybe you could also improve my looks just a bit," Elliot amended. "Clear up this acne, remove twenty—make that thirty—pounds, and make me a couple inches taller. When people look up to me, I want them to look *up* at me."

"It's a deal, Elliot Grundy," the demon had said. "All of it. And when we are finished you will have no concerns about your looks."

The demon's words echoed in Elliot's mind as he stared down at his left hand, the graying flesh, and the two thick fingers, instead of four, now opposing his thumb. All of the fingernails were gone, having fallen off in the past day. The skin of the hand felt tough, as he imagined sharkskin or elephant hide might feel. "Yunk'sh"—seemed odd to call the demon by its name—"I need to ask you a question about our pact." Elliot held up his hand for display. "It's not quite human anymore," he said. "Really puts a crimp in my keyboarding."

"It will be fine," Yunk'sh said. "What you are experiencing is overlap . . . or transference. I borrow from your physicality and you reflect back my true nature. As the ritual nears completion, there is some spillover from the substance I absorb from my victims."

"So what happens . . . at the end, I mean?"

"I will have real substance, not your borrowed substance, to sculpt my new body. I will pull the combined substance from all my victims back into that new, re-spawned body. You will revert to normal."

"Uh . . . except for those minor physical improvements you promised with the pact. Right?"

"As you wish," Yunk'sh said. "In the interim, you must hide your differences from your kind. Agreed?"

Elliot nodded. A small price to pay for all the power and prestige he would have after it was all over. And except for an occasional fast-food run, he already spent most of his time in the apartment. Had to keep up the disability act, after all. Besides, Shirley felt sorry for him and was always offering to run errands for him, to spare his sore back. *I'll take her up on her offers, that's all. Can't beat having a full-time gofer downstairs.* "I'll be fine," Elliot told the demon. "Just fine."

Angel had spent several hours reading through the case folder for each murder, looking for patterns. If he could see the big picture, maybe he could predict where the demon would strike next. Nine victims so far, including the most recent, Greg Schauer. All basically between twenty-five and thirty-five years old. *That leaves, what?* Angel thought. *A few million potential victims still out there.* Six female to three male victims, indicating a two-to-one preference for women—basically a meaningless statistic. No way of knowing if another man or a woman would be next. All but one had been single, and the exception to that trend apparently had difficulty remaining faithful. Meaning what? The victims were all dating or looking to date.

Some had been killed in their homes, while others had been killed on isolated or dark streets. Statements from witnesses who saw the killer meet his victim in a public place shortly before the murder indicated that the meeting seemed prearranged rather than spontaneous. So the victims had agreed to meet their killer, possibly for the first and last time.

Angel sighed. "Looking for love in all the wrong people." *If you consider demons people,* he conceded.

Doyle knocked on the doorframe. "Look at you, keeping all this fun to yourself."

Angel looked down at the folders and photographs spread across his desk. "Actually, I'm in the mood to share."

"Ah, be careful what I wish for, is what you're sayin'."

"No good deed goes unpunished," Angel replied, gathering the folders into a haphazard stack. "Two heads are better than one."

"In that case, let's make it three heads," Doyle suggested. Then, as he leaned back out in the reception area to be sure Cordelia could hear him, "Although, in Cordelia's case, it would be a *big* head we'd be adding to the mix."

"Better big than thick," Cordelia commented as she joined Doyle in the doorway.

"What exactly are we discussing here?" Doyle asked with a wry grin.

"I don't know, Doyle," Cordelia replied. "Either your drinking problem or your gambling problem."

"Not my way with the ladies?"

"Delusions would fall under the drinking problem."

Angel had the folders tucked under his arm. "I think she has you," he told Doyle.

"A rose with many thorns, that one," Doyle said softly.

Cordelia observed him for a moment, trying to read his expression. Giving up, she turned to Angel. "So . . . pretty gruesome stuff?"

"Take a look," Angel said, dividing the files into two stacks. He practically had the contents memorized, and they needed to get up to speed quickly. Cordelia took her folders and returned to her desk, while Doyle sat in a chair to begin his perusal. "Nine murders. Male and female victims, twenty-five to thirty-five years old. With one exception, all were single and lived alone."

Cordelia held up a color photograph showing a stretched-out, desiccated skin with a tape measure next to it to show the height of the victim. "Okay, somebody is taking crash dieting to a whole new level."

Doyle shook his head. "Whatever this demon is, it sucks everything right out of them, doesn't it?"

"All that remains is the skin and some powdery bone residue." Angel leaned against the wall, arms crossed over his chest, head lowered in thought.

"Sucks out the cream filling." Cordelia shuddered. "Could the demon be feeding off them?"

"Possibly."

"Or maybe the demon's a serial killer gone off the deep end," Doyle suggested.

"These murders seem too . . . premeditated," Angel said. "If this demon just wanted to kill, it could overpower any human it found alone. Instead, it's choosing its victims, setting up meetings. A lot of effort for the thrill of a kill."

"Carefully selected victims," Doyle mused.

"We need to determine what its motivation is," Angel said. "Then maybe we can figure out who or where it will strike next."

"Why," Cordelia said, not making the word a question.

"Well, isn't that obvious?" Doyle asked her. "Helping the helpless and all that."

"No," Cordelia said. "I mean we need to find out *why* it's doing this."

Angel pushed off the wall. "She's right, Doyle. This isn't just premeditation we're seeing. It's *purpose*. This demon is planning something."

"I hate surprises," Doyle remarked.

Cordelia was staring at the tape-measured remains again with a look of disgust. "Maybe it's just trying to disprove the saying: you really *can* be too thin."

"Where's Ginger Marks?" Doyle asked, flipping through the contents of a folder.

"Who's Ginger Marks?" Cordelia asked.

"Victim number eight," Doyle said. "There's no photo of her skin."

Angel frowned. "Somebody stole her remains."

"Oh, that is so gross," Cordelia blurted out. "Somebody stole a human skin?"

"Another *why* we need to answer," Angel said.

"Why? I'll tell you why. It's because there are too many perverted freakazoids running around."

"That may be. But we have to be open to the possibility that somebody has a specific use for the skin."

Cordelia squeezed her eyes shut and shook her head vigorously. "I do not want any mental pictures to form."

Angel smiled. "Relax, Cordelia. I meant a supernatural use."

"Okay . . . amazingly, that *is* better."

"So what now?" Doyle asked Angel.

Angel had an idea. "The demon that appeared in your vision," he said. "Could you describe it?"

"The vision was a little vague," Doyle said. "I just got an impression of tentacles whipping about. What do you have in mind?"

Less than a half hour later, Angel had sketched an image, mostly in silhouette, of the demon based on Doyle's description. Every few minutes, Angel would show the drawing to Doyle and ask him where it seemed off. When he finished drawing the man-shaped demon with a serpentine tongue and fingers that were transformed into tentacles, Cordelia commented, "I've dated a few guys who would fit that description."

Doyle arched his eyebrows. "You've dated demons, then?"

"No, just guys with octopus arms and slobbery tongues."

"Oh," Doyle said, slightly deflated.

Angel glanced at him, knowing the half-demon was looking for any opportunity with Cordelia, since she was anything but an equal opportunity dater when it came to demons, half-demons, or anything listed in the demon column of the species handbook.

Doyle cleared his throat. "I think I might know someone who could give us a lead on this demon. Care to bring your drawing along, with an *after* shot of one of the victims to see what we can get out of him?"

"Fine. But let's leave a copy of the sketch here. Cordelia, cross-reference our research volumes and the on-line database. Maybe we'll find something to match our . . . silhouette."

"Sure," she said. "And I'll research the victims on-line. Try to find something linking them together."

"Sounds like a plan."

Just then the door opened, revealing Chelsea Monroe of *L.A. After Dark*. On her earlier visit she had worn a meticulously tailored gold metallic suit. This time she had opted for silver, with a sheer emerald-green silk blouse. "I'm back," she said. "I think you'll want to hear what I have to say, and I'd like to take you out to a late dinner to discuss it."

Cordelia snatched her purse from the corner of her desk and started to rise. "Great! There's this new place I've been dying to try, and . . . oh, you meant just you and Angel."

"I'm afraid so," Chelsea said with a sympathetic smile. "For now, anyway."

Angel glanced at Doyle, who waved a hand at him. "It's okay. We've got some time. Dink, my associate, he don't come out till after midnight anyway."

"Even so . . ." Angel began.

"A word, if I might," Doyle said, gesturing toward Angel's office.

Angel glanced at the auburn-haired, green-eyed woman who was waiting for his answer with a confident smile. "Excuse us for a minute."

"You know what?" Cordelia said, coming out from behind her desk. "I'll keep Chelsea—I mean, Ms. Monroe—company while she waits."

Once they were inside Angel's office, Doyle said what they were both thinking. "Cordelia's networking."

"What's on your mind, Doyle?"

"You," Doyle said. "And her—Chelsea Monroe. Well, mostly you. I think you should let her take you to dinner."

"Why's that?"

"It's not enough for you to protect and save humans."

"It's not?"

"No," Doyle said. "It would do you a world of good to actually be one of them now and then."

"There's no point, Doyle, she—"

"Maybe she just wants dinner. Maybe she just wants to dance. And maybe she just wants an exclusive interview. You'll never know unless you give her a chance. Besides, all this isolation from human contact isn't good. Listen, all I'm sayin' is, you gotta learn to have a little fun now and then or what's the use?"

"But you know what happens if I have too much fun," Angel said. "If I act too human." Angel still had nightmares about what he'd become, after making love to Buffy. One moment of true happiness and he'd lost his soul, become the destructive, evil Angelus. Jenny Calendar had lost her life because of that one moment in which he'd forgotten his demonic nature. At least then he hadn't known he would lose his soul. Now he couldn't claim ignorance. He'd left Sunnydale and come to L.A. to avoid seeing Buffy all the time, seeing her and being reminded of what they could never be to each other again. He'd owed it to her to let her get on with her life, a normal life. Well, as normal a life as the Chosen One, the Slayer, could expect to have. For him, self-imposed isolation made it easier to forget things that would forever be denied him.

"I'm not sayin' you should walk her down the

aisle," Doyle said, as if reading his mind. "Just take some time to enjoy being human. No harm in that."

"What about you?" Angel asked. "Why haven't you taken your own advice to seize the moment? To tell Cordelia how you feel about her?"

"I'm just waiting for my boyish charm to wear her down," Doyle said. "That way when she learns about my demon half, it won't matter."

"It's not a mask, Doyle. It's part of who you are, and you have to live with that. So will she if you two ever get together."

"Well, it's not the sort of thing you blurt out to a girl, a human girl. It takes time."

Angel suspected it was Doyle who still needed time to adjust. He had never really come to terms with his own identity, being half Brachen demon. After his twenty-first birthday, when he'd discovered the other half of his identity, Doyle's life had spiraled out of control. Angel suspected that Doyle would need to accept himself before he would truly believe that somebody else would accept him for who and what he was. "Someday," Angel said.

"Oh, that will be a day, won't it?" Doyle grinned, a gleam in his eyes. "So it's settled. You'll let the lady take you out for dinner and maybe a little dancing?"

"I'll listen to what she has to say," Angel said. "That's all. Wait for me."

"Can't blame a guy for tryin'."

* * *

"I just love your outfit," Cordelia said. "The whole metallic look. Very bold." Cordelia had placed her chair in front of her desk, angling it to face Chelsea, so she could give the television hostess her undivided attention.

"Thank you." Chelsea had removed the silver jacket and folded it over her arm. Her green silk top was backless, with spaghetti straps.

"So what's it like?" Cordelia asked. "Being Chelsea Monroe, hostess of an entertainment news program?"

"Well . . . you get to meet a lot of interesting people."

"I suppose you have to be bold, to take on the seamy underbelly of L.A. at night."

"It helps."

"What the heck is a seamy underbelly, anyway? Never mind. That's not the glamorous part."

"Not really, no."

"Are there lots of openings for entertainment news types? I mean, you meet a lot of famous television and movie directors, and they probably offer you roles all the time. Right?"

"Occasionally, but—"

"See! I knew it. A great stepping-stone. Once they see the talent, it's just a phone call to business affairs and draw up the contracts."

"It's really not as simple as—"

"I have an idea! Maybe I could audition to be

your guest host? Have they thought of that? Sure they have. You need time off. Vacations. Everyone gets sick, occasionally . . . well, except for vamp— I mean, everyone. Everyone gets sick, right?"

"I suppose so."

"So you could put in a good word for me?"

"Well, they do run *The Best of L.A. After Dark* when I'm unavailable, so I really don't think a guest host—"

"Oh, you're right. Who am I kidding?" Cordelia laid her palm on Chelsea's forearm. "It's not like you've ever been in a halfway decent movie or anything because of that show. You are so right."

"I am?"

"Absolutely! A guest host gig would be a dead end for me. But thanks anyway."

"You're welcome . . . I think."

Angel's office door opened. Doyle stepped out while Angel waited in the doorway. "Ready?" he asked Chelsea.

"Oh, we're done here," Cordelia said. She slapped the arms of the chair, stood up and carried the chair back behind the desk.

Chelsea grinned as she stepped into the office.

Puzzled, Angel closed the door behind her. "Everything okay out there?"

Chelsea hung up her jacket. "I was afraid I had burst her bubble, but I think she burst mine."

"Cordelia is nothing if not buoyant."

Chelsea smiled. "She's like a force of nature."

"Never has a problem filling her own sails." Angel sat down in his chair and steepled his fingers expectantly. With her jacket on the coat rack, Chelsea was showing more skin, if less cleavage this visit. Her skin was smooth and pale, not a sickly pale, just a sunless pale. Because of the nature of her show, she was a fellow creature of the night. Angel imagined that if she sunbathed at all, she'd be prone to freckling on her cheeks and on the delicate lines of her long, graceful neck. And just maybe he was beginning to stare. "I wasn't expecting you."

"I thought I warned you." She chuckled. "Anyway, about the dinner offer . . ."

"A gracious offer. Thank you."

Her smile faltered a bit. "As in, 'thanks but no thanks'?"

"I have to be somewhere tonight," Angel said. "Maybe some other time."

"Rain check logged and recorded," Chelsea said. "Still, while I'm here, mind if I run an idea by you?"

"Run away," Angel replied, then frowned at his choice of words. "Sorry. You know what I mean."

"Of course," Chelsea said. She picked up a business card from his desk, ran a long, manicured fingernail down the edge. "Let's recap. You say you help the helpless." Angel nodded. "Even if the helpless can't afford to pay."

Angel shrugged. "Even lawyers take pro bono cases."

"But they're required to, by the courts," she countered. "You're not."

"Anything wrong with helping people?"

"Absolutely not," Chelsea said. "In fact, I think it's noble."

For Angel, it was a path to redemption. A way to make amends for a hundred and fifty years of crimes committed while he was Angelus, a soulless vampire. Obviously, he couldn't tell her that. "I'm not asking for a plaque from the mayor or a key to the city."

"All the more noble," Chelsea said. She ran her fingernail across her full bottom lip for a moment, sizing him up. "I have an idea for a segment on my show."

"On cheating spouses," Angel said. "And I told you we don't handle those cases."

"No, this would be a different segment," she explained. "On you and your firm. More people should know about you. Truth be told, I think you deserve recognition for your selfless work."

"If I received recognition, it wouldn't be selfless."

She laughed. "Point taken. But not everyone who needs help is penniless. The segment would bring in new business. Face it, this would be great promotion."

"Even without promotion, the helpless manage to find me."

"But your firm could be doing better, right?"

"Of course, but I take it as it comes."

"I could give you more clients than you could handle, Angel." Her smile was provocative this time.

Angel cleared his throat. "I don't doubt that, Ms. Monroe." She was an attractive woman who was attracted to him—and probably for more than just the boost in ratings a segment on him might lend her show. Still, he had to remind himself that what she saw in him was not reality, only the image he projected to the world. And while she might find him physically attractive and his mission laudable, the implicit lie of his real nature and the curse on his soul separated them like a chasm that only he could see or even acknowledge.

"Please, just Chelsea."

Angel nodded. "Chelsea, then. But understand that in my line of work, a low profile works to my advantage. Sometimes anonymity has benefits."

"Anyone else would jump at the chance for the kind of exposure I'm offering."

"Just call me contrary."

"You're unique," she replied. "As corny as this sounds, I really believe you're one of the good guys, Angel."

"The other options aren't too appealing."

Chelsea sighed, then stood up. "Well, here I am, foiled again."

"Careful," Angel said, rising as well. "It could become a habit."

"I'd love to know what makes you tick."

Angel came around the desk as she plucked her jacket off the hook. He held it for her while she slipped into it, then held the door open for her. "Oh, just the usual," he said. "Truth, justice, and the American way."

With a long, manicured finger she reached out and drew a slow *S* on his chest. Her green eyes stayed focused on his face all the while. "Superman, huh?"

"Nah," Angel said. "I never looked good in tights."

"Well, the dinner offer stands, whether we talk business or not. I'm completely intrigued now. I want to know the real Angel."

"Is that the reporter talking? Or the woman?"

She winked. "Let me take you to dinner and find out."

This is an impossible situation, yet I continue to flirt with her, Angel thought. *Am I simply taking Doyle's advice? Is this just part of the human dance? Or do I wish there could be something more here, something real.*

After she walked out the door, Doyle and Cordelia continued to stare at him. "What? What did I do?"

"Oh, nothin'," Doyle said. "Only steamed up a few windows."

"We were just flirting," Angel said. "It was harmless."

Cordelia's eyes were wide. "She totally wants to jump your bones."

"She's just trying to charm a story out of me."

"I think she's expecting a little more than a story after that dinner," Doyle commented. "And I don't mean dessert."

"No dessert," Cordelia was quick to add, a trickle of fear in her voice. "We all know what happens when Angel has . . . dessert."

"You're overreacting," Angel said. "Nothing is going to happen. No dessert, no dinner, or anything else. Doyle, are you ready to meet Dink?"

Doyle frowned. "If that's it for the fun and games, yes. But first we gotta make one stop."

CHAPTER SEVEN

Angel drove down Hollywood Boulevard in his black convertible, keeping his eyes steadfastly forward. Most of the businesses that relied on tourist dollars had shut down for the night. The bustle of daytime sight-seeing crowds had given way to late night stragglers and insomniacs. Angel drove past Mann's Chinese Theatre and the Roosevelt Hotel. High on a hill to his left, the Hollywood sign was floodlit, stark white against the darkness.

Doyle sat in the passenger seat, watching Angel curiously, a white take-out carton balanced on his knee. Finally, Doyle asked, "You all right?"

Angel sighed. "It's not like I have no self-control."

"Of course you do."

"I'm capable of having dinner with a woman, even a romantic dinner, and letting that be the end of it."

"Sure. I meant what I said, about the dance and all that. I think you should do it. You want to make a turn at Vine." Angel frowned, but not at Doyle's instructions. Doyle said, "Don't mind Cordelia. She's overreacting."

Maybe she has good cause, Angel thought. *She was there the last time.* "So why do I feel as if taking that step would be like peering into the abyss."

"A little like playing with fire?" Doyle asked.

"More than that," Angel said. "It feels false, somehow. Even though it would probably never become serious, it's knowing there's a dead end, that there will always be a dead end."

"Havin' a little fun doesn't mean you have to become what you once were. Just know when to say when." Doyle sat up straighter. "Okay, turn here, at the souvenir shop."

"What's this place called?"

"Two places," Doyle said. "Upstairs, Radley's Refreshments caters to the tourists and locals. We're just interested in the basement. It's off-limits to the rank and file of humanity. It's called the Underbar. Take a left here, then a quick right. There should be parking in back."

All but one streetlight had been broken, making the back street a mugger's paradise. Angel parked the convertible in one of several herringboned slots. He noticed several people standing in a rough semicircle, watching a pair of combatants, urging them on. An unusual number of the onlookers wore bulky coats and hats.

Angel pushed his way through the onlookers and saw that the aggressor in the fight was a few inches over seven feet tall and heavily muscled. He was also yellow-skinned with a black topknot. Demon. Gold chains crisscrossed his bare broad chest like bandoliers. Green-and-black camouflage pants and high black leather military boots completed the look. Short hooked claws bristled from the knuckles of his sledgehammer-size fists. His opponent was less than five and a half feet tall in a long gray coat with a wide upturned collar obscuring a pale face. With his small hands held up in front of him, he seemed on the verge of prayer. Not a bad idea, considering he was pressed up against a dark brown–painted cinder-block wall, and the yellow-skinned demon outweighed him by two hundred pounds and had twice his reach. Angel's first thought was *Why isn't the little guy dead?*

As the demon swung a fist in a great arc, Angel learned the answer. The claws scored four white parallel tracks through the cinder blocks with an earsplitting screech. The little guy had ducked under the blow, incredibly quick, with the flitting grace of a hummingbird. But backed up against the wall, he was fast running out of room to evade the large demon's clawed fists.

"Crush him, Gahryen!" a woman called.

Standing beside a fire-engine-red Kawasaki, she was tall, over six feet, wearing a black leather bustier, a matching leather miniskirt, and thigh-high black leather boots with four-inch heels. Her exposed skin was a brighter shade of yellow than her companion's, but her hair was just as black, pulled back and tied severely, almost whip-like, in a pony-tail that hung down to the backs of her knees. Like her companion, she also wore a gold chain criss-crossing her torso, with a multifaceted amber-colored gem in the center, just beneath the cleavage revealed by the bustier.

"This will teach you to be rude to Slyora," Gahryen said, obviously referring to the female demon. Taking her bloodthirsty comment to heart, Gahryen jabbed his left fist toward the little guy's head. Fortunately, the little guy bobbed aside a moment before the cinder block behind him imploded with the impact.

"I wasn't whistling at her," the little guy protested, his voice mumbly. "I sneezed." Angel noticed for the first time a bunch of tendrils sticking out of the little one's mouth.

Gahryen wasn't listening to the excuses. He swung his left leg, dropping his small opponent.

"Doyle," Angel said, "you go talk to Dink. I'll take care of this."

"Slight problem with that plan."

"What?"

Doyle pointed at the little guy curled up on the ground. "That's Dink."

"Then we better keep him alive long enough to find out what he knows."

Gahryen was about to introduce a size eighteen boot to Dink's rib cage.

"Gahryen," Angel called, stepping forward out of the ragged line of spectators, "why not pulverize someone your own size?"

Gahryen whirled around, surprised at the interruption. His wide grin revealed a mouthful of pointed teeth almost as yellow as his skin. "They don't make 'em my size."

Angel spread his arms wide, glanced down. "I'm close enough."

He walked toward the huddled form on the ground while keeping his attention on Gahryen. The demon turned in steady increments to match Angel's progress, like a compass needle tracking magnetic north. "Dink, go to Doyle, over there. I'll take care of Gahryen."

"Your funeral," Dink said, darting out from the wall. Angel frowned. Well, at least he *seemed* grateful. Angel had caught a glimpse of stubby, writhing gray tentacles under Dink's flattened nose and realized he too was a demon.

Dink ran toward the circle of onlookers and looked as if he would have kept running if Doyle hadn't caught him around the throat with an extended arm. "Not so fast, Dinikyllesus," Doyle said.

"C'mon, Doyle! If your friend wants to get himself dead, that's on him. I for one don't need to hang around and watch."

"Have a little faith, Dink. Angel can take care of himself."

"Don't be too sure," Dink said. "Marzekian demons don't just kill you; they make sure nobody can I.D. the remains."

Angel held up his hands, willing to talk his way out of the fight if he could. "This seems to be a little misunderstanding."

"The only misunderstanding is you thinking you're gonna be alive five minutes from now." Gahryen swung his clawed knuckles at Angel's head.

Angel ducked and blocked the blow with his left forearm while drilling his right into Gahryen's bare left side, below the ribs and beside the crisscrossed chain and the amber gem that matched Slyora's. The demon grunted with the impact, but that was the extent of his reaction. "You're right," Angel said. "I'm not gonna be alive five minutes from now." His face morphed into his vampiric countenance, revealing his undead nature. "Then again, I haven't been alive for over two hundred years."

Gahryen seemed mildly surprised but unconcerned. With a shrug, he drove his knee up toward Angel's groin. Angel leaped back, pressed his hands against the wall and swung a kick toward Gahryen's jaw. Proving faster than Angel anticipated, the demon caught Angel's foot and swung it higher, upending him.

Angel wrapped both arms around Gahryen's legs and pulled hard, bringing them both down. He rolled off the demon but felt clawed knuckles rake across his abdomen, tearing through cloth and gouging his flesh.

Doyle saw Gahryen connect and grimaced. The amber gem at the intersection of the crisscrossing chains glinted briefly in the weak glow of the street-light. Doyle turned to Dink. "A Marzekian demon?"

"Yeah. So?"

"Angel!" Doyle called.

A claw-knuckled fist whistled through the air, just missing Angel's face. "I'm kinda busy right now, Doyle."

"He's a Marzekian demon!"

"Thanks for clearing that up," Angel replied as a cinder block shattered beside his left ear.

"All Marzekian demons wear banishment gems."

Angel twisted sideways to avoid a left jab and drove his right elbow into the demon's throat, momentarily stunning him. The banishment gem glittered in the middle of the demon's chest. Angel caught Gahryen's right arm in a lock and brought it up behind his back even as he drove the edge of his foot into the back of the demon's knee. Gahryen stumbled forward, and Angel shoved hard, using the demon's own momentum in combination with Angel's vampiric strength to drive him into the wall. Angel heard the ground-glass sound as the gem shattered against the wall.

Break the gem and banish the demon.

He released the demon, who staggered back, face leaking blood the color of pus. Nuggets of the shattered gem tinkled to the ground like loose change. Gahryen looked down, an expression of horror and surprise on his face. Where the gem had been, a circle of darkness throbbed rhythmically, spreading with each pulse. Fissures began to split the demon's chest, exposing a black void. Gahryen bellowed in outrage. His body began to crumple, as if being crushed by the hand of an invisible giant. A hot wind buffeted bystanders and stirred up dust and debris. Paper food wrappers swirled about. Gahryen was pulled inward into the void, winking out of existence. Abruptly the wind died and an eerie silence fell upon the alley.

Then, behind Angel, a shrill scream.

Doyle called, "Watch out!"

Angel spun around as Slyora charged him, pulling a long dagger from a sheath strapped to one of her high leather boots. She held it overhead, ready for a quick downward strike. Angel braced his left forearm, catching her wrist as the point of the blade stabbed down at his face. "What's good for the goose . . ." Angel said, prying the blade from her hand and slamming the metal hilt into the gem.

"No!" Slyora shouted. But the gem was already fractured. She attempted to hold the pieces in place, a stunned expression on her face.

"I'm sure Gahryen already misses you," Angel said. He waved. "Bye now."

"It's not fair!" she cried. Blackness engulfed her chest, spreading across her body like dark veins. With a rush of sound, she was pulled into the darkness.

"Show's over, folks," Doyle announced.

The onlookers scattered, some departing, others descending the steps to what Angel presumed was the Underbar.

As Angel joined Doyle and Dink, Doyle turned to the little demon. "Insulting a Marzekian demon, Dink? I would have thought you'd have more sense."

"She bumped into me and I sneezed," Dink said in his mumbling fashion, pointing to the ring of writhing tentacles surrounding his mouth. The tentacles were a couple shades darker than his pale gray complexion, and his wide eyes were burnt orange with long, vertical pupils.

"And when you sneeze, it sounds just—"

"Like a whistle," Dink finished.

"Anyway, Dink, I brought you a little present," Doyle said, hoisting the take-out carton in front of Dink's face. "Your favorite."

"Live night crawlers?" Doyle nodded. "Ooh, gimme! Near-death experiences always give me an appetite."

"You have a lot of near-death experiences?" Angel asked.

"Well, just about everything gives me an appetite," Dink admitted. "But I try to stay out of trouble."

Doyle handed him the carton. Eagerly, Dink opened the lid, peered inside, and emitted a contented sigh. "Still squirming in their native soil. Nothing better. No doubt." With two long fingers and his thumb, he fished out a long, segmented worm. Tilting his head back, he lowered the morsel toward his mouth. The ring of tentacles substituting for lips rippled with the hypnotic rhythm of a sea anemone. They clutched at the wiggling worm and stuffed the end into his mouth. He slurped it up like a strand of spaghetti. After chomping on it for a few moments, Dink mumbled, "So what's up, Doyle? You don't bring me worms for nothing."

"Now that you mention it, I need a little favor."

"Exposed!" Dink exclaimed. "Worms always make me thirsty, so it's only fair you buy me a drink."

Dink walked toward the cinder-block building, grabbing the railing beside the steps that led down to the basement entrance. Doyle whispered to Angel, "Everything makes him thirsty."

"No doubt," Angel replied.

A green neon sign mounted to the upper panel of the glass basement door blinked "Underbar" at them. Beneath was a white plastic sign with red lettering: Private Party. Invitation Only. Without hesitation, Dink walked through the door.

Angel glanced a question at Doyle. "If you're demon, or part demon," Doyle explained, "you're invited."

The Underbar had a counter along the right wall lined with a row of three-legged stools. To the left were scattered tables. The place was about half full. Most of the patrons were obviously demons of one sort or another. Even the bartender, who was six and a half feet tall and dark as obsidian, had startling pink eyes and a spiral horn protruding from the crown of his bald head. On a shelf behind the bar, he had a small wire cage filled with live white mice. Occasionally, as if tossing back peanuts, he popped one or two into his mouth.

Completely undisturbed by a single, lazy ceiling fan, a smoky haze filled the long room. As near as Angel could determine, the smoke issued from a gray demon with folds of flesh where his face should have been. The mist spilled from the demon's pores.

Another pair of green-skinned demons played a game involving daggers and quick reflexes. One demon would place his gnarled hand palm down on the table and wait for the other to take a literal stab at it. The idea was to pull the hand back before the blade came down. They took turns, and now that they'd each quaffed a few intoxicating beverages, there were more howling hits than misses. No one else seemed to mind if the pair cut their hands to ribbons.

In the near left corner, looking like a lost exhibit from an Art Deco museum, stood a dusty jukebox with an Out of Order sign taped to the front of it. Beneath the official notice, someone had scribbled with a pen, "Again!" Beneath the sign itself was a gaping hole, obviously the result of a conflict over tastes in music.

Doyle spoke softly to Angel. "Mitch Radley owns both the upstairs and the downstairs. Rumor has it he's some sort of demon that passes for human."

Carelessly weaving his way between tables, Dink scooped another worm out of the white take-out carton and dropped it down among his tentacles. When he reached the table beside the pinball machine, he plopped down, still not taking his eyes off the worms in his carton. He pulled back the hood of his cloak, revealing wide, floppy gray ears. As Doyle and Angel took seats on either side of him, Dink said, "Whatcha get me, Doyle? Looks like a half dozen."

"Special of the day," Doyle said. "Buy six, get one free."

"You're a prince," Dink said, plucking another

worm out of the carton. He looked at Angel with the worm twined between his fingers. "I'd share, but live worms seem to be an acquired taste."

"Definitely," Angel said. *A taste I have no intention of acquiring.*

"Angel's got some pictures for you to look at, Dink."

"First my drink," Dink said. "A vodka and grape juice. Goes great with worms."

"And me without a clue," Doyle said, shaking his head.

While Doyle went for the drink, Angel took a manila envelope out of his inside coat pocket and slid out the picture of the murder victim. He placed it on the table. "What can you tell me about this?"

Before he examined the photo, Dink chomped the worm in half. He waved the other half over the picture of the shed human skin, dribbling worm guts on it. "Ooh, that's totally disgusting."

Angel rolled his eyes. *I couldn't agree more.*

Doyle returned to his seat with a large glass. "One vodka grape."

Dink dipped his mouth tentacles into the glass and produced a horrendous slurping noise while emptying half the glass. Most of the bar's patrons looked his way before shaking their heads.

"Enough stalling, Dink," Doyle whispered irritably.

"Okay, okay," Dink said. "Let's have another

look." He flicked away the worm guts and shook his head. He let out a heavy sigh, fluttering all his mouth tentacles at once. He glanced from Doyle to Angel. "Is this what I think it is? An empty human skin?" Angel nodded. "I thought those stories were just rumors," Dink explained. "If you want me to give this up, I'll need some walking-around money. Fifty bucks. No less."

"Angel saved your sorry hide," Doyle said. "We fill your belly with worms and this is the thanks we get?"

"Fifty, or I ain't saying a word."

"Twenty," Angel said in a voice that brooked no compromise.

Dink gulped. "Twenty works."

"Let's have it," Angel said.

"I'll tell you," Dink replied. "But you ain't gonna like it."

CHAPTER EIGHT

Willem 94 drove the panel truck the Vishrak cult rented. Vincent 74 sat in the middle. And the Omni leaned against the passenger-side door, hands steepled, chanting softly, the whites of his eyes showing. The sorcerer was employing magic to locate the demon named Yunk'sh, while the rest of the cult waited in the back of the truck, sitting in the darkness on three long wooden picnic benches bolted to a slab of plywood.

Willem was afraid to ask Vincent how the Omni's magic worked, especially after the Albert 97 incident. Vincent had taken Albert's own baseball bat and smashed his skull with it. Then he'd ordered several cult members to dump the body into the church basement. At least Albert, the poor bastard, was dead before the rats started gnawing on him. "Let this be a lesson," Vincent had told them afterward. "We must avoid all distractions and stay focused on binding Yunk'sh."

As the Omni had explained to them before they piled into the truck, "The demon must take physical form, substance borrowed from his human servant, to absorb each victim. Now that we have completed the naming ritual, I will be able to sense his presence during these manifestations."

So they cruised through the streets of L.A. waiting for some sign of the demon. And Willem, as instructed, was careful to obey all traffic laws.

The Twilight Club in Culver City was a split-level nightclub with a large bar island surrounded by booths on the lower level and a parquet dance floor ringed by small round tables on the upper level. An exterior wooden staircase led up to a U-shaped rooftop deck. Most of the Twilight Club's business came from the twenty-something, after work, happy hour crowd, who enjoyed the mix of dancing, drinking, and socializing. In the last seven years, the club had changed ownership three times and its name five times, trying to find just the right combination of music, mood, and menu to make it successful.

To escape the throbbing pulse of the dance music inside the club, Hank Stepanski—one of three regular Twilight Club bartenders and just about the last person to see Mike McBain, victim number six, alive—took a cigarette break and led Angel outside.

They stood out of the way, under the exterior staircase. Hank lit an unfiltered cigarette, took a long drag, and shook his head. "The weirdest thing, Mr. Angel," he said as he exhaled. Angel had tried to get the bartender to call him Angel, but it hadn't stuck. "I could've sworn it was Suzette with him."

"Suzette?"

"I see a helluva lot of faces come through here," he said. "Mostly they blur together. But the regulars and the big tippers start to stand out."

"Which was Suzette?"

"A knockout," Hank said, flashing a wolfish grin. "A regular knockout." He chuckled at his pun. "Always dressed to kill. Slinky, flashing a lot of skin. Real looker. Comes in on Friday and Saturday nights hoping to be discovered. See, the Sony lot ain't too far from here. She probably figured the star makers might drift this way after hours."

"What was unusual about her that night? McBain not her type?"

"He was waiting for her at the bar," Hank replied. He'd worked his cigarette about halfway down, and Angel guessed that when the cigarette was done, the interview would be over. "Seemed to recognize each other."

"She normally came in alone?"

"Always," Hank said. "And usually danced by herself too, with this dreamy look on her face. Sometimes you just had to stare. Though I don't think she minded. That was probably the whole idea of the one-woman shows. Oh, she'd talk to people casually, trying to get a read on the room, scoping for players. But this was different, like she had an appointment to meet this guy."

"Maybe she thought he was a player," Angel suggested.

Hank took another drag. "Could be. But it turns out, from what I read in the paper, the poor jerk was just a working stiff."

"What happened after she met McBain?"

Hank examined his cigarette. "Butch is gonna kill me if I don't get in there pronto."

"Just a few more minutes."

Hank nodded. "Sure. But I better get to the weird stuff. I know Suzette. Not personally, but to see her, right? Well, here she sits down right in front of me at the bar and I don't know it's her."

"I don't follow you."

Hank paused as two boisterous couples thundered up the stairs overhead. "Because it don't make sense, at least not to me. She's halfway done with her margarita—a drink Suzette never orders, mind you—and I nearly drop the mug I'm wiping. Because it's Suzette. Bang! Like she appeared right in front of me. The clothes are a bit tame by Suzette's standards, but how could I miss her right there? Before I know it, she and McBain walk out arm in arm."

"Were you busy that night?"

"The usual." He flashed his easy grin again. "You gotta understand, Mr. Angel, this lady is a featured attraction in many of my best recurring dreams. You want weirder? Five minutes after she walks out with this McBain guy, she walks back in again."

"She dumped him?"

"In five minutes?"

"It's been known to happen."

"Well, in five minutes she not only dumped a guy, she also managed to change her outfit. She comes in wearing this white body stocking thing with strategic peepholes all over. Now *that* was a Suzette-type outfit." Hank dropped the cigarette butt and ground it out with his boot heel. "First thing, she comes up to me, leans over the bar, and says, 'Hank, I need a drink to loosen up.' So I ask her if she wants another margarita. Guess what? Suzette hasn't the first clue what I'm talking about. Thinks I'm nuts. Well, I'll tell you what, Mr. Angel, maybe I am nuts at that."

According to the hostess at the Captain's Table, Jill Gonczi's date was the hot male stripper who had danced at her best friend's bachelorette party the previous weekend. "It was either him or a dead ringer," the hostess told Angel. "His name was Aaron. Do you think they use their real names?" She went on to explain that she'd told the police the same information, along with the name of the stripper's employer, Steel Studs of America. Sounded like a union slogan.

Janis Howe, the twenty-two-year-old waitress who had served drinks to Jill and her date, had a different story. As she talked to Angel in the employee lounge, she had the nervous habit of stroking her blond ponytail. She wore black pants and a white cotton blouse with narrow red stripes. The stripes were actually embroidered lobsters, crabs, and fish in a repeating pattern. "He was my boyfriend."

"Your boyfriend?"

"Brian, my ex-boyfriend," she elaborated with a slightly embarrassed smile. She spun a little silver ring on her right ring finger. "He gave me this ring. I still haven't taken it off. He never asked for it back, so . . ." She shrugged. "We both go to UCLA, so I still see him around sometimes. When I walked up to the table, I thought for sure it was him. I even dropped the menus on the floor."

"You recognized him, but he didn't recognize you?"

"He smiled, but it was a polite smile, like I was a complete stranger. I really thought he was pretending not to know me. They left money for the drinks, but walked out without ordering." She shrugged. "Guess I made him uncomfortable."

"You're sure it was him?"

"At the time, I really thought so," Janis said.

"Now . . . I don't know. He seemed not to know me at all. And Brian would never kill anyone."

"But you gave his name to the police?"

She looked down for a moment, then back up at Angel. "I just told them he looked like my boyfriend." She rolled her eyes at her mistake. "I mean ex-boyfriend."

"Did the police question him?"

She nodded. "He was in a stage production at the college that night. Lots of witnesses. Guess it was just one of those freaky coincidences."

"I don't suppose your ex ever worked for Steel Studs of America?"

Janis laughed. "You've been talking to Nancy, the hostess." Angel nodded. "She described that stripper guy to me—Aaron?—and he looks nothing like Brian. Believe me, my Brian is a sweet, average guy. But nobody would mistake him for a Chippendale."

Angel had to be sure. "Sounds like you miss him."

She nodded briskly, dabbed at a tear in the corner of her eye. "Little bit." Her voice was tight with emotion. "He's a senior, already has a job lined up back home in Philadelphia, and doesn't want to be involved in a long-distance relationship. Said it was better to break up now, before graduation. Easier on both of us, he said."

Angel squeezed her hand and thanked her for talking to him.

• • •

Cordelia had called for reinforcements. The thousand-page books promising to make Web design easy had only made it easier for her to exhaust her supply of extra-strength Excedrin. The whole Web design project was turning out to be more involved than the do-it-yourself guides had led her to believe. Designing a site that would actually dazzle people and lead them to Angel's office involved a soup-to-nuts approach. She could write the text, but creating graphics and programming were the type of Willow Rosenberg zones into which Cordelia dared not tread. Instead she called Willow for advice and got the names of some local sites offering Web design services at a price Angel Investigations could afford. Cheap.

When Arnold Pipich agreed to do the work with video games as compensation, Cordelia decided she'd found her man—except that her man turned out to be fifteen years old and video games turned out to be more expensive than she had imagined.

"Fifty, sixty dollars apiece, easy," Doyle had informed her.

"Fifty dollars is a lot of quarters," Cordelia said. "I guess Visa and MasterCard are big at the arcades now."

"You buy the games for your home," Doyle had explained. "Play them on a TV."

Cordelia had stared at him. "Why?"

"It's supposed to be fun."

Now Arnold Pipich was standing beside her chair, leaning over her desk, staring at her work in progress on the computer monitor. He was pudgy, wearing a green shirt printed with a circuit board pattern over baggy jeans. His dark hair looked as if it hadn't been washed or combed in at least a week, and he wore eyeglasses with distressingly thick lenses. "Kinda pathetic," he commented.

"That's why you're here, kid," Cordelia replied angrily. "The books lie. The wizards suck big-time."

"I'll start from scratch. Should be a piece of cake."

"Really?" Cordelia asked, considering. "So that would make it a one-video-game piece of cake?"

"I'm thinking three."

"Two," Cordelia countered. "And that's final."

Behind the thick glasses, one of Arnold's highly magnified eyes winked suggestively. "Maybe we could work something out with just two games."

"Arnold! That's my knee, not the keyboard!" She slapped his hand away from her bare knee, wishing she'd worn jeans to work.

"How about this? I give you a killer site, state-of-the-art scripting and graphics and all I ask in return is one game and a date . . . someplace where my friends can see us."

"Sorry, kid. Geek chic doesn't work on me."

"Ouch," Arnold said. "Two games it is."

Cordelia looked up as Doyle stepped into the reception area. "Doyle, this is Arnold. He'll be designing our Web site. As soon as he stops hitting on me."

"Am I interrupting something?" Doyle asked.

"Just a case of juvenile sexual harassment."

"Keep your hands off the lad, Cordelia," Doyle joked. "Try to fondle someone closer to your own age. Like me, for instance." When Cordelia refused to take the bait, Doyle said, "So we're on the video-game payment plan, then. So much for your fancy wizards."

"Well, he's a wizard or a hacker or something. Aren't you, Arnold?"

"I'm whatever you need, baby."

"Get over yourself, hacker boy," Cordelia said. She handed him a ballpoint pen and a steno pad. "Take notes so you get this right the first time."

"You might want to wrap this up, Cordelia," Doyle said. "Angel's coming."

Before she could reply, Angel stepped through the door. He frowned. "Who's this?"

"This is Arnold," Cordelia answered.

"Arnold would be . . . a client?"

"A contractor."

"Little young for a contractor."

"Apparently younger is better," Doyle observed.

"For computers," Cordelia amended. "He's helping with our computer."

"It's broken?"

"Not exactly," Cordelia said, grimacing. She sighed. "Okay, I decided we need a Web page."

"We do?"

Cordelia explained her idea of attracting business over the Internet through a Web presence. "And I thought we could have a subscription for information on that special interest database stuff we collect."

Angel shook his head. "I don't know about this, Cordelia."

"Just give me a chance," Cordelia said quickly, before the ax could fall on her project. "One month. Once you see all the clients coming through that door, you'll want to give me a big fat raise."

"Make it two weeks."

"You won't regret it," she replied, flashing a broad smile.

Angel was beginning to regret it already. "Cordelia, you need to hear this. Will you be long with Arnold here?"

"Grab a coffee," Cordelia said. "Give me two minutes."

Five minutes later, Cordelia joined Doyle in Angel's office. She sat down beside Doyle and asked, "So this Dink guy panned out?"

"Worth every worm," Doyle said.

Angel began. "We believe the murders are the work of a Vishrak demon with the power to use glamour to seduce its prey."

"That's not what you told Kate," Cordelia said.

Angel cleared his throat. "Kate's taking the cult angle."

"Cult?" Cordelia said, looking between them.

"There's a cult all right," Doyle explained. "But that comes later."

"So how is this demon glamorous? Usually they're just icky."

Doyle frowned. "The glamour is the demon's ability to make you see what you want to see."

"An illusion?"

"More than that," Angel said. "This is real magic, not simply sleight of hand. Think of it as . . . as empathic pheromones."

"Pheromones?" Cordelia asked. "Flashback to biology class. You mean chemicals? Sexual attractants? Drugs?"

Doyle answered. "Basically, but with supernatural magic instead of drugs. We're talkin' about pure evil here."

Angel continued. "The victims and, more recently, the eyewitnesses are seeing someone who is attractive to them. And the effect seems to be getting stronger. I talked to the bartender who last saw Mike McBain, victim number six." Angel explained how the bartender saw the woman with McBain transform almost before his eyes. "But the witnesses who last saw Jill Gonczi never talked about a gradual or sudden change. They immediately saw someone they were attracted to or had recently fantasized about. That means the demon's full powers are almost restored. It has nearly finished its cycle."

"Cycle?" Cordelia asked. "What are you talking about?"

"The demon was improperly slain," Doyle explained.

"Improperly slain? Isn't that like being a little bit pregnant?"

"Killing certain demons requires complicated rituals and such," Doyle said.

"Doyle's right," Angel said. "Killing a demon doesn't always mean that it's banished forever."

"Demonic loopholes," Cordelia commented.

"And this one's a doozy," Doyle said.

"Through these body absorptions, essentially human sacrifices, the Vishrak demon is attempting to acquire a new body, to return to our physical plane."

"And twice-spawned demons are particularly nasty buggers," Doyle added.

"So it wants to have the perfect body? Same as everyone else in L.A."

Angel shook his head. "Not a particular body. A series of bodies. It's trying to complete its ritual, a re-spawning cycle."

With a leap of understanding, Cordelia said, "So it needs the complete set to finish its collection, and then it gets a new body."

"Essentially," Angel said. "Yes."

"So how does it complete the set?"

Doyle frowned. "That's what we don't know."

"And what happens if it finishes the cycle before we stop it?"

"A lot more people are going to die."

CHAPTER NINE

"I'm confused," Cordelia said. "If the demon has no body, how does it meet and kill its victims?"

"With a willing human accomplice," Angel explained. "Somehow the demon borrows some of the human's body . . . his physicality to complete each kill. We're not sure what happens to the human during this borrowing process, but it's probably unpleasant. The demon exists in a state of flux, changing from an active, dangerous-matter state to a resting psychic state."

Doyle added, "And it's only vulnerable in its borrowed physical form."

Cordelia frowned. "So we have to catch it in the act?"

"Catch, kill," Angel remarked. "It's a fine distinction."

"But this is where it gets complicated," Doyle said.

"Let me guess," Cordelia said. "The cult?"

Angel nodded. "They also want to catch the demon in the act."

Cordelia held up her hands, palms out. "Wait a minute. The cult's on our side for a change?"

"Not exactly," Doyle said, frowning. "They want to bind the demon and its powers to their will."

"A pet demon?" Cordelia asked.

"And you thought pit bulls were dangerous," Doyle commented wryly.

"Apparently the cult has an ancient order of sorcerers who learn arcane rituals and magic to locate and bind the demons," Angel said. "However, to bind the demon, they must confront it in its borrowed physical state."

Cordelia nodded. "So they have to catch it in the act. Literally." Doyle nodded. "How much of this have you told Kate?" Cordelia asked Angel.

"Only about the cult," he replied. "That we believe a cult is harvesting organs for some ritual."

"Which isn't far off the mark," Doyle added, "if you combine the demon, his human servant, and the cult into one, uh, menace."

Cordelia brightened. "If this cult knows how to find the demon, maybe they can lead us to it."

"First," Angel said, "we have to find the cult."

Walking down Sunset Boulevard, Christine Foust was enjoying her first ever cup of Arabian mocha java, while Stefan sipped at the Gold Coast blend. Chris was on a mission to try every coffee flavor that Starbucks offered. She could always go back to her favorites later, after her experimentation.

She had light brown hair that fell almost to her shoulders, watery blue eyes, and a slightly uneven tan, evidence of an outdoor lifestyle rather than idle hours spent sunbathing. She wore a sleeveless white loose-knit sweater and stonewashed jeans over fresh hiking boots. To her mother's dismay, she had never been comfortable in a dress, skirt, or heels of any elevation. Stefan was also dressed casually, in a blue and gold striped shirt, jeans, and loafers.

Naturally excitable, even without the jolt of fresh-brewed coffee, Christine walked faster than Stefan, who seemed content with a more leisurely pace. She kept turning to face him, walking backward as they talked. Stefan was several inches taller than she was, with light brown hair, deep blue eyes, and a square jaw. Broad across the shoulders with a trim waist and muscular legs, he looked like the outdoorsman he had claimed to be in their e-mail and chat room discussions. Both of them had declared themselves to be better at scaling mountains than navigating computer keyboards, yet the computer, strangely enough, had brought them together.

On their second date, they planned to hike up one of her favorite trails, but for this first meeting Chris had chosen the coffee shop, a safe public location. Within minutes they had clicked. She felt so right, so natural, with Stefan. He seemed like everything she'd been waiting for in a guy. She just wanted to gobble him up.

Growing up with three brothers and no sisters had played a significant role in her sensibilities. Consequently, she was as likely to ask a guy out on a date as he was to ask her. She had suggested this face-to-face meeting with Stefan, and she was about to take it to the next level.

"A personal question, Stefan?"

He took another perfunctory sip of his Gold Coast blend. "Fire away."

"How do you feel about public displays of affection?"

"You mean, like holding hands while strolling through the park?"

"I was thinking of something more affectionate."

He stopped walking, forcing her to pause in mid backstep. "Really? Should I be intrigued?"

"Oh, if I were you, I would definitely be intrigued." She glanced down the side street, which was momentarily deserted, gathered the front of his striped shirt in her hand, and tugged him in that direction. He let her lead him out of the glare of streetlights and passing cars. "Is this secluded enough for you?"

"That depends on what you had in mind," he replied, looking around for passersby.

"Just . . . this," she said, pulling his face down to hers.

"I never complain when a woman makes the first move," he whispered against her lips.

"Good to know," she murmured, opening her mouth to him.

She heard his Gold Coast blend splash on the ground, thought, *Oh, what the hell,* and let her own cup fall behind him.

She felt the tip of his tongue, his hands sliding up her arms to her bare shoulders, pushing against the edge of her sleeveless sweater. Something sharp jabbed into her throat. As she tried to cry out, his tongue went deeper into her mouth and became something else. She tried to scream, but her throat was being ripped open, her back, neck, and chest pierced. Biting down on the thing in her mouth proved futile, like trying to gnaw through steel. She pounded on his arms with her fists, kicked at his shins with her hiking boots, but none of her efforts loosened his hold. Worse, she could no longer breathe.

She heard a distant screech and thought it might have come from her throat, but all too soon total darkness and utter silence claimed her.

The Omni pounded the dashboard of the panel truck. "Faster! The Vishrak is near! The time for caution is past! Go! Go!"

Willem 94 floored the accelerator. After more than an hour of aimless driving through the city, the Omni had ceased his chanting and turned his head to the right. "Yunk'sh has manifested over there," the Omni had said, his voice quavering with excitement.

"Over there" had been fifteen minutes and ten miles ago. The Omni had used the chanting ritual to attune his mind to the demon's presence. Vincent had described it as a kind of psychic sonar. The signals rippled out and came back in a continual stream, revealing nothing until, finally, the Omni sensed the physical manifestation of the demon, which meant that Yunk'sh was about to claim his next victim.

Vincent had explained their strategy. "The demon masquerades as a human, a wolf in sheep's clothing. He will want to lead his human sheep away from the flock, to a place of isolation, before beginning the absorption. That is all the time we will have to intervene."

"Turn here," the Omni instructed.

Willem braked slightly as he swung out onto Sunset Boulevard, swerving slightly to get back into his lane. From the back of the panel truck, Willem heard several cult members tumble from their seats and bang into the sides of the truck. Muffled cursing erupted. Horns blared at Willem's reckless driving.

The Omni opened his wooden case and a vial of green salve within it. He dabbed a spot of salve on each fingertip of his left hand, then closed the vial and put it back in the case. He steepled his hands so that the salve would be on all ten fingertips. He looked down Sunset, his head darting from side to side like a bird's. "Faster!"

Willem weaved in and out of lanes of traffic to avoid an accident.

The Omni's fingertips had begun to glow a pulsing emerald green. "Turn left here! Now!"

Willem slammed his foot on the brake and spun the large steering wheel, cutting across several lanes of traffic. All around the truck, car tires squealed as drivers fought to avoid collisions. Nevertheless, glass shattered and fenders crumpled as speeding cars stacked up like accordion folds. The panel truck, however, made the turn off of Sunset without any damage, other than to the cult members flung around in back.

"There!" the Omni shouted triumphantly.

Willem's jaw dropped as he drove the panel truck right over the curb before bringing it to an abrupt stop. In the dim light of the side street, he saw a tall, muscular man leaning over what obviously had once been a human being but was now just a long, withered skin inside a pile of collapsing clothes. Only the man was not a man, but a demon, with long whipping tentacles where his fingers should have been, each tentacle segmented and tapered to a dangerous point. From his mouth sprang another tentacle, dripping with blood and gore. Although Willem had seen sketches of a Vishrak in its feeding state, still he was unprepared for the reality.

Vincent pounded on the wall behind him, loud enough for the rattled cult members in back to hear and shouted, "Go! Now!" The back door trundled up on its track; then the truck began to shake as cult members poured out. The Omni pushed open his door, careful not to wipe the glowing salve from his fingertips. Vincent shoved Willem to break him out of his stunned trance. "Out! Move it!" Willem fumbled with his door, but Vincent had already jumped out the other side by the time Willem emerged.

The exhilaration Yunk'sh experienced after the absorption was short-lived. Another sensation intruded. A pressure building within his skull, an itching beneath his false human scalp. Claustrophobia and panic filled him with an overwhelming need to flee. Instinctively, he sensed a power attempting to bind him to its will. *The cult!* he screamed silently.

Dropping the empty skin of Christine Foust to the ground, he looked over his shoulder just as a panel truck swerved toward him, jumping the curb and screeching to a stop. Cloaked figures poured out of the back, but Yunk'sh was more interested in the figure who first stepped out of the passenger side of the truck, a bald man with fingertips glowing a bright green. Their sorcerer, he realized. Their Omni, drinker of Vishrak blood, binder of Vishrak demons.

The Omni's hands were like the doors of a cage, closing around him. Yunk'sh knew without knowing *how* he knew that if both hands touched the flesh he now inhabited, he would be bound for eternity to the Omni and his cult, forced to submit to their will, be their servant. Yunk'sh backed away.

"Yunk'sh," the man called in a deep voice, a voice that reverberated with the power of magic. "I bind you to our will and to our purpose. You will live to serve us."

"Never!" Yunk'sh shouted at the man, but seemed frozen before the cult members, almost mesmerized. "I will not play cobra to your mongoose, mortal."

The Omni strode forward, hands outstretched, fingers bathed in the emerald glow. "I bind you now. Live to serve."

Yunk'sh stepped away. He could not let the Omni get close enough to touch and thus complete the binding. Wearing identical black robes with crimson linings, the other cult members fanned out to surround him. One of them crossed his sight line, momentarily blotting out the glowing hands. In that moment, Yunk'sh felt his will return. Avoiding the hypnotic hands of the Omni, the demon glanced left and right. With the exception of the Omni and the oldest among them, they all seemed nervous. Yunk'sh retracted his tongue and finger tentacles. Until he completed the re-spawning ritual he could not risk absorbing a random human. Each sacrifice in the re-spawning ritual had to be unique within the cycle. A duplication would nullify the whole ritual and all would be lost. He would have to wait almost two hundred years in a psychic limbo, before he could attempt the ritual again. *Unacceptable!* he raged.

While he couldn't risk another absorption, there were many other ways to kill mere mortals. As the Omni filled in the last gap in the circle of cloaked cultists, Yunk'sh looked around hastily and targeted the smallest among them. Even though his demonic life force endowed his current borrowed form with the strength of several men, attacking the weakest link in the chain was the most expedient route to escape. His fists curled into the cloak of the short cult member and hoisted him up in the air. But the face looking out at him from the hooded cloak was that of a woman.

"Let us bind you, Yunk'sh," the woman said, grinning fatuously. "It will be glorious."

"Imbecile," the demon roared and hurled her into

a brick wall to the sound of pulped flesh and shattering bones. *The fool,* he thought. *Doesn't she realize that what she offers is an eternity of enslavement?*

Approaching sirens filled the night.

"Gary! Samuel! Grab him!" the elder shouted.

Overcoming one fear in the face of another, both men approached.

Yunk'sh felt their hands on his arms. He drove his fist into the face of the first man, squashing his nose flat against his face. Screaming, the man dropped to his knees. Yunk'sh grabbed the other one and hurled him at the dangerously close Omni. Both men fell back in a heap. The demon turned, darted through the gap in the circle behind him, and fled down the street.

In a few moments his mind calmed enough to allow him to will himself out of the physical plane, out of this location. The shadow his body cast weakened to palest gray, and his heavy footfalls faded to whispers and then to silence. Once again he became psychic energy floating in the ether and let his link to Elliot—a lifeline and a homing beacon—pull him home. The memory of the Omni's glowing green hands chased him all the way.

"Get off me, you moron!" the Omni shouted at Gary.

Gary climbed to his feet and backed away from the sorcerer, then helped Samuel to his feet.

Vincent called to the others. "Everyone back to the truck! The police are near."

"Dora's dead," Willem told Vincent.

"Leave her," Vincent instructed. His face was drawn in harsh lines, his fists clenched in frustration over their failure. They all piled back into the truck. Willem drove them away from the approaching sirens.

Pressed against the passenger door, the Omni held his hands in front of his face. The salve smeared on his fingertips no longer glowed.

Vincent turned to the Omni. "That wasn't the last sacrifice, was it?"

"No," the Omni admitted. "But I sensed he is very near completion. Two more sacrifices, no more."

"So we will have other opportunities."

"Know we were very fortunate to catch the demon this night. With only two opportunities remaining, we must have a contingency plan ready."

"We follow as you lead us, Omni."

CHAPTER TEN

Elliot Grundy was an Ultimate Quest level-twelve shaman, the only magic user in his group, engaged in magical warfare with a level-four mage in the Forest of Splintered Doom. Should have been no contest. *I'll toast the little twerp,* Elliot had been thinking—right up to the moment the level-four mage hit him with a dissolution spell. Just like that, two months of campaigning down the tubes. Elliot slammed his mouse down on the desk, cracking the molded plastic case. Dissolution meant no corpse, no possibility of his group taking the body to a forest temple to petition for resurrection. His carefully crafted character was lost forever.

Inevitably, the messages began to appear on the bottom of his screen, the first from Jason, the barbarian swordsman in his group. "Elliot, you butt-wipe! You just got fragged by an eleven-year-old newbie!" Another, from Billy, "You are such a total loser." And from Milton, "Hey, Grundy, you spaz, I'd accuse you of hacking into level twelve, but hacking takes brains!" Finally, from Curt, "Hey, maybe the kid can take Grundy's place."

Elliot typed back his own message before quitting the game, "Like I need you morons!"

As Elliot cursed and ripped the pages of his shaman's profile into confetti, the walls of his bedroom began to vibrate. At the same moment he felt the telltale pain in his head begin to swell, from throbbing nuisance to splitting headache.

The desk trembled, the fractured mouse jittering across its Marvin the Martian mouse pad. Several panes in the bedroom window cracked. Books tumbled from his one freestanding bookshelf. And the only picture hanging in his bedroom—an acrylic painting of various fantasy creatures looking in awe upon a gargantuan medieval castle—fell off its hook and the glass panel shattered. Shirley had given him the painting when she found out how involved he was in on-line fantasy role-playing games.

The air in the bedroom shimmered before his eyes. Elliot staggered, thrusting out his malformed left arm to catch himself against the wall. The arm was coarse and gray, wrinkled like an elephant's leg from his shoulder down to the thick thumb and two fingers. Also, because the demon sucked vitality out of him whenever he manifested in physical form,

Elliot felt as if he hadn't eaten or slept in days. The demon was about to appear again, but something was wrong.

Shimmering air coalesced before him, becoming a thick mist, then a soupy evening fog. Limbs and a head appeared with the consistency of cotton candy. Features began to resolve as the shape stretched and gained an appearance of weightiness. Yunk'sh solidified as Stefan, the last form he had taken, which required less energy, but some of the features were *off*. Not that anyone but Elliot would have noticed. Yunk'sh was already slipping back into his neutral state. Something had weakened him.

"What happened? Was it the cult?" Elliot asked.

Yunk'sh staggered before catching his balance, then nodded. "They appeared as I finished the sacrifice. One of their sorcerers spoke the binding words."

Elliot dropped down on the bed, fearing the worst, his headache completely forgotten. Yunk'sh had said that if he was bound by the cult, their first order of business would be to kill Elliot. Had Yunk'sh arrived in his bedroom to carry out that assignment? "What does that mean for you—for us?"

"For now it means nothing," Yunk'sh said. "I resisted his touch."

"That's good. I mean, hell, that's great!"

"Hardly," the demon replied. "They have their

sorcerer and their magick ready. They know the ritual. All that remains is the binding touch and I will be their servant."

"But you were expecting them," Elliot said. "And you outmaneuvered them."

"I had hoped their knowledge and preparation would be incomplete, that even if they found me, they would not know how to contain my power. A foolish assumption, I now realize. They are indeed dangerous."

"Only two more sacrifices and you won't have to take any crap from anybody." *And neither will I,* Elliot thought.

A musical knock on the door: shave and a haircut. Elliot rolled his eyes. It could only be Shirley. "Wait here," he told Yunk'sh. "If I don't answer the door she'll think I had an accident and call the paramedics."

As he rushed out the bedroom door, his foot connected with his high school yearbook and it skidded across the floor, rebounding off the doorframe. He picked it up, and it fell open to the page he'd bookmarked with clippings from the school newspaper. Centered on the lefthand page was a picture of blond Julie McGraw, head cheerleader, with her arms above her head forming a big *V* for victory. Under her picture she'd written, "Have a great summer!" with a little smiley face under it. It had taken every ounce of his courage to approach her, to ask her to sign his yearbook, and she hadn't even included his name in the bland message. He wondered, not for the first time, if she had even known his name. After four years of high school, had he simply remained a faceless, nameless geek to her? That would all change after he was through helping Yunk'sh. When he was rich and powerful the Julie McGraws and Trudy Ryans of the world would all take notice of Elliot Grundy.

Rapid knocking intruded on his thoughts. With a sigh, he shelved the yearbook, closed the bedroom door behind him, and called, "I'm coming."

So that he would be prepared to hide his deformities when he answered the door, he'd tossed an athletic bandage and a roomy bathrobe on a nearby chair. In about twenty seconds, he was able to wrap hand, wrist, and forearm nearly up to his elbow. Then he slipped into the robe to hide the rest of his arm. With a sigh to calm himself, he flipped the dead bolt, unhooked the chain, and opened the door. "Hi, Shirley."

Looking ready for a country-western concert in a checked flannel shirt and denim overalls, Shirley bobbed her head at him. "Hey, Elliot!"

As cheerful as ever, Elliot thought, *but at least she didn't come empty-handed.*

She held a large covered green Tupperware container. "I couldn't help but notice you've been living off fast food lately."

Elliot glanced over at his small kitchen and all the empty fast-food bags and wrappers there. "Guess you don't have to be Sherlock Holmes to figure that one out."

She chuckled. "Thought you might appreciate a home-cooked meal. I was on my way up with this when I heard something crash. Are you okay?"

"I'm fine. I was . . . hanging a picture in the bedroom and I dropped it."

"Oh, my God! Your hand! What happened?"

"Nothing. I was trying to make my own home-cooked meal and got a little too close to the boiling water."

"Oh, my!" Before he could offer a protest, she slipped by him and walked toward the kitchen with her container. She set it on the small table, then turned back to him with a concerned frown. "Let me have a look."

"No! Really, it's okay. The doctor already treated it. It's gonna be fine. No scarring, nothing."

"But, Elliot, athletic bandages are for muscle strains, not burns."

"I did this. Extra padding over the bandages. That's all. In case I bump into something." *And I need to move this along,* Elliot thought, with a nervous glance at his closed bedroom door. *Be patient, Yunk'sh. I'll give her the boot. I promise.*

"Okay. Well, for tonight at least, you're safe from further kitchen mishaps. I brought enough lasagna for two. Thought we could have a friendly dinner together, you know, talk about things down at the store."

"Hey, that sounds . . . great. It's just that I had a little bit of a dizzy spell hanging that picture. I think I should get some rest, maybe wait till later to eat."

Shirley's ever-present smile crumbled a little bit around the edges. "Oh."

"Don't worry. The food won't go to waste. I'll reheat it in the microwave."

"If it's not too late, give me a call. I'll come up and keep you company."

"Don't wait up, though," Elliot said quickly. "Could be real late."

"Right," she agreed with a nod. A little of the sparkle had gone out of her eyes. She clasped her hands together, a nervous gesture, as if she wasn't quite sure what to do with them.

Elliot walked her to the door and held it open.

"Oh," Shirley said as she backed into the hallway, "if you cover the lasagna with plastic wrap, be careful pulling it off. Steam burns are nasty."

"Sure. Thanks again for the grub."

"No problem. Well . . . I guess that's everything," Shirley said. "See ya."

Elliot shut the door, flipped the dead bolt, put the chain on, and sighed. Eating lasagna would have been fine. Sitting across the table from a babbling Shirley was more than he could stomach. *Why can't she be more like Julie McGraw?* he wondered. *Would it kill her to wear a dress once in a while? To put on some makeup and do something with that hair?* But comparing Shirley to Julie gave him an idea. Once he had his power and a fortune, he could afford to have someone track down Julie and find out if she was still available. *She'll be mighty impressed at the new and improved Elliot Grundy.*

He tossed the robe on the chair and unwound the athletic bandage from his arm. Elliot scratched the back of his neck, his fingers trailing down across rough, scaly skin. "Well, this is new." Little bumps, forming evenly spaced ridges from his hairline down to the middle of his spine. "Oh, hell," he whispered, shaking his head. He'd have to start wearing high-collared shirts or turtlenecks. "Damn! What next?"

From the bedroom, he heard Yunk'sh call his name.

As he rubbed the ridges along his spine, Elliot thought with new resolve, *Maybe it's time to find out exactly how Yunk'sh is gonna make my dreams come true.*

Cordelia opened the door to Angel's office carrying an oversized leather-bound tome with brittle yellow pages that were all too willing to abandon the security of the old binding. "I found something," she said, excited. Then she flashed a disapproving frown. "Would it kill them to put an index in the back of these things? It would save us all a lot of time."

"I bet they wish they'd thought of that," Doyle teased.

"And the smell gives 'musty' a bad name," she added for good measure.

"What have you found?" Angel asked.

Cordelia laid the old volume of demon lore down on his desk, opened to a smudged page near the back, which showed a small lopsided woodcut image similar to the sketch Angel had made from Doyle's vision. "Without that picture, it probably would have taken me a week to find this small entry."

Angel and Doyle leaned over the desk to get a look, but Angel was looking at the text right side up. "Not much information. Just speculation. It says the Vishrak demons' re-spawning cycles are tied to the moment of their initial spawning."

Doyle stepped around the desk and glanced ahead. "Believed to be based on planetary alignment. But how? Could be anything. Days of the week. Phases of the moon."

Angel read from the text, " 'The greater the number of sacrifices in the ritual cycle, the more powerful the Vishrak demon will become in its second-spawned form.' "

"Nine sacrifices so far for this one," Doyle reminded them.

"Nine seems like a lot," Cordelia commented. "Which can't be good."

Angel shook his head.

The telephone rang, startling them. Cordelia picked it up, gave her regular greeting, then mouthed "Kate" and gave the handset to Angel.

Doyle and Cordelia only heard his side of the conversation, but that was ominous enough: "Where? Two of them? Both women? In a cloak? I don't suppose any of the drivers caught the plate number on the truck? Okay, I'm on my way." He hung up the phone and said, "Better make that ten victims."

"You mentioned two on the phone," Cordelia reminded him.

"Only one was skinned. The other was thrown against a brick wall hard enough to break most of her bones. My guess is she interrupted the sacrifice intentionally. She was wearing a hooded black cloak."

"Standard cult issue," Doyle commented.

"Don't leave the compound without it," Cordelia added.

"Go through the case folders again," Angel instructed them. "See if you can find a pattern to this cycle. If we know the cycle, maybe we can figure out who the next victim will be."

"What if ten completes the cycle?" Cordelia asked. "What if that's all the demon needs?"

"If what we've heard about twice-spawned demons is true, pray that it's not."

Doyle raised his eyebrows and nodded. "Amen to that."

The remaining cult members had gathered in the burned-out Trinity United Methodist Church again, minus Gary and Samuel. Fearing the wrath of the Omni and Vincent, Gary had been all too willing to drive Samuel to the hospital to have his crushed nose examined. Even with the failure, the group was excited by the proof of their faith. It was the first time any of them had been in the presence of a Vishrak demon—or any demon, for that matter. Vincent and the Omni, however, could only lament the agonizing failure after being so close.

The Omni said, "There is another way to bind Yunk'sh."

"Speak it," Vincent said, eager to make amends for his group's bungling of the first attempt to bind the demon.

"As with binding the Vishrak demon during the sacrificial absorption, this method too must be accomplished before the second spawning is complete. According to our ancient teachings, we may yet beguile a binding."

"Beguile?"

The Omni nodded. "When the ritual sacrifices are complete, after the demon attains his second body, his true demonic form—not the feeble borrowed essence we have witnessed this night—he must yet walk one day and one night within that form before it is truly his. This is called the settling time."

"What must we do?" Vincent asked.

"We must locate the demon's last true demonic form, what we call his remnant corpse. Since the demon was improperly slain and thus never banished from our realm, the corpse still has influence over the demon's psyche. During the settling time, if we possess the remnant corpse we may be able to beguile a binding."

"How will we find this remnant corpse?"

"I have placed a name to the demon and touched the flesh he has touched. I have seen his borrowed form—his physical manifestation—within our binding circle. If fate favors us, the contact we have made so far will be sufficient to locate the remnant corpse. Choose three of your number to travel to San Francisco."

"Why San Francisco?"

"The Omni Council had reports ninety-five years ago of a Vishrak demon operating in San Francisco. Then silence. At that time, they could only hope the demon had been improperly slain and not banished."

"And you believe that remnant corpse was the first demonic body of Yunk'sh?" Vincent asked.

The Omni nodded. "This is what our lore tells us," the Omni explained. "As the moon holds sway over the tides, so too do the outer planets determine when improperly slain Vishrak demons may reemerge. We believe that the detached psyche of an improperly slain Vishrak demon must wait until the celestial alignments approximate those of the demon's initial spawning, that the demon is therefore ruled by a particular planet."

"But how can we know when the demon was first spawned? And how the planets were aligned at that moment?"

"The Omni Council tracks the planets as they move from one astrological sign to the next. We watch for a year or more for signs that a demon's psyche has reawakened, marking the commencement of a ritual cycle. Because the demon's psyche may take over a year to awaken, a demon spawned with Jupiter as his ruling planet has little chance of re-spawning, as Jupiter moves through all twelve constellations in a dozen years. Before a Jupiter-ruled demon psyche is fully aware, Jupiter has already fled the demon's spawning constellation and the psyche remains impotent."

"Then how—" Willem asked.

The Omni ignored his interruption. "Neptune, however, takes one hundred and sixty-five years to complete its circuit of the heavens, spending over thirteen years within each constellation. More than enough time for a Neptune-ruled Vishrak demon's psyche to awaken, enlist the aid of a human servant, and begin its re-spawning cycle."

"Is Yunk'sh Neptune-ruled, then?" Vincent inquired.

"In 1998, Neptune entered Aquarius," the Omni said. "A year has passed, and Yunk'sh's psyche, now awakened, hurries to complete his cycle to awaken once more in a demonic body more powerful than his first."

"So Yunk'sh was initially spawned when Neptune was in Aquarius?"

"That is our belief," the Omni said. "As we believe that the Vishrak demon who raged in San Francisco almost a century ago was improperly slain and that his remnant corpse, assuming it has survived, awaits us there even now."

From Willem 94, "If that demon was Yunk'sh, why wouldn't he reemerge in San Francisco instead of Los Angeles?"

Vincent frowned at Willem's impertinence, but the Omni took the question in stride. "A demon's detached psyche may drift in relation to our physical plane. Reemergence may occur within a several-hundred-mile radius of the demon's near-death.

"I must now prepare for the Divining of the Remnant Corpse ritual. Afterward, Vincent, I will create a tool that your chosen three will carry to San Francisco to help them locate the remnant corpse.

Time is critical. They must hurry back with the remnant corpse before Yunk'sh's cycle is complete. Best if they leave tonight and return here by late tomorrow.

"Gentlemen, we must not be found wanting now. Our time is at hand!"

With his deformed left arm resting on the back of his desk chair, Elliot picked at the rough skin and ridges that had begun to protrude from his neck and spine. He was stalling, trying to think of a diplomatic way to ask the demon for proof that he could make good on his promises, that he could make Elliot the next megabillionaire techno-god. So far, all he had to show for his pact with the demon was a case of elephant hide and some fused fingers.

The demon stood near the foot of the bed, his human features slipping back into the anonymous pod-person mode that somehow made the average mannequin appear animated.

Finally, in frustration, Elliot asked, "Can't you drop in on these cult bozos when they're least expecting it and do a number on them?"

"Just as he uses magic to locate my physical manifestations, the sorcerer can mask their presence from me, at least for as long as I am stuck in this in-between state. This is why we must accelerate our schedule and complete my ritual before they complete theirs."

"We're already moving very fast," Elliot said. "I've lined up ten victims for you in about three weeks."

"Once begun, the ritual must be completed within one lunar cycle."

"Why the moon?"

"Cycles within cycles," Yunk'sh said. "My kind are only spawned during the night within the day, under the dark eye of the moon."

"A full solar eclipse?"

Yunk'sh nodded. "If my ritual is not finished in one lunar cycle, I must wait through another cycle of my ruling planet to begin again. Almost two centuries."

"And I'll be worm food by then."

"Precisely," Yunk'sh said. "I hope that is sufficient motivation."

Elliot saw his opportunity. "Speaking of motivation, I've set up a lot of people for you to consume."

"You feel no remorse?"

"Look, nobody ever cut me a break," Elliot said, letting anger creep into his voice. "Life ain't fair. Believe me, I learned that lesson the hard way. You gotta take what you can get, any way you can get it."

"Then what is your concern?"

"It's just that I . . . I was kinda wondering how you'll be able to make me king of the technology mountain, you know, when your cycle's complete."

"You doubt my word?" Yunk'sh asked, enraged. "Or merely my power?" The demon's booming voice rattled the walls.

"Not doubt," Elliot added hastily. "I'm just curious . . . and excited about getting what's coming to me, you know, and seeing what shape it will take."

"Observe," the demon said, pointing a spatulate hand at Elliot's computer screen.

Elliot watched as the screen filled with what looked like object-oriented programming code. He knew enough about programming to know what it looked like, if not how to code it himself. In a moment, the code began to scroll up his screen so fast it blurred before his eyes, thousands, maybe millions of lines of it. "What are you— What is it doing?"

"Creating what you would call the next computer operating system, a universal operating system that will work with all that has come before it."

"It's backward compatible?" Elliot asked, a little awed. "Even with Mac and Unix?"

"With all of them," Yunk'sh explained. "At a fraction of the size and requiring a fraction of the computing power to run. Vastly powerful yet simple to use. Its features will include all those ever desired by every computer user, and it will never crash."

"What will it be called?" Elliot asked.

"It is your creation, Elliot," Yunk'sh said. "You should be the one to name it."

"EOS," Elliot whispered. "The Elliot Operating System. No, GOS, the Grundy Operating System."

"As you desire."

"Can I try it now?"

"Restart your computer," Yunk'sh said. "It will run one time only and only on this machine as a token of my good faith. You will see that your patience and your dedication to my cause will be well worth it. But wait till after I am gone to experiment with it."

"Why?"

"Do you wish me to be found?"

"That's right," Elliot realized. "What's to stop the cult from finding you when you manifest here, in my apartment?"

"Nothing," the demon replied evenly. "Which is why I dare not stay long."

"Then go hide wherever it is you go," Elliot said, his gaze pulled hypnotically back to his computer screen. "I'll find you your next victims. We'll do this."

"My re-spawning and your life depend on you finding them quickly."

"Trust me, I know," Elliot said. "When I need your face for the camera, I'll call."

"Call and I will come," Yunk'sh said. "But do not dally too long with your creation. It is not over between us."

Elliot nodded, hardly aware as the demon vanished. He rebooted the computer and laughed with joy as the new operating system came up in the blink of an eye. In a few flashing screens it learned everything attached to his system. It was graphical, but so quick he felt no lag at all, launching programs in an eye-blink, even the ponderous photo manipulation software that was usually so slow on his system. Little touches, grace notes, everywhere, had him practically cooing over his old computer. *I love it,* he thought. *People will love GOS. Mr. Gates will be an obscure footnote in all the technical journals. Ha!*

GOS cast its spell over him, but ten minutes after he began experimenting with it, a brownout hit his building. He screamed in frustration as the screen went black. His one-time trial over, the computer system rebooted normally and GOS was gone.

CHAPTER ELEVEN

With Detective Kate Lockley standing nearby, Angel knelt beside the body of nineteen-year-old Dora Epstein. The medical examiner had found severe trauma to the body and head with massive internal bleeding. Angel was making his own assessment. The damage had been caused by her impact with the wall. Whatever had thrown her was too powerful to be human. Kate, of course, would not see that. Almost commenting to himself, Angel said, "To inflict this much damage required incredible strength."

"Or access to PCP," Kate responded.

Well, there you go, Angel thought. The situation was easier for her to grasp at a rational if no less violent level.

"How do you see this playing out?" Kate asked.

Simple, Angel thought. *The demon was taking his*

tenth victim when the cult arrived and attempted to bind him, whereupon the demon inflicted grievous bodily injuries upon one cult member, either to scare the others off or merely to open an avenue of escape.

"A division in the cult, maybe," Angel said. "A struggle for power, and Miss Epstein was on the losing side."

"Or she had a change of heart and tried to stop them before they killed victim number ten," Kate suggested.

"Possibly," Angel conceded, strictly for her benefit.

Bitterly, Kate said, "Maybe we'll get lucky and they'll all kill one another. Or become a suicide cult. Spiked punch for everyone."

"Stranger things have happened."

Kate flashed a wry smile. "You're just trying to cheer me up. I don't suppose you've heard any other whispers on your mysterious grapevine?"

"Not yet," Angel said. *At least nothing I can reveal.* "I suppose division in the ranks of the cult would be an improvement."

Kate pursed her lips, thoughtful. "That would explain the truck's reckless driving along Sunset—it was rushing to get here, not rushing to get away. While one faction of the cult is making this sacrifice, the other rushes to stop them." Kate looked from the shed human skin to the pulped body. "It's a theory," she said. "But still not an improvement."

* * *

Doyle and Cordelia had spread the case folders on the floor in the reception area. Not the height of professional methodology, Doyle realized, but he wasn't about to complain about any time spent in close quarters with the young and fetching Ms. Chase. Now and again, as he leaned near her to read something in one of the files, he caught a fleeting whiff of her perfume. "Multiple Fridays and Saturdays," Doyle said in as professional a manner as he could manage while sitting on the floor beside her. "So we can rule out a days-of-the-week pattern for the killing cycle."

"Ditto on phases of the moon," Cordelia said. "Our demon is nowhere near that patient. Also, he's basically an equal-opportunity slayer."

"Geographical location scattered, but some overlap," Doyle said, then sighed. "There's gotta be a pattern staring us in the face, you know?"

Cordelia shook her head in frustration and ran her hands back through her hair. Captivated by the simple gesture, Doyle realized he was staring at her. "I don't see one," Cordelia said. "None of these people even have the same sign."

The line of her neck is so . . . Doyle shook his head. "What did you say?"

"Nothing. Just that none of them have the same—"

"Zodiac sign!" Doyle finished. "He's completing the zodiac wheel!"

Cordelia was excited at her indirect discovery. She grabbed Doyle's forearm. "Astrology, not astronomy. That means ten down, two to go."

"The zodiac," Doyle whispered. He grabbed Cordelia by the shoulders. "I could kiss you, darlin'."

She placed a hand on his chest. "Think better of it."

"Right," Doyle said, looking down. "Got a little carried away there."

"Okay, maybe a hug." She grabbed him in a quick hug that thrilled him. It ended before he had time to react. From a distance she smiled and said, "I did good?"

"You certainly did," Doyle replied. Maybe he was even talking about the zodiac business.

At that moment, Angel stepped through the door, stopped, and looked down at them. "New filing system?"

Doyle wore a broad grin. "Then I say we keep it. Cordelia figured out the demon's cycle."

"She did?" Angel frowned at his own incredulity. "I mean, that's great."

Doyle nodded. "Our demon uses astrology to pick his victims."

Cordelia shuddered. "Talk about a horrorscope."

Angel helped them gather up the scattered folders. "That means he needs two more victims to be re-spawned. And we have no idea how he finds them."

Cordelia frowned. "We've narrowed it down to the two remaining zodiac signs."

"That's what? Eight percent of the population?" Angel commented. "We need to know how he's contacting victims to set up the meetings."

Doyle decided to attack the problem from a different angle. "What did you find at the murder scene?"

"Another human skin, belonging to Christine Foust. And a nineteen-year-old female cult member, bones crushed, internal organs ruptured. The demon's handiwork."

"So the cult members found the demon while he was still in his borrowed physical form," Doyle surmised. "Probably right after he finished vacuuming the contents of the young lady's body."

Cordelia glared at him. "Was it really necessary to paint that picture?"

"Sorry," Doyle said. *So much for the precious moments together.* "But what if they completed the binding?"

Angel shook his head. "This had all the markings of a botched effort. But I don't doubt they'll try again."

"So we not only have to stop the demon," Doyle commented. "We have to stop the cult from stopping the demon."

Cordelia frowned. "One tall order coming up."

* * *

Angel took word of their discovery to Kate. She was quick to latch on to the astrological pattern, but not too optimistic about their chances of using the information effectively. "Any suggestions on how to proceed with this knowledge?" she asked.

"We know they contact the victims beforehand to set up meetings. Now we need to talk to the friends, family, and neighbors of the victims to find another pattern."

Kate nodded. "To tell us how they all managed to hook up with the killer—or killers, if we assume the whole cult takes part in the murders. Generally, our victims are young single people looking for love, or at least companionship."

"In a bar, a club, a community, or a singles group."

Kate sat up straighter. "What about on-line? I've been in the homes of all the victims. They all had computers, some of them pretty elaborate setups with scanners and those little round cameras."

Angel had a vision of Arnold Pipich helping Cordelia set up a Web page for the business. While Cordelia knew it could be done, she lacked some of the requisite skills to get the site up and running. *The human servant,* Angel thought. *He or she is locating suitable victims on-line and sending the demon out to meet and kill them.* With the demon's power of glamour, they would basically be going to meet the man or woman of their dreams. Angel said, "That would certainly be an efficient way to find victims. With millions on-line, just keep looking for the right sign for your sacrifice."

"Let's assume the initial contact is made on-line," Kate said. "The Internet is vast."

"Look for common sites that all of the victims visited."

"I can check their computers," Kate said. "And talk to the aforementioned neighbors, friends, and family, just in case they talked about any budding on-line relationships."

"How can I help?"

"Leave this part to the professionals," Kate said. "I can't have you running around the city impersonating a police officer."

"That thought only crosses my mind when you bring it up."

Kate smiled. "Good-bye, Angel." As he stood up to leave, she added, "And, thanks."

"Glad I could help."

The next day, Angel and Doyle were searching again through the old volumes of demon lore. Since they now had the Vishrak name to go with Angel's sketch, they hoped to find a scrap of information that might help them defeat and ultimately destroy the demon, either before or after the completion of the ritual cycle.

Cordelia focused on astrology texts, seeking a

celestial clue as to how and when the demon chose its victims. "We might have a lunar cycle after all," Cordelia told them. "This says the moon takes about two and half days to move through each astrological sign. And the demon is averaging one murder every two to three days."

Angel looked up from an oversize leather-bound volume about obscure demons. "It's possible the demon has to complete its ritual cycle within one lunar cycle."

"What about the order of the signs?" Doyle asked.

Cordelia flipped back and forth between several pages. "The order of the murder victims' signs doesn't match that of the moon's passage through the constellations."

"Let's assume a twenty-eight-day time limit and start the lunar clock ticking with the first murder," Angel said. "That leaves the demon about a week."

"With the cult breathin' down the demon's neck," Doyle said, "I doubt he'll take the whole week to finish the ritual cycle."

The telephone rang. Cordelia answered, then passed the handset to Angel. "It's Kate," she informed him.

At that moment, Arnold Pipich, Cordelia's Web guru, arrived. Angel said, "I'll take it in my office."

Angel walked into his office, closed the door, then picked up the blinking line.

Ever direct, Kate said, "Chat rooms."

"Chat rooms?"

"I concentrated on the last couple of victims. What I'm hearing from their nearest and dearest is that these people talked about spending evenings in computer chat rooms. One of our techies will look through the computers and see if they had any particular chat rooms in common."

"Chat rooms provide immediate information. A few casual questions and the killers know if they have a potential sacrifice." Angel mused aloud. "This has possibilities."

"Angel, don't get any ideas. This is a courtesy call, not a cry for help."

"I'll keep that in mind," Angel replied before hanging up.

Angel had faith that Kate could put the pieces together. Yet she would never suspect a demonic killer. And that blind spot in her logic could get her killed. Besides, they couldn't afford to delay. The demon only needed two more victims to become re-spawned. Doyle was right: following the close call with the cult, the demon would probably accelerate his schedule to deny them another chance at binding him.

Then Angel had an idea: *If we can't find the demon in time, maybe we can arrange for the demon to find us.*

* * *

Beaming, Arnold carried an accordion folder tucked under his arm. He wore an olive-green T-shirt with a stereotypical almond-eyed alien head silk-screened in white on it, threadbare jeans, and battered sneakers. "Ask me what I'm so happy about."

Doyle guessed, "CompAmerica is giving away free mouse pads with every purchase?"

"That was last week," Arnold said dismissively. "This is way better."

"You asked a hacker girl to the prom and she said yes?" Cordelia guessed, the tease almost completely hidden behind the smile.

"No," he said, blushing a bit. "I can't dance."

"Color me unsurprised."

Arnold giggled. "I bet you could teach me a few moves."

"Not even for an audition with Steven Spielberg."

Arnold turned to Doyle for support. "Won't she give a guy a break?"

"You're askin' the wrong man, Arnold."

"Enough," Cordelia said. "You'd better be here about our Web page."

"Prepare to be dazzled."

"Just show me what you've got, Pipich."

Arnold dropped his folder on her desk, then stood near Cordelia, who promptly rolled her chair back to put some distance between them. *Geek boy's a little too aggressive with those sweaty mitts.*

Dramatically cracking his knuckles before placing his hands on the keyboard, Arnold typed with the speed if not the grace of a touch typist. The modem squawked, squealed, and pinged. "Okay, we're connected. Now I'm accessing the new, improved, and I must say awe-inspiring Angel Investigations Web site, designed by yours truly."

Cordelia planted her elbows on her knees and leaned forward to see the screen. From the computer speakers came the pattering sound of steady rain. Cordelia's eyebrows rose. "Doyle, come see this." Doyle came around the desk, sandwiching Arnold between him and Cordelia, who asked, "What is it?"

"Flash animation," Arnold said, arms crossed. "You really need a killer image to get attention. Watch this!"

The computer screen was black until a jagged fork of lightning flashed, revealing black buildings in silhouette against a dark, stormy sky. A rumble of thunder spilled out of the computer speakers. Atop the leftmost building, the dark shape of a man stood braced against the night. Although he was still, a long coat billowed around him with each gust of the wind. After another flash of lightning, the word "Angel" faded in, a ghost image of fractured letters. Another bolt of lightning, a sharp crack of thunder, and the word "Investigations" appeared, almost like an afterimage on the retina. A deep voice said, "We help the helpless." Finally, contact information appeared on the bottom of the screen, resolving out of mist into block letters.

"Whose voice is that?" Cordelia asked.

"Mine," Arnold replied proudly. Cordelia frowned. "You can do some amazing things with software."

"Apparently," Doyle quipped.

"So that's it?" Cordelia asked.

"Tell me that's not cool."

"It's great, Arnold. But it doesn't do much. It's a . . . mini-movie business card."

"That's just the front door," Arnold replied. "Click the logo in the center and you're into the belly of the beast."

Interesting choice of metaphors, Cordelia thought. "Show me."

Arnold clicked on the logo and the next page loaded: black background, silver buttons, white text. "Basically dark, monochromatic," Arnold explained. "I noticed your boss favors dark clothes, so I figured the stark look would appeal to him. I used the content you gave me."

"Content?"

"Text," Arnold explained. "I put in an e-mail link, but you should probably put in some related links—LAPD and whatnot. It's customary. And look, down here you've got the link to subscribe to your demonology database. The rest is self-explanatory."

"What's that number at the bottom?"

Arnold seemed embarrassed all of a sudden. "Garden-variety hit counter. Tells you how many visits the page has had. You'll eventually want some hidden tallies that only you can access, but expect to pay a small fee."

"Doyle, look!" Cordelia exclaimed. "Seventy-five hits already." When Arnold cleared his throat, however, she smelled a rat. "What?"

"The seventy-five are, um, just from me testing the site."

"What about all those millions of Web surfers out there?" Cordelia asked. "I thought this was like, build it and they will come. Where are they?"

"Millions of Web sites go up every day," Arnold explained. "You gotta register with search engines, link to other sites, get them to link to you."

"You mean promotion, right?" Doyle asked. "As in advertising?"

"Sure, that helps. Having cool stuff helps. Like that Flash animation. Funny stuff, weird stuff. And freebies, naturally."

"Weird stuff's not a problem," Cordelia said. "Can you do all that? The registering and linking and everything?"

"Well, advertising costs money, but I'm good at the other stuff," Arnold said. "However, I'll need at least half of my fee before I do any more work."

"We're good for it," Cordelia assured him.

Arnold looked around the very-not-busy office and shook his head. "Just the same . . ."

"Fine. You want half, you'll get half," Cordelia said. "What's that, one video game, right?" Arnold nodded. "Give me the name, and I'll find the best deal on it."

"Pricing is pretty standard."

"I'll be the judge of that, you little hustler. Name?"

"Ghoul Academy Three," he said. "Or, if you can't find that, Vampire Vixens. That's supposed to be hot."

Cordelia sighed. "You know, Arnold, maybe you should just take the money and spend it on dance lessons."

"Will you be my instructor?"

"That was Ghoul Academy Three, right?" Cordelia said, jotting the title down on a slip of paper. Maybe it was too late for Arnold to get a life.

Angel stepped out of his office, nodded to Arnold.

Cordelia said, "Angel, come look at this. Arnold, play the movie again."

Angel watched impassively through the animation. "That's supposed to be me, right? Why am I wearing a cape?"

"It's a coat, not a cape."

"Looks like a cape."

"That's for dramatic effect," Arnold said. "It's supposed to look cool."

"It's meaningless," Angel said.

Arnold shook his head vigorously, perhaps trying to dispel images of his payment vanishing. "Cool gets attention, so it's not meaningless."

"Even so . . ."

"Besides, it's symbolic," Arnold interrupted, scrambling for the right thing to say. "It's you, standing there alone in the dark, through the stormy night, unafraid, undeterred."

"Those are all good symbols," Cordelia said. "Right?"

"I guess so," Angel conceded. "Good work, Arnold."

Cordelia asked, "Want to see the rest?"

"Not right now," Angel said. "Kate believes our . . . suspect is trolling chat rooms to find his victims and—"

"Hey, is this about the murder that was on the news last night?" Arnold asked. "The serial killer? They said he's killed several people."

Angel frowned. "Arnold, this information is confidential. Are you about through here?"

"Yeah," Arnold said, disheartened at the dismissal. He picked up his folder and headed for the door.

"Wait a minute, Arnold," Angel called. "We're paying you as a computer consultant, right?"

Arnold smiled. "Web designer, computer consultant," he said and shrugged. "I wear many hats."

"Tell me about chat rooms."

"Most of the time chat rooms are filled with mindless gabbing. Bunch of simultaneous conversations. But they can be completely anonymous. You pick a name, an identity, sometimes even a screen avatar. Half the time, nobody knows who you really are." He laughed. "I've heard of fifty-year-old guys pretending to be teenage girls."

"Thanks, Arnold," Angel said. "You've been a big help."

After Arnold left, Doyle said, "You're thinking we could stalk the stalker on-line?" Angel nodded. "But how?"

"This is Los Angeles," Cordelia said. "People lie about their age. They lie about their looks. Why not lie about a zodiac sign?"

"So we set a trap for the demon," Doyle said.

"It's a good plan," Angel said.

Doyle nodded. "Oh, definitely."

"Who's the bait?" Cordelia asked.

Both Doyle and Angel looked meaningfully at her, neither saying a word.

CHAPTER TWELVE

"Oh, no! Not me!"

"It makes sense," Angel said.

"And you won't be in any real danger," Doyle added.

"Stop right there," Cordelia replied, spreading her arms, palms up. "I'm not sitting around in a bar waiting for the Hoover deluxe demon!"

"You'll meet in a public place," Angel assured her. "Doyle and I will be there to watch over you."

"This demon takes both guys and girls," Cordelia said. "One of you can meet up with the lady demon version."

"We could," Angel conceded. "But Doyle and I make better bodyguards than you would. And the demon won't try anything in a public place."

"I won't have to be alone with him?"

"Only for as long as it takes to lead him outside to us," Angel said.

"This sounds like a bad plan," Cordelia said. "It might sound fine on paper, but out in the real world everything could go wrong and the ingenue could end up as victim number eleven."

"Ingenue?" Doyle asked.

"The young innocent starlet," Cordelia explained. "And no wisecracks about my innocence."

"Wouldn't think of it," Doyle said. He picked up some case folders and started to flip through them.

"We'll watch you meet him," Angel said, "and we'll stay right up till the moment you leave with him. Then we'll step outside ahead of you and wait."

"Next you'll say nothing could possibly go wrong."

"No, I won't."

"Oh, my God," Cordelia said and dropped into her chair. "You're serious, aren't you?"

"I won't let him hurt you, Cordelia."

She looked into Angel's dark eyes for a moment and saw the determination there. While she couldn't be sure of much in her life, she knew that if push came to shove, Angel would be there to shove back, to risk his life for her. She could count on him. "I know."

Doyle looked up from an open folder. "You should be perfectly safe, Cordelia."

"Why's that?"

"The demon doesn't need you for his collection." Doyle indicated the file. "He's already killed someone with your zodiac sign. You don't fit into his cycle."

"You're saying that if he kills me, he'll be real broken up about it?"

Doyle pretended to ignore the icy sarcasm in her tone but couldn't help smiling. "Worse. He'd probably have to start the cycle all over again."

"I'll feel so much better knowing I foiled his plan," Cordelia replied. "No. Wait a minute. I won't feel a thing. Because I'll be dead!" She looked at Angel and frowned. "No offense."

"None taken," Angel replied.

"I want hazardous-duty pay," Cordelia said. "I've had my eyes on a pair of red shoes. Problem is, they're a little out of my current price range."

"You'd risk your life for a new pair of shoes?" Doyle asked.

"Hey! Dead guy here said I'd be safe," Cordelia said, jerking a thumb toward Angel.

"Okay, now I'm starting to take offense."

"Do I get hazard pay or not?"

"How about a small above-and-beyond-the-call-of-duty bonus?"

"These are *really* sweet shoes."

"We'll work something out."

"Okay, I'm in," Cordelia said. "Where do we start?"

"Kate's checking the victims' computers looking for common chat rooms, but I think that's a dead end," Angel told them. "Each time the demon met one of his victims in a public place, the location was different. I'm betting the demon or his human servant stalks a different chat room each time."

"Lots of chat rooms out there," Doyle commented. Shrugging off the look they gave him, he added, "Or so I've heard."

"Right," Angel said. "So we need to look for astrology themed chat rooms, especially ones local to L.A."

"Let's do it," Cordelia said. She frowned. *Note to self. Right after I buy those shoes, I need to have my head examined.*

Willem 94 and his Taurus wagon were called into service again for the six-hour drive to San Francisco. Terrance 90 sat in the passenger seat. Clifford 98 sat in the back, but hung over the front seat with crossed arms. As senior member, Terrance 90 was in charge.

The Omni had given Terrance the slender foot-long stick he called a divining rod. But they weren't driving to San Francisco in the middle of the night to find water. They were looking for Yunk'sh's remnant corpse. As the Omni explained, the stick had been carved from the wood of a lightning-struck oak tree, then stained with a diluted mixture of Vishrak blood and other ingredients the Omni was forbidden to disclose. Finally, the Omni had anointed the tip of the rod with the green salve to attune the rod to Yunk'sh, or rather his remnant corpse. It was effective within a fifty-mile radius.

The Omni Council believed Yunk'sh had manifested in San Francisco days before the great earthquake of 1906. Further evidence indicated that Father Brian McGrath of St. Ann's Church had become aware of the demon's presence in the tenements in the South of Market District. McGrath had made every effort to destroy the demon, but was himself killed on April 18, either during the earthquake or the resultant fires. Sometime during the four-day tragedy that had destroyed much of the city, Yunk'sh's original body was burned. Whatever the ultimate cause, Yunk'sh had been improperly slain, therefore escaping banishment. His psychic energy was left free to roam beyond the physical plane, where he could bide his time, awaiting the right celestial alignment to seek a human servant and begin his re-spawning ritual.

In the darkness of early morning, well outside the San Francisco city limits, the tip of the divining rod began to glow. "Look!" Clifford shouted.

"I'm not blind, Clifford," Terrance replied. "But thanks to you I'm now deaf in one ear. And your surprise indicates a lack of true faith."

"Wave it around," Willem told Terrance.

"Keep your eyes on the road, Willem." But Terrance did as Willem suggested. When the rod was pointed south the glow faded altogether. As it was brought forward, the greenish aura returned. "Looks like we're in business, boys!"

The divining rod, the Omni had explained, worked like a compass with the remnant corpse serving as magnetic north. Yet before the naming ritual, the Omni would have been unable to attune the divining rod to Yunk'sh. The demon's reemergence had given the cult the key to imprisoning him.

With the arrival of dawn, they had narrowed the apparent location of the demon's remnant corpse to a few city blocks in the South of Market District. Willem suspected a condemned lot filled with mounds of debris, surrounded by a chain-link fence topped with barbed wire. But the magick powering the divining rod was magick of the dark, and with dawn the green glow faded. Willem parked the car a couple hundred feet from the lot.

In a voice hushed with awe, Terrance quoted the Omni, " 'Where the remnant corpse lies, the land will exude an aura of pure evil, so that only the most faithful among us may approach while all others cower in fear.' "

"Well, we're stuck here till night," Willem said. "Why not check into a motel, get some sleep, then round up whatever equipment we'll need?"

"Agreed," Terrance said.

Near midnight the three men returned. As soon as the street seemed deserted, they left the car, dressed in dark gray pullovers, canvas work gloves, black jeans, and black military-style boots. Terrance and Willem watched opposite ends of the street while Clifford used the bolt cutters to open a flap in the chain-link fence. Terrance held the divining rod and a small utility shovel. Holding a crowbar in each hand, Willem had a vague sense of dread, not because of what they might find but because of where they were. Unease wafted up and down the street like an unpleasant odor. The small hairs on the back of his neck stood at attention. No wonder foot traffic was so light. For the first time he noticed that many of the streetlights were burned out and the few that remained cast only meager illumination, as if the oppressive darkness leeched away any human attempt to dispel it.

The men slipped through the fence, Terrance in the lead, divining rod held out before him like a torch lighting the way. The green glow flared bright. "Do you feel that?" he asked, strangely excited. "Like spiders crawling all over my body." The others nodded. As Clifford shuddered, Willem fought the urge to slap the back of his neck. First dread, now loathing. *The sane reaction would be to run screaming into the night, as far from here as possible,* Willem decided. *But overcoming the fear is what separates the masters from the servants.*

When Terrance pointed the rod downward, it flared brilliantly, bathing him in unearthly light. He yelped in pain and dropped the stick. The green light winked out, leaving blotchy retinal afterimages.

Willem squatted down on the other side of Terrance and poked at the charred and crumbling stick. "I guess *X* marks the spot."

Terrance looked to each of them. "Let's do it."

All three men bent down and began the task of clearing away the debris, mostly crumbled stone and brick. Deeper, strips and chunks of wood were wedged in with the stone. A wheelbarrow or a hand truck would have come in handy. A flat piece of charred wood crumbled in Willem's hands, the remains of the dedication plaque for St. Ann's. Had Father McGrath battled Yunk'sh in his own church? One more fire in all the fires that raged through San Francisco on that fateful day? McGrath had been crushed outside under falling debris, so the truth was unknown.

Clifford hurried over to help Terrance move a split beam, but fell to one knee, gagging. Terrance hissed at him. "It's a test of your faith! Only the unfaithful need fear this place."

"Told you to skip that third chili dog, Clifford," Willem said.

That was enough. Clifford spun around, staggered a few steps and vomited all over his boots and the nearby debris.

"Feel better now?" Open scorn in Terrance's voice.

Clifford nodded unconvincingly, his face ashen.

From that point on, the work proceeded smoothly. Eventually, they cleared a hole deep enough to stand in without being seen from the street. Willem noticed a dark gap at the bottom, leading down into a protected chamber. Willem had a penlight on his key ring and offered it to Terrance. Crouching down as much as he could in the confined space, Terrance shone the light into the pit beneath them. When next he glanced at Willem, the look in his eyes was one of uncontained excitement. "Do we have anything brighter?"

"Big flashlight. In the trunk of the car," Willem said.

Terrance unclipped the penlight from the key ring and shoved the keys into Willem's hand. "Get it!"

Willem climbed out of the pit and felt a little better with each step he took away from the lot. With a heavy sigh, he retrieved the flashlight and returned to the pit. A rising line of bile scalded his throat. "I will not let the fear control me," he whispered. Back at the hole, he quickly asked Terrance. "Where's Clifford?"

"I ordered him into the pit," Terrance said. "To reaffirm his faith."

Clifford called up from the darkness, his voice strained with fear, higher-pitched than normal. "I . . . I think I found it. But this light is dying. I need a stronger beam. Hurry!"

"Take the flashlight down," Terrance instructed Willem. "If he's truly found the remnant corpse of our demon lord, he will need assistance bringing it up."

Swallowing a protest, Willem complied, reassured by the heavy-duty flashlight beam, which cut quite a swath through the darkness. Long and lanky, Willem had no trouble, physically at least, sliding down into the pit. His feet caught on a mound of rubble and he eased backward into the darkness. The flashlight beam caught Clifford's distraught face. "You're a little green around the gills, Clifford."

"Shut up and shine that damn thing behind me!"

Willem played the beam across the floor behind Clifford and initially mistook the body for a patch of deeper darkness. He tracked the light backward and saw the charred remains, nearly seven feet long. Arms raised above the chest, away from the body, as if warding off blows . . . or flames. Human corpses, when burned, tended to curl into the fetal position. But nothing about this burned corpse seemed natural or human. They had found the remnant corpse of Yunk'sh. If only for a moment, Willem's awe overcame his profound unease. "Will you look at that . . ."

But Clifford was frantic. "Can't you feel the walls closing in on us?"

"That's impossible, Clifford. It's just your imagination playing tricks. Besides, there aren't any walls."

That was not completely true. They were in the remains of some sort of room, but the floor and walls had been twisted into carnival fun-house angles. Despite his assurances, Willem noticed that the bright beam of the big flashlight had faded. He batted the case against his palm, and it flared back to life. Spooked himself now, Willem said, "Let's do it."

As Clifford scrambled over to the charred corpse, lifting it by its shoulders, Willem shouted, "Careful!" He scrambled up the mound of debris and extended the flashlight to Terrance. "Hold this. I need my hands free."

Willem grabbed the feet of the demon's corpse. They were hard and fibrous but possibly brittle. "Could be worse, Clifford. There could be rats."

Clifford smiled just a bit at the gallows humor. "Oh, man, I hate rats more than anything." In the darkness behind him, something squealed. "What was that?"

"Nothing." But Willem had heard it too. Could this be a place where fears became reality? The thought alone spurred Willem along. He propped the corpse's feet against the wall and pulled himself up through the gap. Terrance backed out of the way.

While Terrance was changing his position, Willem had crouched down, then dropped to his stomach to extend both arms into the darkness and pull the demon's feet up through the gap. Given its length, the corpse seemed to weigh less than it should have—a result of the loss of all bodily fluids, Willem reasoned. By the time he had his trembling arms around the corpse's hips, Clifford's pale face had emerged from the darkness.

Squeals sounded from below. "Rats," Clifford wailed. "Lots of them."

Seeing that Clifford was about to lose his composure, Willem yelled, "Stay focused! We're almost done!"

Panicked, Clifford shoved the corpse up through the gap. The left arm snagged and spun the corpse awkwardly in his hands.

More squeals. Too many. Clifford screamed, "They're biting me."

Terrance moved the flashlight about. "There's nothing down there!"

Clifford was beyond reasoning. He would have scrambled through the gap if the corpse hadn't been blocking him. Willem tugged as Clifford shoved the shoulders of the demon's corpse, and the left arm shattered into thousands of bits of black debris. Terrance pulled the corpse clear so Willem and Clifford could climb up after it without causing further damage.

The black particles floated around Clifford's face like dust motes, but larger. Willem climbed out of the hole, then looked back when he heard buzzing. What seemed like hundreds of flies darted around Clifford's face. Willem blinked away the image, shook off the sound, but Clifford thrashed about, swatting at the particles. Angry red welts appeared across his face. He began to wail, a low keening sound growing louder by the second.

Dropping into the hole, Terrance raised a crowbar over Clifford's head. "Faithless bastard, you'll ruin everything!"

Though Willem turned away, he could still hear the sickening crunch of the crowbar splitting Clifford's skull, followed by the muffled sound of his body tumbling back into the dark pit. Then the rubble and larger debris shifted around them with a shriek of metal and stone grinding against stone. "Cave-in," Willem warned.

Terrance tossed the bloodied crowbar into the deeper pit, then clambered up out of the hole. Together he and Willem dragged the demon's corpse toward the fence.

The whole mound sank a few inches, pausing for a brief moment before everything started to crack, groan, and collapse, and a sinkhole began to form. Tons of debris collapsing into the open chamber where the demon's corpse had waited for almost a hundred years.

"Get the tarp," Terrance ordered. "We have a long drive ahead of us."

CHAPTER THIRTEEN

With the passing of another day, Elliot's deformities had progressed. His left leg had become thicker from thigh to ankle, the skin gray and leathery, while his foot had become wider. He'd had to slit the sides of his left sneaker just to wedge his foot inside it. Some masking tape wrapped around the sneaker managed to hold it together. The only clothes he could pull on over his legs now were baggy pajamas, Bermuda shorts, and fleece sweatpants.

Elliot was bothered more by the leg deformity than he'd been by the left arm and hand, mainly because it affected his mobility. He now walked with a sort of one-sided bowlegged gait. His brief vision of GOS—the wondrous Grundy Operating System he would soon bring to the world—was enough to keep him focused on helping Yunk'sh finish the ritual cycle, and almost enough to make him forget about the innocent twelve who must be sacrificed so that he, Elliot, could become rich and powerful.

During the course of the day, the demon had appeared only for brief periods, long enough to gauge Elliot's progress in finding the next candidate for the ritual, but not long enough for the cult's sorcerer to fix his position.

Elliot's search for a suitable candidate was limited to what he could do during the day. Most of the preliminary acquaintances he'd made in the chat rooms had day jobs and so were unavailable to be lured to a physical meeting. True, he had found a few online, but when he insisted on a meeting that evening, he'd scared them off. Either they sensed his desperation or the increasing number of news reports about the murders made them cautious. Fortunately, the press seemed ignorant of the gruesome nature of the killings so the reporting hadn't been too sensational . . . yet.

After Elliot had scared off the umpteenth potential candidate, his head flared with pain and a wave of nausea roiled through his stomach. The air rippled beside him and he turned to greet the demon. "No luck," Elliot said, before the demon could even ask the question.

Yunk'sh now resembled an animated mannequin, a noticeable improvement over the runny wax face. As he talked and gestured, the motion of jaw, mouth, eyebrows, and forehead all appeared natural, but the skin was smooth, without blemish, like molded plastic or rubber. Of course, this was just Yunk'sh in his improved neutral state. When he took the form of a real human, the disguise was perfect.

"This delay is unacceptable, Elliot."

Something in the neck muscles underneath the skin was wrong. Maybe because the demon's shape was unsupported by even a facsimile of human musculature or skeletal structure. *Molded from demonic clay,* Elliot thought. "There's not much I can do until these people get home from work."

But the demon was focused on something else now, his gaze distant. "I sense danger."

Elliot stumbled out of his chair. His deformed leg was a real hindrance. "What kind of danger?"

"Unclear," the demon replied. "But question not my premonitions. We must hurry."

With a nervous glance at his wristwatch, Elliot said, "Give me a little more time. That's all I ask. You still need two candidates. And you can't do both in one night."

"When next I appear, Elliot, be sure you have good news."

With that warning, Yunk'sh vanished in stages, from solid to translucent to transparent to ghostly, leaving behind a swirl of air to mark his passage.

As Elliot's headache eased, he sighed. *Gotta find number eleven.*

* * *

"Any luck?" Angel asked Cordelia.

"Oh, there are plenty of horny guys on-line," Cordelia replied. "But none of them seem to have actual horns just yet."

"In other words, no demons?"

"None," Cordelia replied. "I found a couple of possibilities. Each time they wanted to meet up close and personal, I suggested one of the killer's former meeting places and they agreed. Since our killer avoids return visits to the crime scenes, I blew them off."

"Did you spend a lot of time weeding them out?"

"At first. But then I had a flash of inspiration." Cordelia flashed one of her dazzling smiles. "I decided to use a computer for what it was meant for." Angel shook his head, unwilling to play a guessing game. "Multi-tasking," she explained. "For the last hour, I've had four separate chat room windows open at once. I'm pretending to be a different person in each window. It's actually cool. Like improvisational acting, making up all these different characters and playing them." She frowned. "You can't develop multiple personalities from this, right?"

Sitting in a chair beside her, Doyle rubbed his forehead. "No, but I'm getting a god-awful headache trying to follow all your chat room conversations."

"I've had years of practice flirting at crowded parties," Cordelia boasted. "Who knew that could turn into a job skill?"

"You're keeping it local, right?" Angel asked.

Cordelia nodded. "And I'm including the missing zodiac sign names in each screen alias."

"That should put a bit of chum in the demon-shark-infested waters," Doyle commented.

Angel handed Cordelia a folded piece of paper he'd been holding while they talked. "Maybe this will help."

Cordelia scanned the page. "A list of chat rooms? Good, I'll use them right away."

"You're supposed to *not* use them."

Cordelia rapped her knuckles against her head. "Okay, maybe there is some mental impairment at work here. I thought you just gave me this list and said not to use it."

"Exactly."

"Okay, so you're the one losing your marbles," Cordelia said. "Doyle, I feel so much better now."

"You and me both, Cordelia."

"Kate compiled this list of chat rooms from the victims' computers," Angel explained.

"So why shouldn't I use them?"

"Because I promised Kate we wouldn't."

"Then shouldn't you wink when you tell me not to use the list?"

"That's not where I'm going with this," Angel said. "Kate only gave me the list after I promised her I wouldn't attempt any sort of entrapment in any of the chat rooms."

"And she believed you?"

"Kate's baffled by this, more than she wants to admit, I think. It's hard for any human to fit this kind of predator into a rational worldview."

"She should move to Sunnydale," Cordelia commented. "She'd either get lots of practice deluding herself or a whole new worldview."

"It's no secret she wants my help. Just a question of how far she's willing to let me . . . interfere."

Doyle reasoned, "Why give you the list, unless she really wants you to work it?"

"Maybe. But I wanted the list for a different reason. To eliminate certain chat rooms from our surveillance."

"Eliminate them?" Cordelia asked.

"Just as the human servant never sets up a face-to-face meeting in the same location twice, I believe he'll avoid picking more than one victim from the same chat room. Regulars in a chat room might overlook one person dropping out, but if several disappeared without word, they might suspect foul play and notify the police."

Doyle pursed his lips, nodded. "Makes sense."

"The list Kate gave me confirms it. Only one duplicate chat room."

"That's the one the police will target," Doyle surmised.

"Probably. But I think the duplicate is pure coincidence, a blind alley."

Cordelia had been comparing the list Angel handed her to the chat room windows on her computer screen. "Two matches," she remarked.

"Drop out of them and look for two that are not on that list," Angel advised. "If the demon is nervous about the cult binding him, he may sacrifice some of his caution for a quick kill."

"Speaking as the bait in this entrapment scenario," Cordelia said, echoing Angel's words, "could we avoid words like 'kill,' 'murder,' and 'mutilate'?"

Elliot sat up straight in his chair. What caught his attention was a woman's chat room name. The screen alias included the name of one of the two missing signs, specifically the sign Yunk'sh said would be the most powerful one to acquire next in the cycle. Whenever possible, Elliot had selected a victim with one of the astrological signs the demon said would be most beneficial for each stage of the cycle. Usually the demon gave him three or four to choose from, and they weren't in any perceptible order. And now that they were down to two signs, the demon had stated his preference for one over the other, and that sign was staring right at him.

He typed a question, asking the woman if the sign in her screen name was her actual sign. When she replied that it was indeed, he took the easiest New Age shortcut that came to mind. He typed, "My psychic told me I would meet an important woman in my life and she would have your sign."

She took the hook and ran with it, asking him if he could possibly be an Aries. He smiled and typed, "Born April tenth. How'd you guess?" *Add a little detail and they never question it.* Already she was thinking they were destined to be an item.

When Cordelia's chat room session marathon entered its third hour, Angel returned to his office to examine the case files one more time, hoping something new would come out of another pass at the 911 transcripts, the witness statements, and the police and medical examiner reports. Having watched Cordelia type messages for over two hours, Doyle picked up one of her Web design books, shaking his head anew with each turn of a page. He nearly jumped when Cordelia grabbed his hand. "I've got a live one!"

Doyle stared down at her hand clutching his, and for a moment he was spellbound. He felt as if he were in another time and place, where they had gotten past all the obstacles to an actual relationship and it just felt *right*.

Cordelia realized he was staring at her hand and said, "Oh, sorry." She pulled her hand away, and he resisted the urge to grab it again, if only for a moment. "I just got a little excited."

Doyle's voice was a little thick around the lump in his throat. "No apology necessary." He cleared his throat and examined the computer screen. "What's happened?"

"Right off, he asked if that was my sign in my screen name," she explained.

Doyle put the book aside and leaned forward. Having an excuse to increase his proximity to the lovely Ms. Chase was a bonus.

"So I guessed his sign," Cordelia went on, "and know what?"

Doyle flashed a wry grin. "You won the Kewpie doll."

"Bingo!" She frowned. "Or whatever it is they say when you win the Kewpie doll. So now he's inviting me into a private room." Cordelia clicked a button and said, "Yes."

"He'd better not be thinking cybersex."

Cordelia gave Doyle a withering stare. "He's not interested in cybersex. A private room means no chat room witnesses."

"Right."

Cordelia spoke as she typed. "My real name is Cordelia. What's yours?" She waited. "Says his name is Richard. But he prefers Rich."

"Does he, now?"

"Why are you getting bent out of shape?"

Doyle realized he was being foolish and shrugged. "No reason."

"Oh . . . he's already asking to meet me somewhere. In public, of course, somewhere safe."

"Ah, the proverbial moment of truth."

"Where we separate the lonely men from the disgusting demons."

Cordelia didn't catch the way Doyle flinched when she said "disgusting demons," but in all fairness to her, the particular demon responsible for the skinny murders was nothing if not disgusting. He just hoped she wouldn't paint all demons or—specifically, half-demons like him—with the same broad brush of loathing.

She typed her suggested meeting place into the computer. "How about CyberJoe's?"

Doyle's fists were clenched. "Come on, Mr. Demon Servant, you don't want to go back there again, do you, boy?"

Cordelia clapped, excited. "He says the ambience is too cold there. He's suggesting a dance club, asking if I like to dance." Cordelia typed and spoke simultaneously again. "I love to dance."

Doyle looked at her. "Really?"

"That part's true," she admitted, without looking away from the screen.

Doyle nodded, filing the information away. It might come in handy someday. "You're doing great, Cordelia. Keep it up."

Angel came out of his office, a thick manila folder under his arm. "What's up?"

Doyle said, "Looks like we hooked one demon servant."

"Okay, he suggested a place"—she looked down at a sheet of paper—"and what do you know, it's not on our list!" She looked from Doyle to Angel. "Do I agree to meet him?"

Angel shook his head. "Not so fast. It's nearly midnight. If you look too eager, you might scare him off."

"Not if he's as desperate as we think he is," Cordelia reasoned.

"True," Angel agreed. "But let him be more desperate than you are. Wait . . . That didn't come out right."

"It's okay. I know what you meant. Besides, it's not me; it's just a character I play in chat rooms."

"Right," Angel said uncertainly. "Tell him it's late; maybe you should meet tomorrow."

Cordelia typed the message and waited. She read back the reply. "He says, it's fate that we should meet tonight. He's willing to be impulsive if I'll meet him halfway. This is one desperate demon boy!"

"Vacillate," Angel said. "Give him a chance to convince you."

Cordelia typed and spoke her response again. "I don't know . . ."

She waited a moment and laughed. "He says, if we are meant to be together, just think of the story we could tell years from now."

Cordelia typed as Angel dictated. "He's swayed you, but it won't be an official date, just a brief encounter."

Cordelia frowned. "Okay, but you're making me sound flaky."

"Not you," Angel said evenly. "Just the character you're playing—a hopeless romantic."

"He wants to know how we'll recognize each other." Cordelia had a mischievous gleam in her eye. "If this demon really can look like whoever I want, I think I'll put him through his paces."

"Be casual about it. You don't want him to suspect a trap."

"Spoilsport." She typed again. "Describe yourself." She waited and smiled. "He's telling me to describe my dream guy so he'll know how he measures up. Ha!"

"The hard sell," Doyle commented.

"He'll be too good to be true," Angel said grimly, "unfortunately for his victims. Now's your chance, Cordelia."

She rubbed her hands together, then typed rapidly. "A cross between . . ."

". . . Brad Pitt and Jean-Claude Van Damme . . . and Jude Law," Elliot's speakers said in an electronic female voice. The current chat room was text only, no caricature avatars, but he'd still assigned computer voices to screen names.

"Oh, gimme a freakin' break," Elliot said. He typed, "Big shoes to fill, but I have similar vibes."

The electronic woman spoke again, "Ha-ha . . . can you prove it?"

Elliot said, "Oh, I'll prove it all right." He called to his demon, "Yunk'sh!" He typed, "This chat room doesn't support live Web cams, so I'll send a photo."

Electronic woman said, "Okey dokey."

"Dammit! *Yunk'sh!*" Elliot winced with the sudden pain. Blood dripped out of his nose. The air in the room wavered. A ghost image appeared and solidified: Yunk'sh in neutral mannequin mode. "Hot prospect," Elliot told him. "You can meet her tonight, but I gotta send a picture, quick."

"How am I to appear for this one?"

"Standard hunky surfer boy—blond, six feet plus, muscular but not bulky."

Yunk'sh transformed himself, his flesh and features moving with the grace and fluidity of quicksilver. It was almost frightening how fast Yunk'sh could now alter his appearance. "Satisfactory?"

Elliot appraised the demon's appearance, firing off suggested revisions to his new look. With each request, the demon's skin and hair changed without delay. "Good, but lose some of the tan. Cool. Now make the hair a little darker. Stronger chin. Little more to the nose, I think the chin's overpowering it. Great. Let's see, something's missing. Ah, stubble. Let me see some five-o'clock shadow. Not quite.

Add another day. Excellent. Oops, we better put a shirt on your back. White, casual . . . make it silk, good, nice contrast with the rough stubble look. Add a gold chain. You told her you were an Aries, so put a ram's-head pendant on it. Terrific! Now smile for the camera." Elliot held up his Web camera and set the software to snap a digital still image of the demon's face and upper body. "Wait a minute . . . you forgot teeth! Thank you. And . . ." *Click.* "Perfect."

Elliot turned to the computer and clicked on the Send Photo button. "That should impress her." He typed, "What do you think?"

The electronic woman said, "Wow! I think I've had naughty dreams about you."

"Out of the ballpark!" Elliot exclaimed, pumping his fist in the air. Then he typed, "I showed you mine. Now show me yours."

Cordelia looked up from the screen. "He wants a picture of me. What now?"

Doyle glanced at Angel, who shrugged.

"Thanks for all the help," Cordelia remarked. "I'll need to wear something to stand out in the crowd." She typed her response, saying it aloud for their benefit. "Sorry, no camera or scanner here. So look for me at the bar. I'll be wearing a short red dress and black heels." She frowned and told them, "I'd better make that black flats. If I have to run for my life from the vacuum demon, I am so not doing it in high heels. I'd wear my black Sketchers, but I think he'd get suspicious."

"He might," Doyle agreed. "But you're in jeans, not a red dress, let alone a short one."

"I'll change on the way," Cordelia said. "We have to drive by my place to get to the club anyway."

"Set up the meeting," Angel said. "One hour from now."

Cordelia nodded, then turned her attention to the chat room screen. She began typing the final arrangements.

"What about Kate? Should we involve her in this?" Doyle asked softly.

Angel shook his head. "We'll only have a few minutes to catch and kill this demon while he's in human form. Kate would try to make an official arrest."

Doyle nodded. "And while she's readin' him his rights, he'll simply vanish out from under her."

"Right. And she's not likely to stand by twiddling her thumbs while I chop off the demon's head and burn the body."

Doyle flashed a wry grin. "The police frown on civilians performing public executions, do they?"

Angel nodded. "It frightens the tourists."

Cordelia signed out of the chat room. "What are you two babbling about?"

Doyle cleared his throat. "Um, we were just talking about security arrangements."

Cordelia poked a finger in his chest. "It's simple, Doyle. You let me die and I'll come back and haunt you forever."

"What?" Doyle indicated Angel. "This one's off the hook, then?"

"If I die, Mr. Brood over there will torment himself plenty without my help. I'll save all my rattling chains and bloodthirsty shrieks for you and you alone." Doyle had his hands up, palms out. Cordelia shuddered as real fear gripped her. "Seriously. You guys won't let me die, will you?"

CHAPTER FOURTEEN

"All set, big guy," Elliot said. "Number eleven in about an hour."

"Excellent, Elliot! I—" Yunk'sh roared in agony, doubled over, and pressed his hands against his head so hard that flesh squeezed out between his fingers like tan Play-Doh.

Elliot stumbled out of his chair. "What's wrong?"

His breathing ragged, Yunk'sh whispered, "The cult." With effort, he straightened up, but his face was a mess, a real-life Picasso. "They have found my remnant corpse."

"How? You said the body was destroyed almost a hundred years ago."

"Burned, made uninhabitable, but not destroyed. It lies in San Francisco. The sorcerer must have directed the cult members to it."

"But it's just a corpse. It's worthless to them. Right?"

Yunk'sh twisted his neck and concentrated on re-forming ears and the sides of his head. "In the right hands—a sorcerer's hands—the remnant of my past life still has power over me."

"How?"

"After I complete the ritual cycle, one day and one night must pass before the newly spawned body becomes permanent, before my psyche can adjust to it. A certain spell cast during that period would confound my psychic energy, make it believe it still inhabits the old, ruined body."

"They could use the burned corpse to bind you by proxy?"

Yunk'sh nodded. "But the spell only works if the body is in close proximity. They must bring the remnant corpse to this city to complete the binding."

"That buys us some time. Wait, you said this spell only works after the cycle, while you are settling into the newly spawned body."

"If one binding method fails, they will try the other."

"Unless you kill the sorcerer or destroy the remnant corpse?"

"Yes," Yunk'sh replied. "But the wards their sorcerer has cast still cloud their location, at least while I exist in this crippled in-between state."

"What happens when you get the new and improved body?"

"Before they know I truly live again, I will penetrate the wards. And when I find them, for presuming to bind me, I vow to destroy them all."

"I'm with you, big guy," Elliot said, displaying more confidence than he actually felt. "But first things first. Number eleven is waiting. Not to belabor the obvious, but you gotta kill this one fast."

Cordelia's glance darted around the bar and dance floor of Cloud Nine before settling on Angel, standing beside her. She took a tentative sip of her Coke and held the glass in front of her mouth as she said, "Promise me I'm not about to die for a really cool pair of shoes."

Angel leaned close to her. "Cordelia, I won't let you out of my sight," he promised. "I'd better give you some room, though. I don't want to frighten him off."

"Oh, no, wouldn't want that," Cordelia said with some irony. "Wait—where's Doyle?"

"By the exit," Angel informed her. "If I should happen to lose you in the crowd—and I won't, but just in case—he'll pick up the tail at the door. We need to get this thing outside to . . . you know . . . finish it."

With that, Angel faded into the crowd of twenty- and thirty-somethings who were energetically dancing, drinking, or flirting, sometimes all three at once. Once one entered the place, one almost had to cross the wide dance floor, which was down a step, to reach the bar or one of the small booths and tables. Obviously, the emphasis was on getting people on the dance floor. Cloud outlines were attached along the railing that overlooked the dance area, and every few minutes they drifted back and forth ever so slowly, almost hypnotically. *If you're using a cloud motif,* Cordelia thought, *the dance floor should be elevated, not down in a pit.* To be fair, the place had small elevators for transporting dancers to elevated cloud platforms about six feet above the main dance floor. *Those women up there in the short skirts must have an exhibitionist streak in them.*

Cordelia twirled a swizzle stick in her Coke, wondering how she had let herself get talked into being demon bait. *The shoes,* she admitted. *I really want those shoes.* But she was starting to think the shoes had been just an excuse. Working as Angel's receptionist had turned into something more. Just as dating Xander Harris had gotten her involved in the Scooby Gang, if only as an auxiliary member. Ignorance had been bliss, because once she learned that monsters were really out there, it was hard to pretend she was one of those three little monkeys. She couldn't just cover her eyes, ears, and mouth anymore. Angel needed her help to stop this demon. If she refused, would she be able to look at herself in the mirror every morning, knowing another person had died because she'd been afraid? The bigger unknown was what would happen if the demon completed its sacrificial cycle. Their research pretty much confirmed they would not want to be around with a twice-spawned demon on the rampage.

She nearly knocked over her soda glass as someone tapped her on the shoulder.

Cloud Nine was located on La Cienega, south of Wilshire Boulevard. Yunk'sh, however, materialized behind the dance club, in relative darkness. Since the cult would be out hunting him as soon as he manifested, Yunk'sh arrived a few minutes after the appointed meeting time to ensure that his eleventh sacrificial victim would be ready and waiting. Several couples and clusters of young men and women milled around outside the club. Yunk'sh slipped through them without hesitation. Even so, his passage caused gazes and double takes. Male or female, they saw in him what they wanted to see.

While in this temporary form between demonic incarnations, Yunk'sh had the ability to mold his physical matter, borrowed from Elliot's body through their link, in any way he chose. Unlike these actual physical transformations, which weakened him, his glamour was a more powerful tool to lure prey. This close to the completion of his ritual cycle, his glamour was potent, perhaps even more so than it had been in his first body. Every human within twenty to thirty feet of him would be fooled into seeing someone attractive to them, an object of desire. Sometimes just a type, but often it would be someone they knew or had known. What better way to lure prey than by appearing to them as someone they trusted and loved? Judging by the reactions, the glamour now took less than ten seconds after he was within the effective range of any humans. Early in the cycle, it had taken a few minutes. If he hurried past them, they would look once, maybe a second time, but then he would be gone and, eventually, forgotten.

After Yunk'sh attained his new demonic body, he would have more control over the glamour, including the ability to project the effect to whomever he chose, to single out specific victims and exclude the rest. While in this borrowed form, unless he made a conscious effort to subdue the effect, he emanated glamour in all directions, like a strong, intoxicating cologne.

The exterior walls of Cloud Nine were metallic silver. Blue neon cloud shapes flanked the double glass doors. Stepping through the doors into the throbbing bass of dance music, Yunk'sh gazed down across the ring of tables and the long dance floor with its hypnotic mass of dancing bodies, to the bar island beyond. And that was where she waited, wearing a short red dress as promised.

As he took a step forward, a young blond woman in a glittery silver midriff-baring top and black satin pants over stiletto heels, caught his arm. "Don't I know you?"

"I'm afraid you're mistaken," he replied without meeting her eyes. Direct eye contact increased the potency of the glamour. With a sigh, he strode through the ring of tables down to the dance floor. When his ritual was complete and his new life began, he would have the luxury of absorbing any victim at any time he chose. For now, though, succumbing to a feeding whim meant he would never achieve the newly spawned body. As Elliot so aptly said, "Keep your eyes on the prize."

Yunk'sh crossed the dance floor, taking care not to touch any of the dancers' bare arms or hands as they whipped around in the rhythmic frenzy of the synthesizer dance track. Touching the exposed flesh of a human would also accelerate the effect and power of the glamour.

The demon approached the woman in red from behind, reaching out with the energy that fed his glamour. Yunk'sh's current physical dimensions and features were as Elliot had molded them in his bedroom—the type of man Cordelia desired. But types were a compromise. To be certain she would be attracted to the image he presented, Yunk'sh allowed the glamour, feeding off her unspoken desires, to reshape his body. As he took the final steps toward her, he lost some height, his hair darkened, and his complexion became paler. *I am now what she secretly desires,* Yunk'sh thought as he reached out to her.

Three guys had already offered to buy Cordelia a drink. Two others had asked her to dance. So when someone else tapped her shoulder, she was about to tell him in no uncertain terms to buzz off. She spun around, finger pointing, mouth gaping just a bit . . . and aborted her outburst before it began. "Doyle? What are you doing down here?"

He stood next to her, leaning his elbow casually on the bar. "I . . . I just wanted to talk to you, Cordelia."

"Why aren't you watching the exit?"

He frowned. "Watching the exit?"

"Angel said you're supposed to follow us out. Is any of this ringing a bell?"

"Angel," Doyle said as if he'd never heard the name before. "Where is Angel? Right now, I mean? Do you see him?"

Cordelia surveyed the crowded dance floor. "No, not right this second. But he's around, watching from the other side of the club." Cordelia shook her head, angry. "This is no time to start changing the plan, Doyle. The you-know-what will be here any minute. Don't screw this up. I meant what I said about haunting you forever."

Doyle appeared incredulous. "So Angel hasn't told you?"

"What are you talking about?"

"About a minute ago. Angel saw the you-know-what leaving with another woman."

"Another woman? Why?"

"Another woman in a short red dress. Mistaken identity. We need to get out there, so you can lure . . . it away from her. Angel's waiting. He told me to hurry."

"Show me," Cordelia said. "I don't believe this. Rushing to be the victim." But she took Doyle's arm and when his hand slid into hers she felt a strange tingle.

Doyle sat alone at a table near the exit, drinking a glass of Murphy's Irish Stout, the only decent import the club offered. He'd already lost Angel in the crowd a couple times, but all he had to worry about was Cordelia, and she would be easy to spot in that fabulous red number. Since he was posted near the exit and she would need to pass this way with the demon, he wasn't concerned when the occasional press of bodies obstructed his view of her at the bar, where she awaited the demon.

The demon was late, but nothing in the dusty tome had guaranteed a Vishrak demon's punctuality. Generally speaking, demons frowned on order and thrived on chaos. Doyle would gladly blame his demonic heritage for the mess he'd made of his own life. If nothing else, helping Angel's cause had given him hope of recapturing his self-respect. Knowing he might actually accomplish something worthwhile before the end of the day made a welcome change to a rudderless existence.

Making the lovely Cordelia's acquaintance had been an unexpected bonus. Yet she remained unattainable, just out of reach for a half-Brachen-demon. The last time she had seen his quilled blue-green demon face she had hit him over the head with a serving tray. True, she hadn't known it was Doyle under all those quills and he'd been quick to revert to his human face before she realized whom she'd struck. But there never seemed to be a good time or a good way to show her what he looked like when he let his father's side out. Each day that passed only made it harder to come clean.

Doyle tipped back his glass and drained it, then looked back toward the bar. Again the crowd obstructed his view of Cordelia. After a brief moment of panic, he caught a glimpse of red, off to the side. He turned and saw Cordelia in her short red dress, flashing lots of thigh as she hurried up the steps toward the exit. Rather he saw Cordelias—plural—rushing toward the exit. Two Cordelias, dressed exactly alike! Doyle knocked over the empty glass and his chair as he ran to intercept them.

• • •

As of about ten minutes ago, Angel had estimated that the dance club was in violation of fire code regulations involving maximum occupancy. Still, they kept coming. And he was having trouble keeping Cordelia in his line of site. Complicating matters was his desire to remain inconspicuous. If the demon showed and noticed somebody continually watching her without approaching, he might suspect surveillance and a trap. So Angel had been forced to keep some distance between them.

In the past fifteen minutes he'd had several offers to dance from attractive women deciding to take matters into their own hands. Angel politely declined drink and dance invitations, along with the occasional invitation to something even more intimate. Naturally, after watching others abandon their halfhearted attempts, a freethinking young woman decided he was a special challenge.

She was a tall, slender brunette in a sleeveless lavender silk dress, with an amethyst-and-diamond necklace and, on her wrists, an assortment of silver bangles. "My name's Ashley," she said. "What's yours?"

"Angel," he replied absently.

She planted herself right in his line of sight. "Angel, hmm? That's perfect. Hard to miss a gorgeous guy standing here all alone."

"I'm . . . waiting for someone," Angel explained. He glimpsed Cordelia, still facing the bar, nervously swirling a swizzle stick in her Coke. Still no demon. Good. Or maybe not good. *What if the demon sensed a trap and found an innocent victim?*

"Why not have fun while you're waiting?" Ashley countered. She ran her finger down the sleeve of his shirt. "I bet you're a terrific dancer."

"You might lose that bet."

"Care to prove me wrong?"

Angel leaned back, noticed a woman beside Cordelia, striking up a conversation, her back to Angel. She was a blonde. That was all he could see from this angle. Cordelia was behaving as if she knew the woman. Another aspiring actress? Angel wondered.

"One dance," Ashley said, turning his face back to her. "I'm not such a bad dancer myself."

"I really don't . . ." Angel's voice trailed off. Cordelia was no longer at the bar

Angel tried to move around Ashley, but she stepped in front of him again. "Listen, if you don't care to dance, let's go outside?"

Angel looked across the dance floor, saw Cordelia hurrying through the rows of tables. The blonde woman was holding her hand, leading her out of the dance club. "I have to leave now," Angel said.

"We could go back to my place," Ashley offered, talking quickly. "I have a magnificent view of—"

Angel slipped by her before she could elaborate on the view. By the time he reached the tables, he saw

Doyle jump out of his seat, knocking over his chair in the process. "Doyle!" Angel called, but Doyle was too far away to hear him over the loud music.

When they stepped outside the club, Doyle squeezed on Cordelia's hand so hard she yelped. "Doyle! You're hurting me."

"Sorry, but we gotta hurry."

He steered her through the small crowd and led her around the side of the building. "Where?"

"After Angel."

Someone behind her shouted, "Cordelia!" And that someone had Doyle's voice.

She stopped in her tracks, forcing Doyle to stop or drag her.

"That was Doyle—I mean, that was *you!*"

He circled around behind her, blocking her view. "It's a trick. C'mon!" He gave her a little shove and she stumbled.

"Stop it!" Cordelia examined Doyle's face and saw something in his eyes, something feral. "What's gotten into you?" Over his shoulder she saw a figure running toward them. It was Doyle. But she was staring right at Doyle. "Wait a minute . . . You're not really Doyle, are you?" But she wasn't about to wait for an answer. She tried to run around him, but he caught her around the waist and dragged her behind the building, then shoved her against the wall.

Dazed, she managed to remain standing only by leaning against the wall. Doyle transformed in front of her, becoming the man whose image had been transmitted to her computer. "I knew it! You're that Vish—Vishrak demon guy."

"Call me Richard."

Doyle hurtled around the corner, off-balance and unprepared for the demon's forearm, which caught him across the throat and dropped him to the ground in what amounted to a clothesline tackle. As Doyle choked and gasped for air, the demon transformed again, his fingers extending into whipping, segmented tentacles, tapered down to hollow points. His mouth opened and sprouted a tongue almost as long as the fingers. "I've subdued my glamour," the demon told her, his deep voice distorted by the serpentine tongue. "You no longer see that which you desire, only what I want you to see. And I want you afraid. Now—open wide!"

"Wait! You can't kill me."

"Why not?"

"It was a trap. I'm not your sign. I mean, I'm not the sign you need. We knew about you, so I pretended that was my sign to trap you."

"Thanks for warning me," the demon said. "And you're right. I cannot absorb you."

"Because that would ruin your cycle . . . thingy."

"But, for interfering where you do not belong, I will kill you."

Doyle rolled onto his hands and knees and attempted to rise, one hand pressed to his throat. His voice came out a croak. "Leave her alone!"

Cordelia tried to stall. "If you suck out my insides, you'll have to start over. Right?"

The demon hissed, "There are many other ways to kill a human."

Cordelia's voice was very small. "Other ways?"

The demon nodded. His tongue retracted to human dimensions, but the finger-tentacles remained. The demon wrapped them around her throat and began to squeeze. "Strangulation has its charms."

"Don't." Cordelia tried to shake her head, but the tentacles only became tighter. She was starting to see spots.

"Choking you will not compromise my ritual," the demon explained. "It will, however, give me great personal satisfaction."

"Doyle," Cordelia croaked. Her hands pried at the demon's wrists, but to no avail. If he had been human, she might have tried latching on to a little finger and pulling it back until it broke, but the finger-tentacles were wrapped completely around her throat and she couldn't get a grip on them.

Darkness enveloped her.

CHAPTER FIFTEEN

Angel rushed out of the Cloud Nine dance club and peered up and down La Cienega, looking for any sign of Doyle or Cordelia and the blond woman. No one on the other side of the street. No sign to the north or south. Only one other place left—behind the dance club.

As soon as he entered the side street, he heard voices, one of them Cordelia's. He followed the sound, running hard. If the demon was there he wouldn't have much time to save Cordelia. He pulled up short and saw a man pinning Cordelia against the wall, his hands around her neck. *Not hands, tentacles!*

Nearby, Doyle was staggering to his feet, looking as if he'd already lost the first round.

"Let her go!" Angel shouted.

The demon's head whipped around to face Angel,

but he continued to throttle Cordelia. Angel leaped toward them, clenching his fists and clubbing the back of the demon's neck. The demon grunted but refused to release Cordelia. Although he had enough strength to snap her neck, the demon had decided to inflict a slower, more frightful death by strangulation. Even so, time was running out.

From a sheath inside his boot, Angel pulled a gleaming twelve-inch blade—the knife he'd brought to decapitate the demon. *No time like the present,* Angel thought. He held it in a two-handed grip and raised it high.

Immediately, the Vishrak demon uncurled its tentacled hands from Cordelia's throat and backed away. She gasped and sagged to her knees, one hand reaching out to the ground to stop herself from falling flat on her face. Doyle crouched beside her to offer his support.

"You must be the one called Angel," the demon said in a deep voice.

Angel took a couple of steps forward, knife held high above his right shoulder. When he saw an opening, he intended to behead the demon with one stroke. "You have me at a disadvantage."

The demon took a step back. His hand tentacles retracted with a wet, squishy sound to resemble human fingers again. "There is power in names and I will not give mine away."

Angel shrugged. "Oh, well. I suppose it doesn't

matter if we haven't been properly introduced, since I have to kill you anyway." He lunged forward, but the demon was just as quick, blocking Angel's wrists with his forearm. Surprise at the sheer force of the blow flashed in the demon's eyes. With his right arm, the demon shoved Angel back. Planting his left foot, Angel unleashed a snap-kick aimed at the demon's right kneecap. The demon leaped back, just out of reach. They circled each other, waiting for an opening.

"The cult knows my name," the demon reasoned. "Therefore, you are not with them."

"Never was much of a follower."

"Then why involve yourself?"

"It's a dirty job, but somebody's got to do it."

"Altruism is an outmoded concept. Besides, you are not human."

"Guilty as charged," Angel said.

"So why defend humans?"

Angel feinted a low kick with his left foot, then swept the blade across the demon's stomach. The razor edge of steel sliced through clothes—or the appearance of clothes—and into the flesh, but the flesh did not bleed. And the cut hadn't gone deep enough to hinder the demon. Angel twisted into a backhanded blow with the knife, arcing higher, aiming for the demon's throat. His wrists slammed into the demon's forearms so hard his hands went numb. A knee drove painfully into his rib cage; then the demon chopped down on his wrists and the knife dropped from nerveless fingers.

The demon stepped forward to press his advantage. Angel flicked his wrist and felt a wooden stake dart forward into his hand. His foe wasn't a vampire, but in demonic combat, a well-placed stake was never a bad idea. Angel used the demon's own momentum against him, driving the stake up into the demon's gut, just below the ribs. He gave it a powerful twist, although he doubted the demon had a heart or any vital organs in this pseudo-human body.

As the demon staggered back, Angel scooped up the blade and held it in both hands for a vicious downward stroke. The demon ripped the stake out of its body and looked up abruptly, as a white panel truck jumped a curb and weaved toward them. "We'll have to continue this another time, Angel," the demon said. He turned and bolted down the street.

Doyle pressed Cordelia back against the wall. Angel dived to his right, rolling out of the way of the careening truck as it bore down on the demon. "Are you both okay?" Angel shouted to Cordelia and Doyle.

Cordelia nodded, one hand pressed to her throat.

Doyle said, "We'll live."

Angel ran behind the truck, faster than any human. Since the truck was not actually attempting to run the demon down but merely to catch up to him, Angel was able to gain on both. The license plate of the truck had been intentionally caked with dirt or mud to prevent identification, though Angel had no doubt about who was driving the truck.

Moving abreast of the truck, Angel glimpsed the demon, whose footfalls were now silent. With a ripple like a heat mirage, the demon flickered out of existence. The driver of the truck pounded the horn in frustration. Angel leaped onto the driver's-side step, catching the frame of the side-view mirror with his left hand. He spun the knife in his right hand and slammed the butt against the window, shattering the glass.

Wide-eyed with sudden fright, the driver cursed in fear. He floored the accelerator and swerved the truck toward the back of the nearest building, intending to scrape Angel off at fifty miles per hour. Deciding not to test the limits of his vampiric healing, Angel released his grip on the mirror a second before it struck and shattered against the stone wall in a squeal of tortured metal, a shower of sparks and a rain of glass.

Angel tucked in his head and rolled several times before his momentum played out. Bits and pieces of metal and plastic bounced off his clothes and arms. He climbed to his feet in time to see the truck careen around a corner and slip out of sight.

First the demon had escaped, and now he had to contend with the cult. Back to square one.

With his human right hand, Elliot scratched the pointed ridges rising from the curve of his spine. The itching was confined to the boundary between his human skin and the new gray leathery hide. Occasionally he could peel off long strips of his human skin, as if it had been toasted by a bad sunburn.

He squeezed his eyes shut as sudden pressure swelled inside his head. *Here's . . . Yunk'sh*, he thought, and would have laughed at his joke if his head wasn't throbbing in excruciating pain. The air in the bedroom swirled into a ghostly viscosity, and seconds later, Yunk'sh was solid again, still in his Richard form, but not exactly basking in the afterglow of absorption.

Yunk'sh looked as if he wanted to hit someone, looked, in fact, as if he already had and wanted to repeat the experience. "It was a trap," the demon roared. "They tried to kill me."

"Damn! It was too good to be true." Elliot sighed. "She was a cult plant?"

"No, the cult came later. This . . . Cordelia was working for another individual, an extraordinary individual called Angel, who possesses superhuman strength and agility. I decided to take his measure in this form. And let's just say it is fortunate for us that he is not with the cult, although he wished to destroy me, not bind me."

"How could he destroy you?"

Yunk'sh stared at Elliot long enough to make him uncomfortable. "While I am in this physical form, I can be bound by ritual or destroyed by decapitation. Yet decapitation is a half measure. He would then need to burn this body before I could dematerialize. Yet the shock of decapitation might be enough to prevent me from dematerializing fast enough."

Elliot sat in his computer chair. "Even though this Angel guy has figured out how I find your sacrifices, he won't help the cult."

"It matters not. I must find another victim. Tonight."

"But I couldn't possibly find another—"

"Not your way," the demon said. "I will hunt out there, on the streets, all night if necessary. I will not fail this close to re-spawning! I only returned to prepare you for your ordeal."

"Ordeal?"

"Simply this. I will need to materialize and dematerialize several times in quick succession. While this will weaken me, you will be sickened."

"More headaches?"

The demon nodded. "And you may become physically ill. Also, your deformities may accelerate."

"I wish you had warned me about the deformities before I signed on."

"If I had, would you have declined my offer?"

Elliot heaved a long sigh. *It's not like I could*

renege now, and besides, it's almost over. "Since it's only temporary, I guess not."

The demon laughed, the rumbling sound of approaching storm clouds. "Good, Elliot. Because one way or another, we are in this to the end."

"As my mother used to say, 'If life gives you lemons, make lemonade.' "

When the demon vanished in a swirl of air, the pressure behind Elliot's eyes eased, but the reprieve would be short-lived. With a minute or two to get settled, he rounded up the Advil, a two-liter bottle of Coke, and the party-size bag of cheese curls before returning to his bedroom. Finally, he placed an empty bucket beside the bed.

Early in the morning the streets were fairly deserted, which meant fewer potential victims but also fewer witnesses and complications. Yunk'sh appeared first in Santa Monica, close enough to the pier to find pedestrians but far enough away to avoid lingering crowds. Immediately he altered his appearance, making himself short with a slender build to seem harmless, and giving himself long, dark hair, pale blue eyes, pierced ears, and a goatee to appear a bit exotic. A large crystal pendant, a silver shirt, a black jacket embroidered with silver stars and moons, and matching pants completed his new persona. First he would try a subtle, if deceptive, approach. Granted, his costume was anything but subtle, but he couldn't absorb the life essence of a corpse, so he needed to determine the astrological signs of humans who were still alive. He stopped a young couple walking hand in hand and told them he was a young psychic practicing his gift and would pay twenty dollars if he could correctly guess their birth sign.

The man, who had short-cropped red hair, laughed. "Should be the other way around. If you're right, we pay you."

"Your incentive to help me hone my powers." This way, if he guessed correctly and they wanted the money, they'd have to prove their birthday. "I know it's late, but I find my psychic abilities are stronger after midnight." He smiled. "Guess I'm attuned to the witching hour."

The woman chuckled and with it, her nervousness eased.

The couple exchanged a look. Yunk'sh imagined they were thinking, What could be the harm? *If only they knew.* Finally, as if it would matter, the woman asked, "What's your name?"

"Sergio," Yunk'sh said.

"Okay, Sergio, I'll play," the woman said. "My name's Sylvia, by the way, in case that helps. Fire away."

Yunk'sh named the same sign he would have had by now if Cordelia hadn't been part of a trap. He could tell immediately that Sylvia was the wrong sign, even before she shook her head. Yunk'sh turned to the man, "Then surely it is your sign I am sensing."

"Sorry, pal. Guess you keep your money tonight."

Yunk'sh failed again with another couple in the same area, then found concealment in the shadows and winked out, to reappear in Culver City. He saw another pedestrian, followed by a man in a car stopped at a red light. Although he needed to find a victim for his cycle, he could not stay in any one location too long. When he switched locales, he had to reappear far enough from his last location to thwart the cult, on the chance that they were still out searching for him. Next he tried Hollywood, hoping to encounter some restless tourists. On his third try he lucked out, stopping a man in a green-and-white rugby shirt, faded jeans, and gray snake-skin boots as he exited a parking garage.

"You are good, my little mystical buddy," the tall, barrel-chested man proclaimed with an easy grin when Yunk'sh correctly guessed his sign. "This is my lucky day. You nailed it."

"Understand," Yunk'sh said carefully, "before I give you the money, I need to see proof."

The big man looked him over, assessing the threat the diminutive Sergio represented. After a moment the man decided he had nothing to fear and twenty dollars to gain. He opened his wallet and removed a laminated Oregon driver's license, which he flashed for inspection. "Read it and weep."

Excitement flared in Yunk'sh as he scanned the card to be sure the man wasn't attempting a deception. "You are J. Christopher Van Trump?"

"That I am, Mysterio. But you can call me Chris."

"And this really is your birth date, Chris?"

Chris chuckled. "So the state of Oregon tells me. Now pay up."

In a flash, Yunk'sh grabbed the collar of the rugby shirt and shoved Chris back several steps, slamming him into the concrete support of the parking garage hard enough to stun but not kill. Chris had already had a few drinks, so the impact was enough to take away the rest of his legs. Falling hard on his rump, he glanced around, dazed, not sure what had just happened. Yunk'sh grabbed a fistful of hair and pulled the bigger man's head back.

Yunk'sh extended his tongue and forced it down the man's throat; then he extended his fingers and pierced his victim's shoulders and neck. Chris thrashed, his feet drumming a tattoo on the sidewalk, but he could neither cough nor gag and soon there wasn't enough of him left to do much of anything.

When Yunk'sh reappeared in Elliot's bedroom to declare his success, Elliot was retching over a bucket and appeared in desperate need of target practice. On the bedspread was a scattered mound of bright orange powder, like radioactive waste. "Good . . . for you," Elliot said. "Now . . . before my head explodes . . . *please* get the hell out of here!"

"I will need time to process the latest sacrifice," Yunk'sh said agreeably. "Just know that the end is near."

"Speak for yourself," Elliot said, retching again.

Yunk'sh grimaced at the wet, violent sound and dematerialized.

Back in the offices of Angel Investigations, Doyle had pulled a chair up beside Cordelia and had his arm comfortingly around her shoulders. Her voice was still hoarse, and now and then she had a coughing spasm. Occasionally she would shudder with the aftereffects of fear, revulsion, and probably a little bit of shock.

Angel stood in front of her, looking apologetic. "Cordelia, I'm sorry—"

"Forget it," she said. "You promised you wouldn't let me die, and I'm still alive. That was our deal, right?"

"Yes. And you're being good about—"

"No, it's my fault," she added. "I never asked about assault and battery, kidnapping, and near-strangulation."

Angel frowned. He couldn't blame her for being upset, but wasn't sure how to mend the fences, regain her trust. Fortunately, the telephone rang. Angel held up his hand and grabbed it. He listened for a moment, then mouthed a single word, "Kate." Doyle and Cordelia exchanged a nervous glance. He listened a short while longer. "Hollywood? Yes. Yes, that is interesting. Hold on a second." Angel covered the mouthpiece. "Apparently the demon couldn't wait another night."

Cordelia's eyes went wide. "He killed number eleven?"

Angel nodded. "In Hollywood. Different M.O. Looks like he confronted some guy outside a parking garage."

"How'd he know the guy's zodiac sign?" Doyle asked.

"There were signs of a struggle. The police found the man's wallet and driver's license next to the body."

"Go," Cordelia told Angel.

"I don't want to leave you here alone after—"

Cordelia wrapped one arm loosely around Doyle's waist, and he wasn't exactly complaining. "Doyle will comfort me. Won't you, Doyle?"

"I'm your man," Doyle said, sitting up a little straighter.

"If you're sure you're okay . . ."

"I'm not," Cordelia admitted. "But your staying won't help me feel any better. I just need some time to get over the shakes. Now go. Stop this thing."

Angel spoke into the telephone again. "On my way," he said and hung up.

"Angel, what are you gonna tell Kate? I mean, about tonight."

"I'll play it by ear," Angel said. "Whatever I decide to tell her, she's won't be happy about it."

"There's an understatement."

Angel headed for the door. He looked back at Cordelia, still ambivalent about leaving her so soon after she'd nearly been strangled. But she was right: she was safe now, and he had to deal with the bigger problem. Just before he left, he said to Doyle, "Take good care of her."

CHAPTER SIXTEEN

Angel ducked under the yellow crime scene tape behind Kate Lockley, who wore a white cable-knit sweater over jeans with her detective's shield clipped to her belt. Red-and-blue police lights strobed the night. An ambulance was parked nearby, headlights and red flashers on.

A couple of plainclothes detectives and several uniforms milled around the area while the crime scene techs took measurements, photos, and video. The medical examiner finished with the body, ripping surgical gloves off his hands as he spoke to two paramedics. Across the street, a KNBC news truck had already arrived on the scene. Two uniforms kept the reporter and cameraman at a safe distance, nominally to preserve the crime scene. Angel would have to slip by the news crew when he was through.

The wash of light revealed the body, mostly a pile

of clothes doubled over at the waist, translucent skin showing above the collar and cuffs. "Other than the remains of the victim, a completely different M.O.," Kate was saying. "Accosted on the street. Looks like they slammed his head against the support here." She indicated a smear of blood. "Wasn't enough to kill him. Wallet on the ground, no cash or credit cards in it. Since robbery wasn't a motive in the other slayings, we think somebody came along afterward and took anything of value, including the shoes. No way to know if the killer or killers examined the victim's license before or after they killed him."

"Before," Angel concluded. "Otherwise the street would be littered with bodies. This murder fits the pattern. The killer was looking for this specific astrological sign and killed when he found it." *Besides,* Angel thought, *the demon needs his sacrifices alive.*

"Funny you should mention that," Kate said, nothing humorous in her tone. "Two witnesses came forward. Apparently they talked to some street psychic who tried to guess their birth sign. He promised them twenty bucks if he guessed right."

"Pay *them?* Unusual, don't you think?"

"Definitely not your typical hustler."

"If he guessed right, he wanted them to prove it," Angel said. "Witness descriptions match this time?"

Kate nodded. "Small, slender man. Long, dark

hair. Goatee. Black suit with silver stars and moons embroidered on it. Of course that doesn't match any of the other descriptions of the killer, but at least they're describing the same guy now. A definite improvement."

"He wanted to look harmless, maybe a bit eccentric, playing the part."

"A master of disguise?"

"Definitely," Angel said and left it at that. A matching description was a meaningless lead. *Kate wouldn't find the killer by circulating a witness sketch.*

"You know something you're not telling me," Kate said.

Angel nodded and turned his back to the crime scene unit. "I almost had him tonight."

"What!"

"I set a trap," Angel said.

"Tell me you didn't go into those chat rooms," Kate hissed.

"None of the chat rooms you gave me." Angel explained quickly how they had set up false identities in various local chat rooms using the remaining zodiac signs as bait.

Furious, Kate struggled to keep her voice down. "You may have ruined our only chance of catching this guy!"

Angel said nothing. There was nothing he could say that she would understand or accept.

Finally, Kate sighed. She placed a hand on her

forehead and brushed it back through her blond hair, then shook her head in disbelief. When she spoke, her voice was controlled. "Because of your little stunt, he's already changed his M.O."

"He was desperate," Angel said. "The cult only needs one more sacrifice before—"

"Before what?"

Angel forced himself to shrug. "I don't know."

She looked back toward the victim for a moment, made a decision. "When I leave here, you're coming with me. I'm taking a full written statement from you. Understood?"

"Yes."

"Good," Kate said. "Then you're through. I want my files back."

"Kate—"

"I'm serious. If I find out you've been talking to witnesses or looking at crime scenes or visiting chat rooms I *will* arrest you for obstruction of justice and anything else I can throw at you."

Angel couldn't blame her for overreacting. As far as Kate was concerned, his interference had driven the killer in a new, dangerous, and unknown direction. But nothing had changed. The demon had his eleventh victim now and only needed one more. If the Vishrak demon completed his cycle and was re-spawned, Kate's threats of arrest would be the least of his concerns—and hers, as well.

* * *

Cordelia had slipped out of Doyle's grasp.

Instead of sitting in her chair, huddled against him, she was up and pacing the reception area, rubbing her left arm vigorously, as if trying to chase a preternatural chill out of her bones and failing miserably.

"No matter how well you think you know someone," Cordelia said. "Appearances can fool you. Doyle, he looked as normal as you do."

"I can imagine," Doyle said noncommittally.

"Strange, though," Cordelia added. "Why would the demon appear to me as you and not as the stud muffin combo platter I requested?"

Doyle frowned, not at all sure he'd come out of that comparison with the tiniest bit of his dignity still intact. "You really saw me?"

Cordelia nodded. "He must have known who you were, who *we* were."

"How could he?" Doyle asked, hoping she'd come to the logical conclusion and realize what it meant. It would be so much easier for him, for what he had to tell her about himself, if she could only admit she had feelings for him first.

Cordelia tried to reason it out. "Well . . . he's a demon." Doyle nodded, encouraging her. "And he has this glamour thingy—which has absolutely nothing to do with *Glamour* magazine, right?"

"Not in the same context."

"It's just demon magic."

Doyle nodded again and decided to help her along. "The power of his glamour is to make the victim see someone he or she desires."

Cordelia looked at him with sudden comprehension in her eyes. She snapped her fingers. "That's it!"

Doyle stood up. "Figured it out, have you?"

"Of course," she said. "I was nervous, wondering if you guys would be there to protect me, so I really wanted to see both of you."

"Oh." Doyle was crestfallen. She'd missed it.

"Although why I saw you and not Angel . . . I mean he is obviously the better choice in the bodyguard department." She noticed his frown. "Not that you're completely helpless."

"Oh, thank you. You're too generous."

"You know what I mean, Doyle." Cordelia sighed. "You stalled him long enough for Angel to scare him off." She ran a hand through her hair. "Maybe this demon just plucked one of the images out of my mind to trick me."

Doyle tried a different, riskier tack. "You know who I saw?"

"When you looked at the demon?"

Doyle nodded, looked her in the eye, and said, "I saw you."

"Of course you did. I was standing right next to the demon."

"Then I should say I saw two of you. Side by side. Both wearing that remarkable red dress. Like twins."

"That's odd," Cordelia said. "I wonder why you would see me . . . see the demon as me, I mean."

"Why do you think?"

Cordelia shrugged and threw her hands wide. "I don't know. Probably because you were worried about me and wanted me safe."

"Well, I was and I did." *But that's not the half of it.*

She walked over to where he stood and placed a hand against his jaw. "Thanks," she said. "I really trust you . . . and Angel. Otherwise I never would have gone through with this harebrained scheme."

"That demon really shook you up."

"That's an understatement," she said. She held up her hand, thumb and index finger an inch apart. "I was this close to being dead. I saw a tunnel, all right, but no light at the end of it. Everything was dark. Pitch black." She shuddered again and raised her hands to her throat. "Feeling those icky demon tentacles wrapped around my throat. So gross. You can't imagine."

"You know, Cordelia, not all demons wear black hats. I mean, they're not all as evil as this Vishrak. One bad apple and all that."

"Right," Cordelia said. "Some are more evil than others. Except for Angel. He's not evil . . . right now. Well, as long as he stays on the straight and narrow and doesn't have—"

"I mean, besides Angel."

"After tonight, when it comes to demons, I have to say 'shoot first and ask questions later.'"

Doyle felt a sting of bitterness.

By the time Elliot woke later that same day, it was close to evening. Since Elliot was the living conduit that gave the demon substance, Yunk'sh's frantic hunt for victim number eleven, and all the physical manifestations required, had taken its toll on Elliot's body. He fought for enough strength to roll onto his back, away from the foul-smelling bucket. Scratching his chest, he discovered scattered patches of the rough gray skin. Yunk'sh had warned him the deformities might accelerate during his hunt, which made Elliot wonder what else had changed.

He examined his right hand and was relieved that he still had all his human fingers, although the fingernails were cracked. The itching extended to his scalp and he tentatively explored the area; he was slightly alarmed when clumps of hair came away in his fingers, exposing scattered bald patches. Judging by touch alone, the rest of his face had remained human. Looking down his body, he saw that the right leg and foot seemed normal although his kneecap was tough and gray. Not great, but he should be as mobile as the day before.

He swung his legs over the edge of the bed and shoved himself to his feet, waiting for a momentary light-headedness to pass before lumbering into the bathroom, wearing only his Bart Simpson boxers.

Squinting into the bathroom mirror in the unforgiving light, he examined the reflection of his face, grateful that he hadn't sprouted a third eye or a pair of horns. The bald spots were a little unnerving but a baseball cap would hide them.

He gargled vigorously for thirty seconds then spit out the mouthwash. He ran cold water in the sink and splashed it into his haggard face to help rouse him before scrubbing at his eyes to get the sleep crust out. When he blinked at the mirror again, he saw the change. His face had become more alien. His eyebrows were gone. The swirling water in the sink was carrying them down the drain. Peering closer at the mirror, he saw that most of his eyelashes had just fallen out as well.

So now I need a baseball cap and sunglasses. If losing his eyebrows and eyelashes was the worst thing that happened to him in the next twenty-four hours, the last sacrifice would be a cakewalk.

He scratched his belly around his navel with the fingers of his right hand. Well, it would have been around his navel if he still had one. But it was gone. That was the easiest deformity to hide, yet of all the changes to his body, it was the most disturbing, because it made him feel most nonhuman. But in a day, maybe two, he would be back to normal—better than normal—and the Grundy Operating

System, Elliot's revolutionary new legacy to the technological masses, would become a reality. As he'd told Yunk'sh, "Keep your eyes on the prize."

A hot shower made him feel more awake, if no more human. After he stepped out, he was completely hairless, like that odd breed of cat. Also, he discovered that the ridges along his spine extended to his tailbone, which was now protruding a bit, wedge-shaped, and pointing down. "Shit," he whispered. "I'm growing a tail."

With renewed dedication to the demon's cause, he was determined to find the twelfth and final victim in record time. He'd kept a folder with a list of the victims' names, signs, and other vital details. Some of the chat room sessions had occurred over the course of several days before he broached the subject of a meeting, so conversations had overlapped. He'd had to make all of them feel special, man or woman, according to the part he was playing to lure them into Yunk'sh's trap.

A master sheet he'd maintained was a quick guide to the twelve signs, listing purported personality traits and how each sign related to the other signs. This cheat sheet had been a perfect tool, since Elliot wasn't exactly a zodiac kind of guy. He could count on the fingers of one hand—good thing since only one hand still had real fingers—the number of times he'd read his horoscope in the newspaper. While Yunk'sh's respawning window was contingent upon Neptune being in the same constellation it had been in during his initial spawning, the demon needed to complete the wheel of the zodiac because it encompassed—symbolically, at least—all of humanity in a wheel, a cycle, a circle. And much of magic depended on symbolism. Aside from that bit of knowledge, Elliot was astrologically clueless. So he had used the master sheet to mingle with the astrologically inclined and, after each successful sacrifice, had crossed off the pertinent sign. The process had been a macabre "got 'em, need 'em, got 'em" approach to finding victims, but it had been enormously practical. Especially since Yunk'sh dictated which signs he preferred to acquire seemingly at random. And now all but two signs were checked off.

Elliot reached for a pen to cross off the penultimate sign. *Mission accomplished, if not the way we intended.* He drew a big X through the sign. *One sign left,* Elliot thought. *I wonder if he was saving the best for last.*

Elliot waited while his computer booted, then brought up his chat room addresses and cross-referenced those with his file of potential candidates for the last sacrifice. When Yunk'sh appeared, Elliot wanted to have a plan mapped out for the evening. Maybe Yunk'sh would even let Elliot boot up GOS again while he was out completing the ritual. He should know the ins and outs of his own operating system before he sprang it on the world.

He found only three good candidates in his file, and two of those were in the preliminary stages of the on-line relationship. There was nothing altogether special about this last sign, so he should just pick the easiest target, the woman furthest along in his wooing campaign, and try to arrange a meeting for that night. Since he'd slept away most of the day, the easiest target seemed best. *The shortest distance between two points is a straight line,* he thought. While he waited for the chat room software to load and go to the correct address, he tapped the two thick fingers of his left hand, his deformed hand, on the desk.

He stopped tapping the fingers.

The easiest target.

Elliot grabbed the master sheet and looked at all the astrological signs he had crossed off the complete list. One left out of twelve. The last sign was . . . his own.

Standing up so abruptly that his chair fell over, Elliot backed away from the computer as if it had bitten him. "Oh, man," he said faintly, "that double-crossing bastard!" He'd been a fool, a blind fool! The deformities weren't temporary, as Yunk'sh had assured him. As the cycle had progressed, Elliot's own body was transforming—to become the demon's re-spawned body! Elliot would be the twelfth and final victim and then the demon would somehow take over Elliot's altered body. It made sickening sense.

"I am so totally screwed," he said, panicked. *I gotta get the hell out of here!* He dressed quickly in a sweatshirt and fleece sweatpants, cursing vehemently while he taped his sliced sneaker over his wide left foot. He took a Dodgers baseball cap from the closet and a cheap pair of sunglasses from the kitchen junk drawer.

As he reached the door to his apartment, he stopped and banged his head against the wood panel. *There's nowhere to go,* he told himself. *I'm linked to him. No matter how far I run, eventually he'll catch me.*

All his dreams evaporated in the few seconds he stood with his head bowed against the door. The demon had lied to Elliot about everything because he needed a human intermediary to gain the temporary physical form needed to kill his victims. He'd needed Elliot to find victims. All but one. The twelfth victim Yunk'sh had found all on his own. And baited the trap with an irresistible morsel. Without the dreams, all Elliot had left was his life.

And tonight he'll kill me.

Elliot began to pace the living room, banging his deformed left fist into the side of his head as if he could jar loose an idea. "Options, I need options." He sighed. "Okay. Find the cult. Let them have the demon. Right? No, no, no! They'll just hold you down while Yunk'sh kills you, completes his cycle, and falls into their hands. What, then? What—No, not what . . . who!"

Elliot returned to his bedroom and his computer desk. Opening his Web browser's window, he muttered, "The enemy of my enemy," as he brought up a search engine and entered several key words, starting with "Angel."

CHAPTER SEVENTEEN

When the telephone at Angel Investigations rang, Cordelia picked up the handset and gave her usual greeting: "Angel Investigations. We help the helpless. How can we help you?" She listened briefly. "Oh, hi!" Then her eyes went wide. "Oh, no! No, wait a— He's here." Cordelia looked up at Angel, who had come out of his office after the phone rang. "Okay, okay. I'll tell him." She hung up the phone, then scribbled some notes.

"Tell me that wasn't Kate," Angel said. He'd spent several hours yesterday—actually much earlier that morning—telling and retelling Detective Lockley everything they'd done to set the trap for the demon. But that hadn't been good enough, so Kate had had Cordelia and Doyle come down at nine o'clock and explain it all again, separately. By noon she'd finally been satisfied they were telling the truth—which they were, right up to the point where they substituted the word "stalker" or "killer" for "demon."

Doyle stood up, dropping the newspaper account of the murders on the chair behind him. "Anyone but Detective Lockley."

Cordelia shook her head. "No. It was Chelsea Monroe, from *L.A. After Dark.* She sounded nervous, said it was urgent. She needs your help, Angel. At this address."

Angel took the note paper and checked the address.

"Go," Doyle said. "Don't worry. I'll keep looking for the spell or ritual that locates the demon while it's in its borrowed form. And Cordelia here will continue to do the chat room mambo."

"Except this time," Cordelia added, "Doyle's the bait."

"Fine," Angel said. "But, Doyle, don't forget your other sources. We need to approach this from all directions."

Doyle nodded. "If anything develops, we'll call your cell."

The address Chelsea Monroe had given Cordelia led Angel to Armand's on La Cienega in Beverly Hills. He found her one floor up, in the Crescent Lounge, a piano bar. With quick, wary glances, Angel checked his surroundings, attempting to locate the apparent menace.

While the inner curve of the lounge overlooked the wide expanse of the restaurant below, the outer curve faced a wall of floor-to-ceiling glass with a stunning view of the immaculate boulevard, modern buildings separated by orderly rows of palm trees. A stunning modern view, as if someone had just removed the shrink-wrap. *Some sections of the city can fool you into thinking almost anything is possible,* Angel thought.

Chelsea Monroe had been sitting at one of the small tables, a long-stemmed wineglass in front of her. She rose when she saw him, smiled with uncharacteristic hesitation. She wore a shimmering bronze blouse with a plunging neckline, a calf-length burgundy skirt, and matching leather boots. Without one of her expensively tailored suits she seemed unusually casual. She stared at him with her rich green eyes, as if memorizing his every feature. "Angel, I'm so glad you came."

Several other couples had come up to the lounge, to better hear the piano player at the white baby grand and perhaps to distance themselves from the clinking of crockery and stemware in the restaurant below. As if by unspoken agreement, all the couples were evenly dispersed, keeping conversations intimate and, Angel hoped, private.

With one last darting glance around the lounge, Angel stepped forward and whispered, "Cordelia said it was urgent."

"I urgently needed you away from that office," Chelsea said. "I'm starting to suspect you hide behind your isolation. Now please, join me at my table."

Angel frowned but accompanied her back to the table to keep their conversation private. "I thought you were in danger."

"I am," she said. "We are."

"I don't follow you."

"I only wanted to give us a chance."

"There is no us," Angel said adding more firmly, "And you lied to me."

"Forgive my little deception." Chelsea reached out and touched the back of his hand. For a moment, Angel didn't pull away. And, if only for that moment, he entertained a possibility of his own, one that could never really exist, one that faded with only a tinge of regret, best forgotten. "This isn't about my show and hasn't been for a while, although I thought I could use the show as a pretext to spend some time with you."

"Failing that," Angel said, "you pretended to be in danger."

A couple walked hand in hand to the small parquet dance floor and began to sway slowly to a Cole Porter tune tinkling from the piano.

Chelsea quirked a wry smile. "I've got you under my skin."

"Excuse me?"

She nodded toward the piano player. "He's playing the Cole Porter song." Canting her head, she said, "I don't suppose you'd care to dance."

For some reason, he found it difficult to stay mad at her and wondered at his own resolve. He sighed. Looking out the grand windows gave the illusion that anything was possible, but that was all it was—an illusion. The reality of life was a series of hard decisions, sacrifices, and responsibilities. "Chelsea, I'm sorry but this just isn't possible."

"Shouldn't anything be possible?" Chelsea asked him. "If we want it badly enough?"

His cell phone chirped.

Angel pulled the phone from his jacket. "I'm expecting an important call," he explained. With a resigned nod, Chelsea sat down at the table and took a sip of wine. Angel turned away and lowered his voice to answer the call. "Cordelia. Did you find something?"

Cordelia twisted the telephone cord excitedly between her fingers. "No, but something found us. You'll never guess. Okay, then don't guess. We were hungry, so Doyle went for takeout and then the phone rang and it was him. The human servant, that's who! He found our phone number on the Web page. I won't say I told you so, but I told you the Web site was a good idea."

Listening, Cordelia sat in her chair but stood up

again in a moment. She reached for a pen in the round desktop holder and knocked the whole thing over, spilling pens, pencils, and paper clips. "He wants to come over to our side, help us kill this Vishrak demon before it's too late. I believed him because he sounded totally terrified."

Doyle backed through the door balancing a large white bag and a couple of cartons of Chinese take-out.

Cordelia cleared a spot on her desk. "He thinks the demon wants to kill him next. Oh, well, I got his name, address, and phone number. No, I told him to wait there, that I'd call you and send you right over."

Doyle mouthed, "Angel?" And Cordelia nodded. "Okay, okay, Mr. Twenty-twenty-hindsight. I'll call him back and tell him. Here it is." She read the name, address, and phone number to Angel. "I think that's near Culver City. Oh—don't hang up! How's Chelsea? What? A misunderstanding? Well, if you say so."

When she hung up the telephone, Doyle asked, "What'd I miss?"

"The human servant just called. He wants to change teams."

"Because the demon wants to kill him next."

"Oh, you heard that part. Anyway, I told him to wait there for Angel."

"You told him to wait for Angel right where the demon can find him?" Doyle asked.

"Now you sound like Angel," Cordelia said, picking up the telephone handset again. "I'm supposed to call this Grundy guy back and tell him to come here instead." She dialed the number, shaking her head as the phone on the other end of the line continued to ring. "Jeez! Everybody with the twenty-twenty hindsight. Besides, there's a demon after this guy. You really think he's safe anywhere?"

As soon as Elliot hung up the telephone in his apartment he felt the cold knot of dread in his stomach expanding, nearly paralyzing him. The woman in Angel's office had told him to sit tight, that she'd call Angel and have him drive immediately to Elliot's apartment. But as the minutes ticked by, Elliot felt a tide of panic rising within him. The demon would reappear any second and this Angel guy might take an hour to show. Less than five minutes had passed when he decided to run. *Anywhere is better than here. I know Angel's office address. Why not wait there?*

Another minute or so passed while he tugged on his canvas gloves, pulled down the bill of his cap, and slipped into an overcoat. With the taped-up sneaker and the odd assortment of baggy clothing to hide his deformities, he appeared no more unusual than a homeless person. His bowlegged gait and prominent limp would be seen as nothing more than a disability.

He slipped quietly out of his third-floor apartment and hurried, as much as he was able, down the stairs, confident that he could still drive his battered old Chevy Cavalier. Since it was an automatic transmission, he only needed his right leg to accelerate and break, his right hand to change gears.

He heard the telephone ringing. *No way in hell I'm going back now!*

Elliot climbed awkwardly into his car, worked the ignition until the car sputtered to life, then swung out into traffic, trembling with relief. Rush hour was past, and the light traffic gave him time to consider his predicament. Yunk'sh would find the apartment abandoned. Elliot wondered how long the demon would hang around before beginning the search for his human servant—hell, human vessel! That delay was Elliot's only hope of reaching Angel in time. Would Yunk'sh grow weary of waiting for Elliot's return and simply hunt down another random victim as he had the previous night, to complete his ritual cycle? Even if Yunk'sh found a twelfth victim, Elliot had a sick feeling the demon would want to settle accounts.

Moments after the telephone stopped ringing, Yunk'sh swirled into existence in Elliot's bedroom and immediately sensed that his human servant and vessel was gone. In light of the demon's impending triumph, Elliot's absence seemed, at first, a minor inconvenience. But as the minutes ticked by, the demon began to wonder if he'd underestimated Elliot Grundy.

Elliot never strayed far from home. Since he had no social life, he spent most of his time eating, sleeping, watching television, or working at his computer. Uninteresting, unnoticed and most of all, unlikely to be missed, Elliot Grundy was an angry young man with little talent but a lot of envy and absolutely no ambition, at least not in the industrious sense of the word—all of which made him a perfect servant, victim, and vessel.

Yunk'sh walked through the apartment, looking for a note, some indication of where Elliot had gone or when he would return. Nothing. "Where is my greedy little vessel?" Yunk'sh rumbled. He knew the cult now had his remnant corpse in Los Angeles. It was agonizing for him to sense his prior physical remains, yet be blind to its location. While his borrowed human form had its magical limitations, his re-spawned demonic body would allow him to rip aside the magical veil and destroy the cult and his own remnant corpse. But first he needed to complete the cycle. And for that he needed Elliot.

A few more minutes passed and Yunk'sh started to worry that Elliot, somehow realizing his fate, had fled. Returning to the bedroom, Yunk'sh perused the contents of Elliot's desk. He found the list of the victims and details about their personal lives and began to tear all the documents into tiny scraps. Next he found a list of all the signs of the zodiac with all but one crossed off. The last one was circled several times in red ink. "So the mortal fool does know what I intend for him." Yunk'sh slammed his hand down on the computer keyboard.

Instantly the animated screen saver blinked off, revealing a dark screen, a Web site for a detective agency. Then he glimpsed the name and shouted it in anger, "Angel!" Yunk'sh slammed his fist through the computer screen. The monitor made a loud pop, followed by a flurry of sparks. Lifting the monitor off the desk, Yunk'sh ripped it free of its connections and hurled it across the bedroom, where it took a large chunk out of the wall, then dropped to the floor with a heavy thud. The stale scent of ozone filled the air.

So he runs to my nonhuman enemy. Angel cannot save you, Elliot. We are linked, you and I. You can run, but you will not escape. Wherever you go, I will find you.

Each time Yunk'sh assumed physical form, he had to tug on the bond between them. Always the link had led back to this place, but Yunk'sh had the ability to follow the link wherever it led, and it would lead back to Elliot.

Somebody knocked on the outer door.

Only one person visits Elliot on a regular basis. Yunk'sh walked out of the bedroom and approached the door, listening but not speaking. His glamour reached out, tendrils of power seeking the human mind on the other side.

"Elliot, open up. It's me, Shirley! I heard a crash from downstairs."

Yunk'sh peered through the peephole. Its fish-bowl lens distorted the frizzle-haired young woman beyond. But she was alone. Maybe if he waited long enough, the meddlesome girl would go away.

"Elliot? C'mon, open up! You and me have to take care of each other, you know. It's fate, right?"

Fate?

"Elliot! C'mon, I'm worried. Open up or I'll call 911."

As he remembered Elliot's varied complaints about this Shirley Blodgett, a smile began to form on Yunk'sh's generic human face. Elliot could never seem to escape her attentions. Not only had they worked together, but she lived right below him and she always made a big fuss about how they had the exact same birth date.

The glamour complete, the demon's smile appeared now on Elliot's face. "I'm fine, Shirley," Yunk'sh said in Elliot's nasal voice and opened the door.

In a green pullover, blue jeans, and black running shoes, Shirley stood with her hands clasped together before her, worry etched on her face until his ready smile put her at ease. "Guess that was pretty dumb, about calling 911," she said. "I mean, you look fine. Even your burn is healed." She reached a hand out toward his. "Can I touch it?"

"See for yourself."

She did a double-take, before nodding with a pleased grin. When she took his bare hand, he could feel a slight tremor in hers. "So, um, what was that loud crash?"

"Nothing. I was cleaning out a closet and some stuff fell."

"Well, the doctor did a great job," she said, releasing his hand.

As she walked into the room, he closed and locked the door behind her. "I've been meaning to tell you, that lasagna was terrific."

She stared at him and frowned. "You were?" She laughed nervously. "I mean, of course you were. Well, you're certainly welcome."

"Next time we should, you know, eat together. It's not fair. I've really taken you for granted all these months. But that's gonna change."

"You sure you're feeling okay?"

"Terrific . . . now that you're here."

"You look a little pale."

With a mischievous grin, Yunk'sh said, "That's easily fixed."

His fingers twitched in anticipation.

CHAPTER EIGHTEEN

Angel swerved the convertible into the nearest parking space, almost jumping the curb in his haste, and ran to Elliot's apartment building. The old three-story building had been converted from a single-family home into three separate units. A small foyer featured a security panel and a locked inner door. Angel pressed the buzzer for Elliot's apartment. After a moment a hushed male voice spoke through the speaker, "Yes?"

"Elliot," Angel said. "It's Angel. You okay?"

"Yeah. But I'm scared. I was just about to leave. Come on up."

The lock release buzzed. Angel opened the inner door and took the steps three at a time, though his footfalls were silent, inhumanly silent. *One of the perks of being a vampire,* he thought. *Stealthy approaches.* Knowing the demon could return for

Elliot at any moment, Angel listened at the door, but heard only silence.

Angel knocked on the door. "Elliot?" Silence. "Elliot, open up."

Soft footfalls approached the door. Calm measured strides that seemed fainter as they neared the door. Caution? A hand fell on the doorknob. But that was all. The knob didn't turn. If Elliot was on the other side, he was waiting for something. *Maybe he wasn't alone.* "Elliot?"

Finally the chain rattled and the dead bolt clicked back. The doorknob rotated counterclockwise and the door swung inward. Smiling at him, as lovely as ever, was Buffy Summers. "Buffy . . ."

A moment's hesitation. But that was all the demon needed.

Beyond Buffy's shoulder, Angel glimpsed a pile of clothes and black sneakers that had been kicked under the sofa. Near them was the translucent sheath of human skin topped with dark, frizzy hair. But in that moment of uncertainty, the implications of those macabre details refused to register.

"Hello, lover," Buffy said and clasped Angel's neck in both hands.

With more raw strength than even the Slayer possessed, the impostor lifted Angel off the floor and hurled him into the room, where he slammed into the wall above the sofa. A remembered image flashed in his mind: *The blond woman in the dance club beside Cordelia—I never saw her face!*

Angel rolled down the back of the sofa, striking a floor lamp with one outstretched arm. The demon, still masquerading as Buffy, strode forward and kicked him in the stomach with enough force to double him over. A second kick sailed toward his face. He recoiled, catching the foot at the heel and giving it a hard shove straight up. The demon fell on its back, arms slapping the floor to absorb the impact.

Angel sprang to his feet, wielding the floor lamp like a quarterstaff. The demon was back on its feet a moment later. Angel feinted a thrust with the lamp, then swung low, clipping one of the demon's knees. With a backward hop, the demon regained its balance, even as Angel charged, holding the lamp parallel to the floor and driving the demon back against the far wall a second after tugging the plug free of its socket.

Buffy's face stared back at him, displaying a rabid expression, equal parts anger and hate. Even when Angel had become the evil Angelus and Buffy had fought him in earnest, with everything she had, she'd never looked at him with that much venom. Determination, confidence, heartache, and regret, but never the mindless hatred the demon brought to the face of the woman Angel loved, perhaps always would love. But the illusion only worked while the victim believed in it.

The demon swung a fist down, bending the lamp pole into a *V* shape, then reached for Angel's throat, nails digging into his flesh. Angel's face morphed into its vampire countenance—convoluted brow, fangs, and yellow eyes. He launched an overhand right, striking the Buffy face square in the nose. The hand around his throat loosened and he pulled away.

"A vampire, then," the demon said. "That explains your strength but not your involvement." The voice was no longer Buffy's and a moment later, as the demon dropped the illusion, its face and body morphed into a gray-skinned, three-fingered demon slightly taller than Angel with ridges down its spine, its outer forearms, and its shins. A leathery tail, lined with ridges, whipped to and fro. The demon strode forward. "Why would a vampire help poor little Elliot Grundy?"

Angel tossed the battered lamp aside. "Moot point," Angel replied with a nod toward the clothes and shed skin. "Since you've already killed him."

"That's not Elliot." The demon smiled, exposing a row of needle teeth. "After Elliot fled, his downstairs neighbor decided to aid my cause." The demon swung an open left hand at Angel's face. Angel leaned back, heard the thick claws whistle through the air, inches from his nose. He countered with a punch under the demon's ribs.

"Elliot thought *he* was your twelfth."

"I only needed his sign," the demon replied. "His neighbor matched—same birth date. Quite a topic of conversation around here. And she served me well. It was glorious! As I sucked the last drop of life out of her, I achieved ritual completion. My borrowed form, the physical essence I had pulled from Elliot, became superfluous. The accumulated life force and bodily matter of a dozen humans transmuted into this re-spawned demonic body. I am only now beginning to feel my new power on this physical plane."

Angel sprang forward, and they exchanged a flurry of punches, but Angel took the first serious hit. Blood trickled down from his left eyebrow. They both jumped back, just out of reach of each other, circling. "If this is your re-spawned body, I have to say I've seen better."

"Do not be misled. My form is yet immature," the demon replied. "I will continue to grow stronger in the coming day. And I am free to feed at will. Elliot will be my next meal, followed, I think, by your pretty little assistant."

He's just trying to goad me into making a mistake, Angel realized, ignoring the tight feeling across his chest. The ritual cycle was complete. No longer a detached psyche, the demon had his re-spawned body. But the re-spawned body could be destroyed and banished forever. *And this time he can't vanish when the going gets tough.* Angel needed a moment to reach for his boot sheath. Closing the distance between them, he waited for the demon to take advantage of his proximity.

Lunging forward with both hands poised to seize Angel's throat, the demon was caught off guard when Angel dropped to a crouch. He hurled the demon back, using his forward momentum to send him end over end across the room. The demon crashed into the kitchen table, smashing it and toppling a chair. A little farther and he would have been propelled right through the kitchen window.

Knife in hand, Angel spun around and surged forward to press the attack. He paused as a crash sounded from below, followed by a rush of footfalls up the stairwell. Not expecting a regiment of the cavalry, Angel had a bad feeling about the new arrivals. The demon scrambled up from the debris of the kitchen table, hoisting a chair in both hands. He was about to toss it at Angel, but when he saw the black-cloaked figures rush through the door, brandishing ceremonial daggers, he turned and threw it at them.

The two men in the middle raised their arms as the chair struck them. Others scattered, stepping around Angel and all but ignoring him as they stalked the demon. Yunk'sh's yellow eyes grew wide as a seventh man entered the apartment—a bald man with hands extended, fingers glowing green. *The cult's resident sorcerer,* Angel guessed.

"Yunk'sh," the bald man intoned, "I bind you to our will and to our purpose."

The demon turned away from the sorcerer and, with two long strides, flung himself through the kitchen window. Somehow Angel knew Yunk'sh would survive the three-story drop.

The sorcerer, standing just behind and to one side of Angel, looked at him, noticing for the first time that Angel was a vampire. "You have interfered, vampire."

"Don't look at me. I want to kill him, not bind him."

"If you would kill Yunk'sh," the sorcerer replied simply, "then we must kill you."

Angel drove his elbow into the man's face, breaking his nose and dropping him to the floor. "Think again."

"Kill him!" the sorcerer screamed, unintentionally smearing green ointment over his split and bleeding nose.

Angel was outnumbered six to one—seven if he counted the sorcerer, who seemed more eager to bark orders than join the fray. All six men had knives and seemed comfortable handling them. They formed a circle around him. Meanwhile, Angel noticed, Yunk'sh, as they called the demon, was getting away.

The sorcerer yelled, "Not with knives! A stake through the heart."

The oldest cult member pointed at the shattered

remains of the kitchen table. "Willem, find a weapon there. Let's end this now."

Angel could not have agreed more. He dropped to a crouch again and swept the legs out from under two cult members. Another jumped on his back, but Angel rolled with the attack, slamming the man to the floor hard enough to knock the wind out of him. Angel came up on his feet, blocked a knife attack with his forearm, and punched the assailant in the stomach with his free hand. In a moment they were all down and groaning except Willem, who had found something wooden and reasonably pointy. With the others groggy or wobbling on hands and knees, Willem seemed less than eager to press the attack on his own.

The oldest cult member shouted, "Kill him!"

Obediently, Willem raised the stake and charged.

Angel picked up the chair the demon had hurled across the apartment and slung it toward Willem, taking out his legs. Willem toppled over the chair, the stake sailing out of his hand.

Minutes later, from a nearby pay phone, Angel made an anonymous call to the police, reporting a violent disturbance at Elliot's address. As far as Kate was concerned, Angel was off the case. Depending on the speed of the police response, they might arrive in time to collect some cult members along with the remains of Elliot's neighbor.

If the demon was true to his word, he would attempt to kill Elliot next, followed by Cordelia. And if Cordelia had followed Angel's instructions, she and Elliot would both be waiting for Angel at his office.

Elliot was babbling and having trouble sitting still. He wanted to run but had nowhere to hide. "He'll kill me to complete the ritual. I'm the last sign, the last one he needs. You gotta believe me."

"He found a replacement, Elliot," Angel said, neglecting to inform Elliot that he was still next on the demon's hit list. If Elliot had any useful information about the demon, Angel needed to hear it before the demon's former human servant had another fit of hysterics.

"What? How could he find another . . . so fast?"

"Your downstairs neighbor."

Elliot's jaw dropped and he sagged in his chair. "Shirley. Oh, God. We are—were—the same sign. And I even told him about it when I was complaining about her. Oh, Shirley . . . I always said she was a pest, but she didn't mean any harm. Why'd he have to kill her?" With a heavy sigh, Elliot pressed his hand to his chest. "That explains it, then."

"What?"

"Since I made the pact, I've felt pressure, in my chest, even when Yunk'sh wasn't using me to manifest in physical form, like something tugging inside me. That feeling stopped on my way here. I just assumed it was relief at having gotten away, but it must have meant that he no longer needed to draw substance from me. That must have been when Shirley . . ." Elliot stared down at his hands—one human, the other demonic. "I'm responsible for this, for everything."

Angel crouched before him. "I need you to focus, Elliot. Yunk'sh said his re-spawned body was immature. Do you know what he meant?"

Elliot looked at him, uncomprehending.

Disgusted, Cordelia reached for the phone. "Detective Lockley's on speed dial. I'm sure she'll be happy to collect this piece of garbage."

Doyle stood beside her, placed his hand over hers. "Not yet," he whispered.

Cordelia frowned. "This goofball helped kill twelve people."

"We need him," Doyle said, softly, but firmly.

"I just want to be human again," Elliot murmured.

Angel grabbed Elliot's jaw, forced him to look at his face. "Elliot, this isn't helping."

"Okay," he said dejectedly. "Look, I'll cooperate. I'll plead guilty, go to jail, and help you kill Yunk'sh . . . on one condition."

"Elliot," Angel said, "you're an accomplice in twelve premeditated murders. That's not a real good bargaining position."

"I know," Elliot said. "But all I want is to become human again."

"You gave up that right, Grundy," Cordelia snapped.

"Cordelia," Angel chided, "you're not helping." And Yunk'sh had Cordelia on his hit list as well. If Elliot knew something that could help them fight the demon, Angel had to find out what it was while the information could still do some good. "Elliot, I'll do what I can."

"Okay," Elliot said. "Thanks. I'll tell you everything I know." He took a moment to gather his thoughts. "For twenty-four hours after he takes his new body, Yunk'sh is in a state of . . . flux or something. During that time he's vulnerable."

"Vulnerable to what?"

"Binding."

"The cult has tried at least twice and failed."

"Not with the remnant corpse," Elliot explained. "The corpse was useless to them before, but now that he inhabits his re-spawned body they have twenty-four hours to bind him by proxy, using the old corpse. That's how long it will take his psychic energy to settle permanently into the re-spawned body. Apparently they have a magic ritual to trick the psyche into being bound through the old corpse."

"The cult has the demon's old corpse? This remnant corpse?"

"They found it last night, in San Francisco. It's probably here in L.A. by now."

"Wait a minute!" Doyle called. He hurried to the file cabinet and brought back a large volume with worn edges. "When I was searching for a spell to help us find the demon, I came across a destruction spell, but I ignored it."

"Why?" Angel asked.

"Because it only works with this remnant corpse he's talking about."

The spell to destroy the Vishrak demon with the remnant corpse could only be performed during the twenty-four hours after the demon's psychic energy inhabited his re-spawned form. Before they could perform the spell, they would need a mystical container similar to an Orb of Thesulah to capture the demon's psychic energy and the remnant corpse itself.

"I'll meet with Dink again," Doyle volunteered. "I asked him to keep his ear to the ground on this cult business. If we find their hideout, we can relieve them of the remnant corpse before they perform the binding spell."

Angel nodded. "Good. I'll pick up the orb. Doyle, as soon as you learn the cult's location, call my cell phone and we'll rendezvous."

"What about us?" Cordelia asked, referring to Elliot and herself. "I'm not staying alone with him, no matter how sorry he is."

"Cordy, go with Doyle. Elliot, you come with me."

"I'll just slow you down."

Angel no longer needed to mince words. "Yunk'sh threatened to make you the first meal for his new body."

"I'll keep up."

"I thought you would."

Before they left on their separate errands, Angel pulled Doyle aside. "Don't let Cordelia out of your sight."

"That won't be a hardship," Doyle said, with a wink. "Wait a minute . . . that's your grim look. What don't I know?"

"Yunk'sh is not the forgiving type," Angel said softly.

"Oh," Doyle replied. "I understand completely."

The white box in Elliot's lap could have held a Christmas tree ornament. Instead it contained an unadorned glass sphere, handblown during a ritual incantation. While it would have appeared uninspired on a Christmas tree, it had the magical power to contain, for about two minutes, the psychic energy of a Vishrak demon settling into a respawned body. Fortunately the proprietor of Incense and Auguries had one of the orbs in stock, the first and only one she'd ever stocked.

"Interesting place," Elliot commented. "Do you shop there often?"

"Now and again." Angel's cell phone chirped, and he answered. After a moment he reached into the glove compartment, grabbed a pen and tablet, and wrote with the pad propped against the dashboard. "Trinity United Methodist." He scribbled down the address. "Got it. Tell Dink I owe him a jumbo carton of worms. Meet you there."

"Worms?" Elliot asked after Angel ended the call.

"An acquired taste."

"It would have to be," Elliot replied. "He found the cult's hideout?"

"Yes. You know, I could turn you over to the police," Angel offered. "You'd be safer."

Elliot thought about it for a moment then said, "No. I gotta do at least this one thing for Shirley. She never should have been a part of this. It's my fault. I didn't mean to set her up, but I did."

"You set up a lot of people, Elliot."

"I know," he said regretfully. "But Shirley actually liked me."

The scorched shell of the Trinity United Methodist Church was located in a depressed commercial district. To the left of the church was a muffler repair shop that had recently failed. To the right, beyond the church's weed-infested parking lot, was a carpet warehouse that had gone bankrupt two years earlier. The nearest viable business was a check-cashing store half a block away. Beyond that stood a pawnshop and a bodega. Several burned-out streetlights in the area had not been replaced.

Angel, Doyle, Cordelia, and Elliot crouched behind the convertible across the street from the condemned church. A few minutes ago the cult's sorcerer had arrived wearing a fresh bandage over his mashed nose and was now ready to perform the proxy binding spell. They were running out of time. Angel held a crowbar, straight end down, chipping at a fissure in the crumbling sidewalk. "Doyle, do you have everything?"

Doyle hefted a canvas gym bag. "Everything but the orb."

Elliot handed the little white box to Doyle, who unzipped the bag enough to drop the box inside. "All set."

Angel turned to Cordelia. "Are you prepared to chant the spell?"

"My Latin's a little rusty."

Doyle gave a dry chuckle. "Whose isn't?"

"You'll only have a few minutes to cast the spell," Angel said. Knowing time would be critical once they had the demon's remnant corpse, Angel had used the crowbar to pry loose the mounting plate of the padlock on what had been the employee entrance to the carpet warehouse. "I'll give you two minutes to get into position."

"How will we know you're in?" Elliot asked.

"Trust me," Angel replied, "you'll know."

CHAPTER NINETEEN

Two minutes later, trusting that Doyle, Cordelia, and Elliot were in position behind the church, Angel crossed the street, carrying the crowbar at his side like an unsheathed sword, almost invisible against his dark clothes. As he neared the double doors at the front of the church, he noticed the right one hung by a single rusty hinge. The door would squeal against the floor of the narthex when opened. *Perfect,* Angel thought.

He paused on the wide top step before the double doors and raised his right leg in front of the damaged door. He kicked the door so hard it ripped free of its last hinge and slammed into the far wall of the narthex, then fell back toward Angel. He slapped it aside, creating yet another crash.

Excited shouting echoed from the sanctuary.

Angel crossed the narthex then stopped, short of

the nave. Most of the arched ceiling of the church had been lost in the fire, but the burned and splintered beams still jutted out like the broken ribs of a giant's rotting carcass. The remaining pews were broken and charred as well, while the floor revealed treacherous gaps, the result of fire and water damage. Black candles flickered in the sanctuary, providing the only illumination.

By the fluttering golden light, Angel counted twelve cult members as they streamed out of the sanctuary, revealing a banquet table with a charred corpse atop it. A couple of the cult members were already brandishing long knives. The bald sorcerer, with his freshly bandaged nose, stayed back. "The vampire!" He turned to the oldest cult member. "Vincent, get the stakes!"

The old-timer reached into a canvas bag in front of the shattered altar rail and pulled out several crude wooden stakes. It mattered not how crude they were; the points were plenty sharp enough. Cult members grabbed them, an eager light in their eyes.

"Some people never learn," Angel said, loud enough for them to hear.

"Circle him!" Vincent yelled.

Since Vincent and the sorcerer weren't all that eager to jump into the fray, the odds were ten to one against Angel. Four came down the wide center aisle of the nave, and two filed down each of the narrow outer aisles. As long as Angel stayed near the narthex doorway, his back would be protected.

The flanks attacked first, but space was limited and they had to come at him one at a time. The one to his left held a stake aloft, while the one on the right had only a knife. Angel lunged to the left and rammed the pointed end of the crowbar into the gut of the first man, who doubled over screaming as blood spilled over his hands, the stake forgotten. Even as that man dropped to his knees, Angel swung the crowbar around behind him, clipping the second man across the cheek. His head rebounded off the wall and he collapsed, moaning.

The next attack was from the four coming down the wide central aisle, although only two could attack at once. Angel swatted away a raised stake, then rammed the crowbar into the teeth of another man. But he had stepped forward into that attack and someone was quick to jump on his back, raising a stake high overhead. At that moment, Angel let his vampire face out. He grabbed the arm of the man with the stake and tossed him over his head into the next two coming from the front.

A knife sliced across his forearm.

Out of the corner of his eye, he glimpsed another stake flashing downward, and he rolled forward away from the attack, slamming into a charred pew. Before he could climb to his feet someone else was on top of him, plunging a knife into his shoulder, scraping bone. As Angel reared back, he saw the sorcerer and Vincent moving down the nave, each carrying a stake. Now Angel had their undivided attention. He noticed movement up in the sanctuary, but he was quick to look away lest he draw attention to the others.

The moment Angel kicked down the front door of the church, Doyle, Cordelia, and Elliot entered through the back door. They passed what was left of the choir rehearsal room and turned down the hallway that bordered the sanctuary. A side door led into the ruined chapel, which was adjacent to the sanctuary and partially hidden from the nave. The door into the sanctuary was missing, leaving a narrow doorway with two steps leading up to where the cult had set up the banquet table and laid out Yunk'sh's remnant corpse. Here they crouched, waiting until the last two members of the cult moved down the nave to join the fight against Angel.

Doyle led them to the banquet table. He grabbed the shoulders of the charred demon corpse, which was missing most of one arm, while Elliot shambled over to lift the legs. Cordelia kept a watchful eye on the fight, and the look on her face told Doyle that Angel had his hands full. Doyle tried to block the thought from his mind. His priorities were to steal the corpse and perform the spell. Besides, the plan called for Angel to take on the entire cult as a distraction. Doyle kept telling himself, *It's all part of the plan. It's all . . .*

Right up until the moment the cult's sorcerer yelled, "Thieves! They're stealing the remnant corpse!"

"Take it," Elliot said, shoving the charred legs toward Cordelia, who grabbed them despite the look of instant disgust on her face. "I'll hold them off."

"Go!" Doyle shouted to Cordelia.

The demon's corpse was surprisingly light for the size of it, and they made good progress down the corridor. Doyle backed into the push bar of the door, which banged open, scraping the sidewalk.

Cordelia dropped the feet of the corpse, then scrambled to pick them up. "This really gives me the creeps," Cordelia said.

"Me too."

"It's missing an arm," she commented.

Doyle forced a grin. "Resurrections usually cost an arm and a leg. I'd say he got off cheap."

He'd left his gym bag inside the carpet warehouse, figuring he'd need his hands free to transport the demon corpse. As they bent low and ran across the back of the parking lot, a large gray shape bounded across the front of the lot. Doyle and Cordelia both dropped to the ground behind some overgrown bushes. The dark shape smashed through one of the boarded-up windows of the condemned church.

Cordelia gasped. "What in hell was that?"

"Out of hell," Doyle corrected, his face pale. "The Vishrak demon. And he looks none too happy." He nodded toward the back door of the carpet warehouse. "Let's go!"

Angel tossed two cloaked cult members off his back and jumped on top of a split pew. Elliot had stayed behind to stop the sorcerer, and there was nothing Angel could do to help him at the moment. He'd lost his crowbar and was currently surrounded by cult members wielding knives and stakes.

Elliot was unarmed, and the cult's sorcerer was merciless. He shoved his long knife up under Elliot's ribs, twisting it to slice as many internal organs as possible. Yet Elliot had one trick up his sleeve, literally—his left arm. It was thick, toughened gray skin with three oversize clawed fingers. He curled it into a fist and clubbed the sorcerer on the side of the head. Stunned, the sorcerer stumbled and fell, knocking over the bare banquet table with a loud clatter. With his human right hand, Elliot attempted to hold in the slippery ropes of his intestines amid a gush of blood, but he was too far gone. All the strength fled his body and he toppled forward.

Angel kicked the nearest cult member in the face,

clipping his chin and driving him backward. The floor beneath the tilted pew creaked, then cracked and began to cave in. Angel jumped clear, throwing his body sideways and taking down two other cult members.

Attempting to free himself from the tangle of limbs, Angel was too slow to block the crowbar as a standing cult member swung at his head. A quick backward jerk saved him from the full impact, but the blow landed hard nonetheless, splitting his scalp and cracking bone. Angel tumbled back, momentarily losing control of his legs. He rolled onto his hands and knees but sensed that he was too slow. Silently he wished Doyle and Cordelia luck.

Plywood shattered, followed by an inhuman roar as the demon Yunk'sh, in his re-spawned and still growing body, crashed through what had been a tall stained-glass window. Stones shattered to accommodate the demon's bulk, and a spray of old mortar billowed into the church in choking clouds. The demon was nearly eight feet tall now, with powerful arms and legs and a long, barbed tail that slammed into the ruined pews with the force of an ax.

"The demon," the sorcerer cried as he climbed to his feet. "There is still time to bind him."

"Your time is at an end," Yunk'sh roared. "You were fools to think you could bind me to your will." To demonstrate the point, Yunk'sh grabbed the nearest cult member by the throat, hoisted him into the air and ripped an arm right out of its socket to the wet sound of skin and muscles tearing. The bones popped and cracked, loud reports in the night. Blood spurted from the stump, spraying another cult member in the face. This one screamed as he wiped at his eyes. Yunk'sh dropped the first man and batted the second one's arms away, grabbing his head in his oversize hands and twisting in one violent motion as he yanked up. The head tore free of the falling body, trailing the ruptured stub of the spinal cord. Yunk'sh hurled the head at the sorcerer, who was pawing through the contents of a lacquered wooden case. The head struck the remains of the altar rail and toppled it.

"Stall him!" the sorcerer shouted to the others.

He needn't have worried. The demon hunted the cult members down one by one, ramming one man's head through a wall, punching his three-fingered fist through the chest cavity of another. To Angel it seemed as if the demon was gaining inches and pounds with each kill, growing before his eyes. The floor groaned beneath his increasing weight, boards cracking and shattering with almost every lumbering step.

Angel pushed himself up to a standing position and was surprised when he staggered. Blood covered one side of his face from his hairline down to his neck. His vision blurred, and he saw ghost images around everything, like bad television reception.

Willem held a knife in either hand and approached the demon cautiously, arms extended, blades up. When he spoke, he couldn't keep a slight quaver out of his voice. "We will bind you!"

The demon's laughter filled the condemned church and rose up into the starry night. Willem raised the knives defiantly. Yunk'sh lunged forward, a blur of motion, catching one of Willem's wrists in each hand. He pulled outward, ripping Willem's arms from their sockets. Then the demon turned the man's severed arms against him, driving both knives completely through Willem's chest and pinning him to the floor.

Only Vincent and the cult's sorcerer remained alive.

Fingers still numb, Angel bent to retrieve his crowbar. As a vampire, he healed quickly, but the process was not instantaneous. He needed time to regain his strength, let alone his wits.

"Where is my remnant corpse, sorcerer?" Yunk'sh demanded. He flung a split pew out of his way. It landed with a resounding crash ten feet away. The demon stormed up the nave of the church.

Vincent stood nervously in front of the sorcerer, a knife clutched in a double grip in front of him. "Omni, are you prepared to bind him?"

"Just a second," the Omni said, applying the green salve to his fingertips. Once all the fingers were coated, the salve began to glow. The Omni stood. "I am prepared."

Yunk'sh blurred forward again, ripping the knife from Vincent's hands. With one quick slash Vincent's throat was gushing blood. He pressed his hands against the flow but stumbled and collapsed.

The Omni reached out with glowing hands and took a step forward. "Yunk'sh, I bind you to our will and purpose."

"You are alone, sorcerer!"

"You will live to serve us. When I place my hands upon you, you will kneel before me!"

The knife flashed lightning quick, a forehand and backhand in quick succession, followed by two thumps as the Omni's severed hands fell to the floor. The green fingertips no longer glowed. Blood gushed from the stumps of the Omni's arms.

"You were meant to serve us," the Omni cried in disbelief, holding his arms out before him. "It is our right!"

"You bore me, mortal," Yunk'sh said. Another brutal forehand and the Omni's bald head slid off his shoulders. The body swayed, then crumpled forward. The demon looked up, as if scenting the air. "I sense the remnant corpse nearby." His voice was the dry rumble of thunder before a storm.

Everything was happening too fast. Had Doyle and Cordelia begun the spell? Would it even work? Angel had to stall the demon long enough to find out. He emerged from the shadows and called to the demon, "You forgot about me."

Yunk'sh spun around to face Angel.

"Ah . . . the vampire, Angel."

"Accept no imitations," Angel said as he assumed a fighting stance, the crowbar held in front of him.

"You are puny. You will never defeat me now."

"Call me foolish, but I'm willing to try."

Yunk'sh charged, thundering down the nave, a one-demon stampede.

"Not my best plan," Angel muttered.

A circle drawn with chalk surrounded them. The flame of a single white candle provided their only illumination.

Cordelia gripped the knife and grimaced as she made a long vertical incision in the desiccated neck of the demon's remnant corpse. As she wedged the glass orb into the incision just above the collarbone, Doyle flipped to the page he'd marked in the frayed tome. He shoved the book over to Cordelia, then removed a meat cleaver from the canvas gym bag. Clutching the handle with both hands, he held the blade about a foot above the orb, to better line up the blow. Doyle whispered, "Read the spell three times. Substitute the demon's name, Yunk'sh, wherever it says '*daemon.*' "

"Anything else?"

"Yeah," Doyle said. "Hurry!"

"What if it doesn't work?"

"We won't be alive long enough to worry about it."

Clutching the book to her chest, Cordelia read the spell three times, her voice becoming stronger, more confident with each repetition. "*Yunk'sh, tibi impero ut in hoc corporem regrediaris. Yunk'sh, tibi impero ut hanc ampullam animes. Yunk'sh, tibi impero ut in hac figura habites.*"

In his own mind, Doyle translated the spell into English: "Yunk'sh, I command you to return into this body. Yunk'sh, I command you to animate this vessel. Yunk'sh, I command you to abide in this form."

They waited, staring at the still dark orb, then glanced at each other. Finally, Doyle spoke, "We're dead."

Angel raised the crowbar, but Yunk'sh barreled right into him, hurling him backward with the collision. Rolling heels over head, Angel knew he only had a moment before the demon would crush him. He was on one knee, crowbar raised, when the floor collapsed under the demon's weight. Yunk'sh's foremost foot crashed through the wood and the demon fell forward. Still, he caught Angel's ankle, dropping him to his back, then grabbed the foot and pulled Angel closer. From a sitting position, Angel held the crowbar in a two-handed grip and shoved the narrow end into the demon's chest.

Yunk'sh roared in pain but continued to tug Angel closer. With his free hand, the demon scooped up an abandoned wooden stake, raised it high and was about to impale Angel with it when the demon's whole body shuddered. "What's happening?" Yunk'sh bellowed.

Angel lashed out with his free foot, striking the demon square in the face. He felt the nerveless hand release his leg and he slipped out of the demon's reach.

Yunk'sh clambered out of the hole in the floor, then shuddered again and was unnaturally still. A green glow bathed his eight-foot-tall body and wafted away like mist. The demon's body began to tremble uncontrollably.

Doyle stared at the dark glass orb, willing something to happen. Finally a pinpoint of green light winked into existence in the center of the sphere. Slowly it expanded within the confines of the glass container until it was almost too bright to watch. The charred corpse began to quiver and vibrate on the floor.

Cordelia shrieked and jumped back. "Do it! Now!"

"My pleasure," Doyle said. Gritting his teeth, he brought the cleaver down through the charred throat and shattering the orb as he severed the head. A loud implosion sounded as green light flared, momentarily blinding them.

The light from the white candle flickered, guttered, and held.

When they could see again, the charred corpse was a pile of ash.

"Is it over?" Cordelia asked. "Is the demon really dead this time?"

Doyle nodded. "Gives a whole new meaning to that old saying, 'If at first you don't succeed . . .' "

EPILOGUE

"So Kate's happy?" Doyle asked Angel.

"Glad it's over, anyway," Angel commented. "When she responded to our anonymous call, she just found the bodies of the suicide cult."

"Whatever happened to the demon's re-spawned body?" Cordelia asked.

"It never had time to establish itself on the physical plane. It just faded away."

"He should've asked for a money-back guarantee," Doyle quipped.

"And after Elliot died—or maybe after Yunk'sh died—Elliot got his wish. His corpse reverted to human form. Hairless, but human."

The telephone rang. Cordelia answered, then displayed a frown that progressively deepened. "What are you talking about? No, you pervert!"

"What was that?" Doyle asked.

The phone rang again. Cordelia answered a little more tentatively this time. "No! And you're a disgusting little creep!"

"Same guy?" Angel asked.

Cordelia shook her head, but the phone began ringing again before she could explain. She picked up and said, "Hold, please." The second line rang and she put that one on hold as well. "What is going on here?"

Arnold Pipich arrived, grinning from ear to ear. "Have you seen? We're up to five thousand hits on the site!"

"What? How?" Cordelia asked. "Wait a minute! These phone calls . . . Arnold, what did you do?"

"First, I registered on the search engines, but that wasn't enough because, you know, there are millions of sites out there. So I started the contest. Win a night of passion with a hot young Hollywood starlet."

Cordelia's eyes went wide. "You what?"

"I, um, borrowed your portfolio, the one you keep in your desk, scanned in some of the eight-by-ten glossies, and posted them on the site. Then I made announcements on various e-mail lists. Mucho traffic!"

"Are you crazy? Every geeky little pervert in L.A. is calling here!"

Arnold winked. "Don't worry. "I rigged it so I'll be the winner."

"Read the fine print," Cordelia told him. "This contest void where you're prohibited."

"Cordelia," Angel said, "I've had my doubts about this Web site from the start."

Cordelia's nod was emphatic. "Say no more." To Arnold: "Pull the plug, geek boy. Now!"

Arnold's shoulders sagged. "All right."

Someone tapped on the door.

Chelsea Monroe. She wore a sleeveless forest-green sweater dress that complemented her auburn hair. "May I have a moment to apologize?"

Angel nodded toward his office. Even with the door closed, he could hear Cordelia's continuing and impressive tongue-lashing of Arnold. Angel gave a little shake of his head, then sat down opposite Chelsea.

"First of all," she said. "I want to apologize for the piano bar."

"Already forgotten."

Chelsea smiled, crossed her right leg over her left, and appraised him for a moment. "I'm a reporter. I have just one question, so please humor me." He nodded. "Why?"

"I don't understand."

"Why are you fighting a natural impulse?" she asked. "I'm attracted to you, and I think you're attracted to me."

Angel sighed. All the obvious reasons remained unspoken: *Because I'm a lie, a fraud. You have this idea about who and what I am. But that's not really me; it's just a mask I wear, a convenient deception that lets me live in your world. You could never accept what I am, and even if you could, it would not be an option.* But Angel thought she deserved an answer, a truthful answer, and finally it came to him.

When the glamour demon had opened the door to Elliot's apartment and showed Angel his heart's desire, it hadn't been Chelsea. It had been Buffy . . . still Buffy. "I'm getting over someone," Angel told her. "Someone who still means a lot to me."

Chelsea looked away for a moment, then nodded, accepting his answer and meeting his gaze again. "She must be something special."

Angel smiled, but it was bittersweet. "She is." *And I will never be with her again.*

"She's one lucky lady," Chelsea replied, then let herself out.

Later, long after Cordelia had dismissed Arnold, Angel stepped out of his office. Doyle and Cordelia stopped talking and regarded him. "You dumped her, didn't you?" Cordelia asked.

"She was only interested in the image," Angel said.

"Angel, you *are* your image," Cordelia said. "And I don't mean that in a phony L.A. way. You may define your entire existence by the fact that you're a vampire. But you're more than that.

You're one of the good guys. You say you help the helpless and you do. That's who she saw. And that's real."

Doyle had a renewed, hopeful gleam in his eye. "She has a point."

And Angel thought, *Maybe she does at that.*

About the Author

John Passarella lives in Swedesboro, New Jersey, with his wife and two sons, Matthew and Luke. His co-authored first novel, *Wither,* won the Bram Stoker Award for Best First Novel of 1999 and will soon be a feature film from Columbia Pictures.

Already an avid fan of the *Buffy the Vampire Slayer* television series, John decided the time had come to write his own Buffy novel after the *San Francisco Examiner and Chronicle* remarked, "*[Wither]* hits the groove that makes TV's *Buffy the Vampire Slayer* such a kick." The result was John's second novel, *Buffy the Vampire Slayer: Ghoul Trouble*. *Angel: Avatar* is his third.

John developed a whole new appreciation for Web site design when he took on the task of revamping (no pun intended) the Horror Writers Association Web site at www.horror.org. Please visit John at www.passarella.com or e-mail him at jack@passarella.com.